CURSE
OF THE
PHOENIX

CURSE
OF THE
PHOENIX

AIMÉE CARTER

MARGARET K. McELDERRY BOOKS

New York London Toronto Sydney New Delhi

MARGARET K. McELDERRY BOOKS

An imprint of Simon & Schuster Children's Publishing Division

1230 Avenue of the Americas, New York, New York 10020

MARGARET K. McELDERRY BOOKS is a trademark of Simon & Schuster, Inc.

For information about special discounts for bulk purchases, please contact Simon & Schuster Special Sales at 1-866-506-1949 or business@simonandschuster.com.

The Simon & Schuster Speakers Bureau can bring authors to your live event. For more information or to book an event, contact the Simon & Schuster Speakers Bureau at 1-866-248-3049 or visit our website at www.simonspeakers.com.

Interior design by Irene Metaxatos

The text for this book was set in Perpetua.

Manufactured in the United States of America

0421 FFG

First Edition

10 9 8 7 6 5 4 3 2 1

CIP data for this book is available from the Library of Congress.

ISBN 9781534478442

ISBN 9781534478466 (ebook)

For the best dad in the world.
And for those who
have lost someone they love.
Grief may never lessen,
but life expands.

1

ZAC

SOMETHING WAS WRONG WITH THE DRAGON'S TAIL.

Zac Hadley squinted at his drawing, tilting his head and holding it at arm's length to try to gain some perspective. The unicorns in the valley looked okay, and he was pretty sure he'd nailed the shading in the mountains. But the longer he stared at the dragon that perched on the words *THE WILDEWOODS SAGA* written in block letters, the more distorted the image seemed, until it didn't look like a dragon at all, but rather a puffy lizard with a tail that was too big for its body. It wasn't right. Nothing he drew was right anymore.

Frustrated, he tossed his graphic novel onto the foot of

his bed. A month ago, he would have already been erasing the tail, determined to start over. Maybe he would have shown it to his mother first and asked what she thought. But now . . .

His stomach rumbled. Glancing at his watch, he realized with a jolt that it was three o'clock. He'd missed lunch. No—his father hadn't called him down for lunch in the first place.

Hungry and confused, Zac plodded across the hardwood floor and into the hallway. Pausing at the top of the stairs, he listened for the clacking of fingers on a keyboard as his father worked from home, the way he had for the past month, but Zac heard nothing. The entire house seemed quiet.

Too quiet.

"Dad?" called Zac. His heart began to race as he scrambled down the steps, nearly slipping on the polished wood. "Dad? Where are you?"

He darted across the living room, narrowly missing a coffee table that was cluttered with pop cans and a greasy pizza box from the night before. The door to his father's office was closed, and he skidded toward it, stopping half an inch from the knob as his chest began to tighten.

It wouldn't happen again. His father was fine. Sleeping, maybe, or wearing headphones and distracted by his work. Everything would be okay.

"Dad?" His voice shook as he knocked on the door. Not waiting for an answer, he pushed it open, and in that split second, he imagined what he would see on the other side. His dad in his office chair, reading a book. Or leaned back with his mouth open as he snored. Or—

The image appeared in his mind before he could stop it. He'd been hungry that afternoon, too, and wondering if his mother had finished lunch yet. He hadn't known then to be afraid of walking into quiet rooms that should have been noisy.

He'd expected to see her standing at the stove and stirring the contents of a pot, or maybe pulling plates out of the cabinet. Instead she had been lying on the floor, motionless.

For an instant, that was all Zac could see as he stood in the open doorway of his father's office. He was cold now, and he could barely draw a breath, but none of that seemed to matter as he relived the worst moment of his life. It had been a month ago now—a month and four days—but Zac still couldn't make himself walk into the kitchen.

"Zac?" His father's voice cut through the fog, and Zac blinked as the present materialized around him again. The curtains in the office were drawn, and his father sat at his desk, a phone held up to his ear. "Is everything all right?"

"I—" Zac tried to swallow, but his throat was too tight now, and he couldn't speak. Stars danced in front of him, and he clutched the knob for balance.

"Merle, I'll call you back," said his father urgently into the phone. Dropping it on his desk with a thud, he hurried toward Zac, hovering over him anxiously. "Are you okay? Do you need your inhaler? Where is it?" He looked around, as if expecting to find it on one of the side tables cluttered with old bottles and documents, but of course it wasn't there.

Zac shook his head. Now that he could see his father and knew he was all right, the tightness was easing. He wouldn't be running any races soon—or ever—but it wasn't a normal asthma attack. This kind had been happening more and more lately, and Zac had a feeling that mentioning it to his father would only result in more trips to the doctor. "I just—didn't hear you call for lunch," he said, his voice hoarse.

"Oh," said his father, and Zac noticed his eyes were swollen and rimmed with red. "Right. Lunch. I thought you had leftovers from last night."

"Yeah, but you need to heat them up for me," he said, sounding pathetic even to himself. His father frowned.

"You're twelve years old, Zac," he said gently. "You can heat up your own food."

Zac pressed his lips together. It was pointless to argue—they both knew why he wouldn't go into the kitchen. But no matter how many times his father urged him, he couldn't do it. Not yet.

His father sighed, his shoulders hunched. "I'll heat them up, but this is the last time, all right? Tomorrow, you make your own—"

"Help!" An ear-piercing cry echoed from the foyer as the front door slammed open, hitting the wall with a resounding crack. "Dad—*help!*"

2

LU

LU HADLEY BALANCED PRECARIOUSLY ON A LOW branch as she glared at the ancient tabby cat perched several feet above her. The cat stared back unblinkingly through his single eye, a silent challenge that made Lu long for a time before he had learned to climb a tree.

"You know you need your medication, Rufus," she said, gripping the rough bark. "We shouldn't have to do this every single day."

Rufus turned away from her and began to groom himself. With her legs wrapped firmly around the branch, Lu grabbed the scruff of his neck and eased him down, swaddling him in her sweater before he could scratch her. "Got you!"

"I don't know why you bother," said her best friend, Sophia Lopez, from the grass fifteen feet below. She sat at the edge of the woods that bordered their neighborhood, and while she untangled a burr from a long-haired kitten's coat, the rest of the homeless cat colony gathered around a pile of fresh kibble nearby. "The infection's probably gone by now, anyway."

With Rufus and the sweater tucked under one arm, Lu climbed down and dropped back onto the ground. "Probably isn't good enough when he only has one eye left." Pulling a tube of ointment from her pocket, she sat beside Sophia and wrestled Rufus onto his back. With enormous effort, she pinned him down and held his good eye open, and at last she administered the single bead of medication he needed.

Rufus darted back up the tree the moment she released him, and Lu sprawled out on the sun-soaked grass, letting herself relax for the first time since breakfast. The last day of school was finally over, much to her relief—though not for the usual reasons. Teachers looked at her with pity now instead of silent exasperation. The other kids avoided her, as if she had some kind of plague they could catch if they got too close. Even her track coach had insisted she take the rest of the season off, despite the fact that she was the fastest one on the team. Only Sophia hung out with her anymore, and as much as Lu dreaded spending the summer with no buffer between her and her twin brother, at least no one would ask how she was holding up for a while.

"I need to go," said Sophia, after she'd untangled the burr. The kitten leaped out of her lap and joined its litter-mates nearby. "Mom will kill me if I'm late for ballet practice again."

Reluctantly Lu rose too, shaking grass out of her dark, shoulder-length hair. "I can still come over tomorrow night, right?"

Sophia snorted. "My mom said you could stay the whole summer if you want."

"Really?" Lu grabbed her backpack, which still smelled like the cat kibble she'd lugged to school with her. "You wouldn't get sick of me?"

"Of course not. You're my best friend." Sophia caught her in a tight hug. "I'll see you tomorrow, okay?"

Lu watched her go, her heart sinking now that she was on her own. But there was no point in making herself miserable, and so she straightened her shoulders and strode in the opposite direction. Summer wouldn't be all bad, she thought, especially if she could spend most of it at Sophia's place. Her dad wouldn't mind, and her brother probably wouldn't even notice she was gone, considering he spent all his time in his room now. But even as she tried to convince herself, she knew that no matter how far from her family she was, it wouldn't change what had happened the month before.

Lost in her thoughts, Lu almost missed the patch of gray-and-white fur half-hidden in an overgrown thicket. With a gasp, she edged closer. There, obscured by weeds and wildflowers, was a young raccoon with deep scratches in its side.

She slowly knelt down, not wanting to startle the poor thing. Its chest rose and fell with effort, and though it stared at her with dull eyes, it didn't move away. Lu bit her lip and looked around. Sophia had disappeared already, and there was no one else on the quiet suburban street. What was she supposed to do?

There was only one good answer to that question, and with renewed determination, she carefully wrapped the raccoon in her sweater. Unlike Rufus, it was limp and didn't fight her. Cradling the injured animal, she stood and hurried down the sidewalk, walking as fast as she could without jostling it. But the quicker she moved, the more the raccoon's eyes closed, and panic squeezed her insides.

Though her house was only half a block away, it felt like a mile by the time she reached her front door. Throwing it open, she rushed inside, desperately clutching the raccoon to her chest. "Help!" she yelled as loudly as she could. "Dad—*help!*"

Footsteps thundered from deep within the house, and as she checked to see how much blood the raccoon had lost, her brother—not her father—burst into the foyer, breathing heavily.

"What's going on?" said Zac, his messy dark hair falling into his eyes. But when he spotted the raccoon, he took an unsteady step backward. "Lu, is that . . . ?"

Every muscle in her body tensed, and she immediately turned away from her brother, trying to shield him from the raccoon. "What are you doing down here?" she said, her panic only growing. "You're always upstairs."

But it was too late. She was covered in cat fur and dander, and no doubt raccoons carried allergens, too. Zac had gotten close—too close—and she could already see him struggling to take a deep breath.

"What's going on in here?" said their dad as he came around the corner. He looked like he'd been crying, and for a moment, Lu stared at him, not knowing what to think. She hadn't seen him cry since the funeral.

"I—" she began, but Zac was wheezing now, the rasping sound growing louder with each breath. "I found a raccoon—"

"You brought a *raccoon* into the house?" Instantly her dad turned toward Zac and gripped his shoulders, as if to steady him. "Zac, are you all right? Look at me, kid."

"I'm sorry," wailed Lu. "It's dying. I didn't know what else to do."

"You know exactly what you should've done," snapped her dad, his face turning red. "Zac, kid—Zac, look at me. You're all right. Where's your inhaler? Where did you leave it? Is it upstairs?"

Zac shook his head, unable to speak now. With her heart racing, Lu started toward the kitchen, but her dad threw his arm out to stop her.

"Don't you take another step into this house until you've put that thing outside," he said. Lu opened her mouth to protest, but Zac's entire body was heaving now. Ducking out the door, she set the bundled raccoon gently on the porch and hurried back inside, furious—though whether at herself for not making sure Zac was upstairs, or with her brother for leaving his room for the first time in a month, she couldn't say.

Sidestepping around her dad, she darted into the kitchen and flung open a worn cabinet. There, still organized by their mother's system, was a mountain of medication, all prescribed to Zacharias Hadley. Without bothering to look at the labels, Lu grabbed a yellow inhaler, a package of pills, and an EpiPen before hurrying back into the entrance hall.

"Here." She uncapped the inhaler and shoved it into Zac's clammy hands. He lifted it to his mouth, pressing on the canister and breathing in the medication. Lu watched him with grim determination, and once she was sure he wouldn't need the EpiPen, she tore open the plastic package and freed a pill.

"What is that?" said their dad, panic catching in his voice. "What are you giving him?"

"It's just a Benadryl," she muttered, not taking her eyes off her brother. At last he could breathe enough to swallow a dose, and he slumped against the wall, panting but alive. "You need to take him to the emergency room. The doctors and nurses will probably only give him a breathing treatment and steroids or something, but you need to go anyway. Mum always did."

Their dad rubbed Zac's arm, his brow knit with both anger and concern. "I want that vermin as far away from here as possible," he said sharply to Lu. "And I want every trace of dander gone too. You could have killed him, Lu. You could've—"

His voice caught, and he hastily wiped his eyes, his face red. Lu swallowed hard. "I was just trying to save it," she mumbled. "I'm sorry."

"Sorry isn't good enough," said their dad roughly. "Not when it's your brother's life on the line." He shook his head, and for a split second, he looked as broken and lost as Lu felt. "I can't do this anymore, guys. I don't know how, not without your mother, and—I can't."

"What do you mean? You can't do what?" said Lu, almost too afraid to ask.

Their dad stood frozen for a moment, his hand on Zac's shoulder. "I'm taking Merle up on her offer," he said at last, his gaze glued to the floor. "I tried. I've been trying. But—I can't, not like this. Not right now. I'm sorry."

"Merle? Who's Merle?" said Lu, confused. But her father hurried Zac toward the car without an answer, and she watched them go, her stomach a knotted mess.

What had just happened?

3

ZAC

LATER THAT EVENING, WHEN ZAC ARRIVED HOME from his umpteenth visit to the emergency room, their father sat them down in the living room and finally revealed who Merle was.

"Your mother's aunt," he said gruffly, his hands clasped. "She lives in England."

"Oh," said Zac, glancing at his sister, who hadn't said a word since they'd returned. "I didn't know Mum had any family."

Lu shook her head. Neither, apparently, had she.

Their father was silent for a long moment, and the tension in the living room grew to unbearable levels. And while Zac didn't know exactly what their father was going to say, he could sense that something was about to change. Something huge.

At last, in a dull, emotionless voice, their father said, "Aunt Merle's invited you both to stay with her for the summer. And I've accepted."

Zac stared at him, waiting for the punch line. It had to be a joke, after all—they'd never heard of Aunt Merle before tonight, and Zac's allergies and asthma were so bad that he couldn't even go to school with Lu, let alone spend an entire summer in a foreign country.

But the pained look on their father's face made it clear it wasn't a joke, and Zac's insides grew hollow. "But—but what about my allergies?" he said, his voice breaking. "My doctors are here."

"They have doctors and hospitals in England, and your aunt knows about your illnesses," said their father. "I'm sorry. I am. But—"

"But you can't do this anymore," spat Lu with such venom that even Zac was taken aback. "You can't take care of your own kids."

Their father didn't answer, and instead he stood without a word and retreated to his office, leaving Zac to bear the brunt of her fury. It wasn't the first time, and he was too shell-shocked to care.

"Mum would never abandon us," said Lu as she paced

the length of the living room, kicking a greasy fast-food bag out of her path. "If she knew what Dad was planning—"

"It isn't his fault," mumbled Zac, feeling like the world had been tilted off its axis. "Mum's gone."

"You think I don't know that?" she said, her hands balled into fists. "She was my mum too, you know."

Zac's face grew hot. "I'm just saying—you saw him today. He doesn't know what he's doing. She's the one who was home with us all the time."

"And *he's* the one who chose not to be here," said Lu. "He could have found a job that kept him in Chicago all week, you know. But he didn't want to. Because he didn't want *us*."

Zac's mouth went dry, and he didn't have the words to argue with her. He'd long suspected *he* was the reason their father had spent most of their childhood traveling across the country five days a week, leaving Monday morning and returning home Friday night. His mum had insisted again and again that he wasn't a burden, and she didn't mind the hospital stays and the endless doctor appointments and the small pharmacy that took up an entire kitchen cupboard. But now that she was gone, there was no one to shield Zac from the very real truth that he was useless. Worse than useless. He was a headache they had to work around, and nothing more.

And this proved it.

⚜ ⚜ ⚜

Their father came home the following morning with new suitcases for both of them. Zac didn't argue—how could he, when he was the problem in the first place? Lu, however, spent the next two days raging and making all their lives miserable. But no amount of pleading, hunger strikes, or angry sobbing changed their father's mind, and he was adamant: they would spend the summer in England with a relative they'd never met, and there was nothing either of them could do about it.

That was why, shortly after midnight Chicago time, Zac was stuck in an airplane between his snoring father and pouting sister, thirty-five thousand feet in the air over the Atlantic Ocean. The cabin lights had been dimmed, and with most of the plane sleeping, it was eerily still.

With little to do and no one to talk to, he pulled out his unfinished graphic novel and opened to the title page, only to see that ridiculous puffy dragon staring back at him once more. He sighed inwardly. Maybe he could take a nap instead.

"What are you drawing?" said Lu, her voice so close to his ear that it startled him. She was leaning over the armrest between them, her gaze focused on the sketch.

Zac shrugged awkwardly, his face growing warm as he hastily flipped to a blank page. "Nothing. It's stupid. It's not even finished."

Lu scowled. "Sorry for asking, then," she muttered, turning back toward the window and folding her knees to her chest.

Zac bit his lip. He couldn't remember the last time she'd asked about his art. He couldn't remember the last time they'd had a conversation about anything normal, either, without it breaking out into a fight. But they were both miserable, and there was no point in making it worse.

Reluctantly he turned back to the title page. Below *THE WILDEWOODS SAGA*, he'd drawn a girl wielding a fiery sword while riding a unicorn. She had turned out pretty good, he thought. Maybe Lu wouldn't notice the dragon. "It's a graphic novel," he said. "Mum and I were working on it together before she . . ." He blinked hard. "It's based on the stories she used to tell us—the ones about the Wildewoods sanctuary? With all the dragons and unicorns and mermaids—"

"I remember the stories," said Lu, her forehead pressed against the window. "You're not the only one who spent time with her, you know."

Something inside him deflated, and he stared at the edge of his tray table. All his life, he had watched Lu do things he couldn't. Play outside with kids from the neighborhood—go to a real school—pet dogs and cats and eat anything she wanted. Creating this graphic novel with their mother was the one thing he had that Lu didn't. The only thing.

"Maybe Dad will change his mind when we get to Aunt Merle's," he said quietly, fiddling with his pencil.

Lu snorted against the window. "Sure. And maybe the sky will open up and it'll rain chocolate."

Zac glanced over his shoulder, making sure their father was still fast asleep. "I mean, it's possible, isn't it? I won't be able to stay if I'm allergic to everything. And old ladies' houses are full of dust and cats and flowers, aren't they?"

Lu said nothing at first, but after a few seconds passed, she twisted around to face him again. "Wait—what if it is?"

She hadn't looked at him like that—like he was her partner in crime instead of someone who would snitch on her—in ages, and a small thrill ran through him. "Then I'll probably have an asthma attack, and Dad will have to take us home," he whispered.

Her eyes were bright now, and she leaned toward him, lowering her voice as well. "I'm not saying you should make yourself sick, but . . ."

"But I could let it happen," he said slowly, his mind whirling with possibilities. "If you need me to."

She hesitated, indecision flickering across her face. "Not enough to hurt yourself or end up in the hospital," she said firmly. "But enough to show Dad you can't stay. Do you think you could do that?"

He considered it. He'd never purposely let himself get sick before, and the thought of it felt like betraying his mother. But this was important. She would understand, he thought. She would want their family to stay together. "Yeah, I think I can manage."

For the first time in a month, he saw Lu smile. Or at least the corners of her lips turned upward in a determined sort of grimace. "Then we might be able to go home after all," she said. "It's risky, but——"

"I can handle it," he promised. Deep down he knew this was a terrible idea, but if it made his sister happy—if it let him be part of the solution for once, instead of the problem—then it would be worth it.

She shifted closer again and peered at his sketchbook. "That's how I always imagined it," she said softly, her sharp edges dulled now that they had a plan. "The Wildewoods, I mean. I used to dream about all the creatures in Mum's stories."

"Me too," admitted Zac, the tip of his pencil tracing over the dragon's snout. "I still do sometimes. I dream that she's there, waiting for us to find her."

Lu was quiet for a long moment. "Is that Mum?" she said, touching the girl wielding the fiery sword.

"Yeah, that's her," he said, and out of the corner of his eye, he thought he saw his sister wipe her cheek.

But after a beat, Lu cleared her throat. "The dragon's tail is too big. It looks swollen."

He pressed his lips together, still staring at the girl

riding the unicorn. "How do you know? Have you ever seen a dragon before?"

"Have you?" she retorted, but when he looked at her, she was smirking. Turning back to his drawing, Zac began to erase the lines, hopeful that their plan would work and the summer wouldn't be a complete disaster after all.

4

LU

LU WAS EXCITED WHEN, SHORTLY AFTER DAWN, THE plane finally landed.

Not because they were in London, of course—she'd never been to England before, even though their mother had been born and raised here, and she had no interest in staying longer than it took to catch a flight back to Chicago. But Lu *was* excited that she and Zac had a plan, and now that they'd arrived, they could put it into motion. She was excited there was still a chance they might go home in time for Sophia to forgive her.

When Lu had told her they were leaving for the summer, she and Sophia had had the biggest fight of their entire friendship. Sophia had accused her of *wanting* to go to England before storming away in tears, leaving Lu distraught and feeling as isolated as she had in the days following her mother's sudden death. All she wanted was to talk to Sophia and make sure they were okay, because right now, Lu wasn't so sure. And she couldn't stand the thought of spending the whole summer wondering if she'd lost her best friend, too.

She trailed her dad and brother through Heathrow Airport, too distracted to be impressed by the fact that it seemed as busy and crowded as O'Hare. In order for this to work, she would have to talk to her dad again, which was unfortunate, since she was currently giving him the silent treatment. But as they made their way through the long corridors and seemingly endless line at customs, he didn't appear to notice anyway. Or if he did, he didn't care.

Their mum would have cared. She would have sat Lu down over ice cream and insisted they talk it out. But their dad was gone so much of the time that up until now, Lu had never really *been* mad at him before. She'd always just been excited to have him home.

As she considered the exact combination of words that would finally make him see how necessary it was that they go back to Chicago, the three of them arrived in the bustling welcome area, where passengers were greeted by friends and family and the occasional chauffeur. Lu was ready to maneuver past them all when their dad stopped suddenly.

"That must be your great-aunt Merle," he said, steering them toward a short, round woman with an explosion of dark, graying curls. She held a sign with the words *Welcome, Zacharias and Tallulah!* written in marker, with tiny flowers decorating their names.

Lu cast Zac a wary look. Why was Aunt Merle picking them up from the airport?

"Merle?" said their dad as he approached her. "I'm Cal Hadley. This is—"

"My darlings! I've been waiting so long to meet you." Aunt Merle sidestepped their dad completely to catch both Lu and Zac in a warm embrace right in the middle of the crowd. Lu tensed. They'd been hugged by plenty of relatives they'd never met at the funeral, but she was sure Aunt Merle hadn't been one of them.

When she finally released them, she immediately took hold of their hands, like she was afraid they'd vanish the moment she let go. And to Lu's surprise, her dark eyes shone with tears. "You must be Tallulah," she said. "You have your mum's nose, and her cheekbones. And you, Zacharias . . ." She shook her head. "You're the spitting image of her."

Lu frowned and studied Zac, trying to spot traces of their mother, but all she could see was him. Wavy dark hair, brown eyes, and a despondent look she'd never once seen on their mum. Lu was the one who had inherited her freckles. And her height.

Their dad cleared his throat. "The twins have one suitcase each, and they should be light. Just clothes. Their other things are in their backpacks. You have my number, the list of Zac's allergies, emergency contacts . . . is there anything else you need?"

"No, no, we'll be just fine," murmured Aunt Merle, gathering Lu and Zac to her. "Don't you worry a bit about us. We'll have the time of our lives this summer."

Wait. *Wait.* "Aren't you coming with us?" said Lu, her heart sinking. Their plan depended on it. "You said you'd stay a few days."

"Had to change my flight," said their dad gruffly, not meeting her eye. "They need me back at work."

"But—we need you too," said Zac in a small voice. They were the first words he'd said since their conversation on the plane, and Lu looked at him sharply, surprised by how close to tears he sounded.

Their dad knelt in front of him. "I'm sorry, kid. I need to get back to Chicago. But I have job interviews lined up," he added, as if this was supposed to be some sort of silver lining. "Ones that will let me work from home so I can help you with homeschool this fall."

Zac's face crumpled, and he threw his arms around their dad. "I don't want to stay here," he mumbled, his voice muffled by their dad's shirt. "I'll be okay by myself at home while you and Lu are gone during the day. You won't have to worry about me at all."

Their dad sighed, and Lu knew there was no point in Zac begging. That battle had already been lost. She had no idea why she'd let herself get her hopes up on the plane—it was only ever going to lead to disappointment.

"I'll be back before you know it," said their dad, but his words sounded empty, and his gaze was unfocused. "And I'll try to visit when I can."

"Sure you will," muttered Lu, but he didn't respond.

"P-please," gasped Zac. "I'll be good, I—I swear." He seemed to be struggling to catch his breath now, and Lu unzipped the front pocket of her backpack, her fury with their dad growing as she searched for Zac's spare inhaler.

"I'm sorry, kid, but you know I have to go." Gently he detached himself from Zac's grip, and though Zac struggled to hold on, he was no match for their dad. As her brother stumbled backward, Lu was there to stop him from falling, and she pressed his inhaler into his hand.

"At least try to remember to call and let us know you're still alive," said Lu darkly. A muscle in their dad's jaw twitched, and he glanced at the ground.

"Lu knows all of Zac's medications," he said to Aunt Merle as he took a few steps back. "Call me if anything happens. I might be hard to reach, especially during the workweek, but I'll return any messages as soon as I can." He hesitated before adding, this time to Lu and Zac, "I love you both. Be good, and try not to cause any trouble."

Zac made a choking sound as their dad turned and walked away, shoving his hands in his pockets. Instantly Lu faced her brother, checking for signs of an attack. But although his face was red and his breath coming in struggling gasps, his eyes were brimming with unshed tears, and he made no move to use his inhaler. He wasn't having an asthma attack. He was trying not to break down and sob. More furious than she'd ever been in her entire life, Lu wrapped her arm around her brother's shoulders as they watched their dad disappear into the crowd, not even sparing them one last wave goodbye.

This was it. This was really happening, and he was abandoning them with an aunt they'd never met before. She wanted to tell Zac that their dad wasn't worth his tears, that maybe they'd be better off without him and his cluelessness. But instead she hugged her brother and, over his shoulder, caught their great-aunt's concerned eye.

"Your father loves you both very much," said Aunt Merle. "That hasn't changed."

"Yeah? Then why is he getting rid of us?" spat Lu.

"He's grieving," she said gently. "You all are. He's lost the love of his life, and he just needs some time." She touched Lu's cheek with her cool hand. "You and Zacharias will be all right. You're together, and you're both on the same team. As long as you remember that, everything will be okay."

Tears stung Lu's eyes, but she refused to cry. Not here. Not like this. And definitely not because of their dad. "We're tired," she said, forcing the words past the lump in her throat. "How long will it take to get to your house?"

"We'll be there a little after lunch, I'd imagine," said Aunt Merle. "I'm sure you'll be able to rest on the train."

She gathered them both to her side. And though Lu was fighting the overwhelming urge to scream and cry at the same time, she didn't protest as their great-aunt led them first to the luggage carousel, and then onward to the place they would call home for the next three months.

5

ZAC

ZAC COULDN'T BELIEVE HE WAS CRYING.

No, actually, he could believe it—he'd been dreading the moment their father would leave them for days now, and the live wire of fear wrapped around Zac's insides had made it impossible not to break down as he'd watched him walk away. He thought he would have more time to prepare. He didn't think his father would bolt like that the first chance he got, with barely a hug goodbye.

The worst part, though, was Lu. Having her fuss over him, embracing him in a way she hadn't since they were younger and still had things in common—it only made him feel more humiliated than he already was.

The rest of the trip to Aunt Merle's house was excruciatingly long. Even once they escaped the claustrophobia of Heathrow, it took several subway changes and a three-hour train ride through the English countryside before they finally crammed into a taxi that took them down winding roads into the heart of the Lake District. As exhausted as Zac was, he had to admit that the views of small mountains and valleys and snatches of lakeshore were spectacular. He'd had no idea a place like this even existed in the real world.

At last the car turned down a dirt road that cut through a forest. Unlike the normal trees he was used to seeing outside his window in the Chicago suburbs, these trees were ancient and covered in moss, and hundreds of blue flowers carpeted the ground around their roots. As the taxi approached a tall wrought-iron fence, the gate creaked open ominously, and Zac shifted closer to the window to get a better look.

In the seat beside him, Lu made a face. "You're practically sitting in my lap," she said, trying to shove him away, but he stubbornly held his ground.

"I want to see too," he said, and as they jockeyed for position, an enormous house appeared. Four stories high, it had rows and rows of windows that looked out onto the front garden, and each side stretched away from the main building in wings that encircled the drive. It was so big that it couldn't even reasonably be called a house—it was a mansion at the very least, or a manor. Maybe even a small palace.

"*This* is where you live, Aunt Merle?" said Lu, her mouth dropping open.

"It most certainly is," she said proudly. "I thought you might approve."

The taxi came to a stop beside half a dozen stone steps that led up to an imposing entrance, and as soon as the car door was unlocked, Lu jumped onto the gravel drive.

"Do you think Mum was royalty?" said Zac as he climbed out after her. "Do you think *we're* royalty?"

"If we were, we'd know it," said Lu, but she didn't sound convinced. Besides, she didn't know any better than he did, and the house was massive. The people who owned it had to be rich.

As Zac eyed the ornate columns on either end of the front steps, a squeal echoed from behind them, and he spun around. A freckled girl with a round face and brown hair streaked toward them, her muddy rubber boots crunching on the gravel and a flashlight tied to her utility belt bouncing as she ran.

Zac stepped aside as she caught Lu in a tight hug. "I can't believe you're here!" said the girl, whose lilting accent sounded so much like their mother's that his heart skipped a beat.

"Neither can we," said Lu, her annoyance obvious to Zac, but the girl didn't seem to notice. Instead she let go of

Lu and looked between them, her smile so wide that he was sure her cheeks had to hurt.

"Look at you," she said. "You're so—so *American*."

"We're from Chicago," said Zac weakly, still reeling. Their mother had been the only person he had ever known with that exact accent, and hearing it again was almost like hearing a ghost.

"Zacharias, Tallulah, this is your cousin Penelope," said Aunt Merle as she pulled their luggage from the taxi. Her accent was definitely English, but it didn't match their mum's. "She's just turned thirteen last month, so you three should get along famously. Penelope, be gentle with them, love. They've had a long journey."

"No doubt," said Penelope, and she hesitated. "I was so sorry to hear about Aunt Josie. I miss her every day."

"You—you knew our mum?" said Zac, startled.

"Of course," she said, puzzled by that. "Surely she told you all about us?"

She hadn't, though. As far as Zac knew, she'd never mentioned—let alone visited—any family at all. He shrugged noncommittally, hoping she wouldn't press.

After an awkward beat, Penelope moved in to give Zac a hug. "It really is lovely to finally meet you," she said, but before she could reach him, Lu stepped between them.

"He has a lot of allergies. Deadly allergies," she added, and Zac could see her eyeing Penelope's overalls. Tiny white hairs clung to the brown fabric, and now that Penelope was closer, Zac could definitely smell some kind of animal on her. "You have to be careful around him."

Penelope's hands flew behind her back, as if to stop herself from touching him. "Aunt Merle mentioned that. I didn't know it was quite so serious, though."

"Very serious," said Lu, squaring her shoulders. "He'll have to go to the hospital if he gets exposed to anything his immune system can't tolerate."

"I can speak for myself, you know," said Zac with a scowl. He didn't normally spend so much time around his sister, and he wasn't thrilled to learn she'd suddenly taken it upon herself to hover over him like he was about to collapse.

"Well, why don't we go inside and see the house?" chirped Aunt Merle as she led the way up the steps. "There's plenty of fun to be had here."

"Especially during the summer," agreed Penelope, picking up both suitcases with ease. "Hiking, biking, swimming—"

"Zac's allergic to five different kinds of trees," said Lu. "And grass. And hay."

"And I can't swim," he added, shooting his sister a glare she expertly ignored.

"Oh." Penelope seemed to consider this as Aunt Merle pushed open the ornate double doors. "Then . . . I suppose you could always explore indoors. There are rooms in the east wing that no one's visited in a century or more," she added brightly, nodding to the right side of the manor.

"I'm also allergic to dust mites," he said. "American *and* European."

Penelope faltered at that, her expression falling. "I didn't realize there were two types."

"You learn a lot when you spend half your life in a doctor's office," he muttered.

As they stepped into the foyer, he was immediately struck with a sense of imbalance. On the one hand, the inside of the house was even more magnificent than he'd expected, with high ceilings, gold-framed oil paintings, and a grand staircase that wound out of sight. There was even a chandelier hanging above them, crystals clinking melodically as Penelope closed the doors, and Zac was relieved to see hardwood floors. Carpet only made his attacks worse.

But on the other hand, as impressive as it all was, it also looked like no one had bothered to fix anything for at least a decade. The sun-bleached wallpaper was peeling in the corners, the wooden steps were dull and scuffed, and to his dismay, he spotted a layer of dust on a small table that held a chipped vase. The manor might have been huge, but it was also in a state of disrepair. Apparently their mother's relatives weren't as rich as he'd thought.

"Would you like the tour now, or would you rather

rest?" said Aunt Merle as she led them up one side of the grand staircase. The steps creaked loudly, and Zac had a sudden mental image of crashing through the floor. If their father had come with them, he would have taken one look around and put them on a plane back to Chicago without a second thought.

A fresh wave of fear and anxiety washed over him. Was their father already on his flight home? Was he flying over the Atlantic Ocean at that very moment? What if the plane crashed? What if—

"I'm exhausted," admitted Lu, but Zac could feel her eyes on him. It was possible she really was tired, but she was only saying so for his sake. Even worse, he couldn't deny it. He hadn't slept on the plane at all, and he'd only managed a light doze on the train, jolting awake with every bump and unfamiliar sound. And ever since his crying jag at the airport, his head had gone fuzzy, and his entire body felt like it was being weighed down by cement. All he wanted was to curl up in his bed at home and sleep for as long as he wanted.

"Penelope can show you to your room, then, while I fetch some clean towels," said Aunt Merle as they turned down a long hallway filled with doors and what looked like the kind of candleholders Zac had seen in video games. Sconces, he thought they were called. Either way, it was creepy.

"*Room?*" said Lu abruptly. "You mean—"

"Aunt Merle wanted to put you two together in your mum's old bedroom, in case your brother gets sick," said Penelope nervously as their aunt bustled out of sight. "Is that all right? It's a big room, really. There are two beds, and it's all aired out and tidy, I promise. We can even hang a curtain down the middle if you'd prefer."

Their mother's room. Zac's stomach lurched, and the tightness in his chest returned. "I don't mind," he said, suddenly afraid Lu would keep objecting and he'd have to stay somewhere else.

"You don't?" said Lu, surprised, and he shook his head.

"This place is full of dust. You know it's going to make me sick, and then you'll be in my room the whole time anyway. You just stick to your side, and I'll stick to mine."

"We don't have many bedrooms ready for use, anyway, so it's either that or share with me or my brother," admitted Penelope as they reached the end of the hallway. "He's called Oliver, by the way. He's in the Wildewoods right now, but he should be back in time for dinner."

It took a moment for Zac to realize what she'd said, and when he did, a chill ran through him. "Wait—the Wilde-woods?"

But before Penelope could elaborate, Lu cut in. "How many people live here, anyway?" she said, apparently oblivious to Zac's excitement. "Mum never talked about her life in England."

Though it might have been Zac's imagination, he could have sworn he saw a flicker of hurt on Penelope's face. "There's me, Oliver, Aunt Merle, Aunt Rowena, and my father, your uncle Conrad," she said as she pushed the door open. "You'll meet them all at dinner tonight."

"That's it? You're the only ones here?" said Lu, but Penelope was already inside the bedroom. Zac followed, opening his mouth to ask about the Wildewoods again. As soon as he crossed the threshold, however, the words seemed to vanish from his mind.

Penelope was right. It was a huge bedroom, nearly three times the size of the one he had back home, and light flooded in from a wide window. The walls were a pale lilac, and someone had shoved two beds into opposite corners of the room, leaving a large stretch of open area in between. Though Zac noted with dismay that the room was mostly devoid of personal touches, there was a yellowing Spice Girls poster hanging above one bed, and in another corner hung a poster of a band called Hanson. Zac couldn't remember their mother mentioning either of them before.

Still, this was where she had grown up. She'd slept in this room her entire childhood, and as Zac inhaled, he thought he could smell a trace of her.

"The chest of drawers is empty and ready for your things," said Penelope. "There ought to be enough room for both of—"

"What on *earth* is going on here?"

Penelope dropped their suitcases, and she spun toward the open door with an audible gulp. Frowning, Zac followed her gaze, only to find a tall, brawny woman with iron-gray hair standing in the threshold, her arms crossed as she glared down her hawk nose. There was a wicked scar running across her cheek, and Zac thought he saw the start of another on her neck just above the collar of her long leather coat.

"Aunt Rowena!" said Penelope, her voice suddenly higher than before. "I can explain—"

"You can explain what your American cousins are doing here?" she said coolly. "Do go on."

Zac glanced at Lu, only to find that she was staring back at him, her eyes wide. Rowena hadn't known they were coming. They weren't invited after all. "Listen, our dad might still be at the airport," he said hastily. "I'm sure if someone calls him, he'll come pick us up and—"

"There's no need for that," said Aunt Merle, maneuvering around Rowena with a stack of clean towels in her arms. "Here you go, my dears. The bathroom's just down the hall, and if there's anything else—"

"What have you done, Merle?" said Rowena. Somehow she seemed even larger and more intimidating than before.

"I've done nothing wrong, and you know it," she said as she set the towels on their respective beds. "Zacharias and

Tallulah are our niece's children. They're family, and this is their home too."

"You know very well why I said no," said Rowena in a harsh whisper, as if she thought that would stop Zac and Lu from overhearing.

"They'll stay in the shop with me. It'll be perfectly safe," said Aunt Merle with a dismissive wave. "What would you have us do? Their father's already on a flight back to the States, and it's only been a month since Josie . . ."

She trailed off, but Zac could hear her implied question: Was Rowena going to abandon them too? This wasn't a family visit, he realized. This was a charity case. He clenched his jaw and shoved his hands in his pockets.

"I'm tired," he said, loudly enough to interrupt the start of Rowena's retort. "If you're going to kick us out, fine. But at least let us take a nap first."

"No one's going to send you away, dear," said Aunt Merle, though there was a hint of steel underneath the warmth in her voice. "Are we, love?"

Beside her, Rowena's face was quickly turning puce. "Fine," she sputtered. "But they're your responsibility, Merle. If anything happens to them, or if heaven forbid, they wander where they shouldn't—"

"They won't," said Aunt Merle serenely. "They're good children, just like their mother. Aren't you, darlings?"

Zac had no idea how Aunt Merle could have possibly

known what they were like, considering they'd just met. But he was too tired to care, and so he shrugged. "Can we sleep now?"

"Of course," she murmured, ushering Penelope and Rowena into the hallway. "We'll wake you for dinner."

As soon as the door closed behind her, however, Zac heard a flurry of whispers on the other side. While Lu claimed the bed beneath the Spice Girls poster, he pressed his ear against the old-fashioned keyhole.

". . . plan on doing if they find the Wildewoods?" said Rowena in a sandpaper voice. "We both know what could happen—"

"It won't," said Aunt Merle soothingly. "This was inevitable. The children will be all right."

"You can't promise that," muttered Rowena, growing quieter as they walked down the hall. "If it was that easy—"

"Will you stop eavesdropping?" said Lu, flopping onto her bed. "I can't believe you let them stick us in the same room. If you snore, I am going to be *so* mad."

"Did you hear what Penelope said? About the Wildewoods?" said Zac, moving away from the door. They were too far away for him to listen now, anyway.

"You really think it's weird that Mum named the sanctuary in her stories after the place where she grew up?" said Lu flatly. "Because I don't."

Zac hesitated. She had a point, as much as he hated to

admit it. But something about the way Aunt Merle and Rowena had spoken about it made him think there was more to it than that. There had to be.

But that wasn't the only strange piece of the puzzle they suddenly faced, and he said tentatively, "Did Mum ever mention her family to you? Or—visiting them?"

"No," said Lu, and he could tell by the way her voice shifted that the question had been bothering her, too. "Maybe they met up in New York."

It was the only time their mother had left Zac—to travel to New York City every August to sell her paintings. She was only ever gone for a week, but those were still some of the loneliest days of Zac's life. Or at least they had been, before he'd known what it was really like to live without her. "Maybe," he mumbled. "It still doesn't make sense. Why wouldn't she mention them? Why were they such a big secret?"

"Maybe they weren't," said Lu. "Maybe she just thought you could never visit, so there was no point bringing them up. Or maybe . . ." She was quiet for a moment. "You heard Rowena. Maybe they just didn't want us here."

"Aunt Merle does," he said. "Penelope—"

"It's pointless trying to figure this out," muttered Lu, turning on her side away from him. "Mum can't tell us anymore, if she was ever going to in the first place."

No, she couldn't tell them, but maybe the answers

were here somewhere—in this dusty old house, or out in the Wildewoods, which were real. The Wildewoods were *real*.

And answers and Wildewoods alike, Zac was determined to find them.

6

LU

LU WAS DREAMING.

In her dream, she was walking through the manor, down a maze of hallways with peeling wallpaper and cracks in the ceiling. She could smell the dampness and feel the cool drafts on her bare arms, and even though she knew it was a dream, it seemed as real as anything had in the month since her mother had died.

She wasn't sure what she was looking for, but something beckoned toward her, and her feet moved of their own accord—down the grand staircase and through another hallway, until she found a pair of double doors with a chain wrapped around the handles. With a trembling hand, she touched the padlock, and the restraints fell away as the door opened, revealing another wing of the manor. The east wing—the one with rooms Penelope said hadn't been explored in a century.

In her dream, Lu felt strangely calm as she strode down the long corridor, which was lined with windows covered in moth-eaten curtains that allowed streaks of sunlight to appear in the dusty air. A dozen doors were spaced evenly along the opposite wall, but she passed them with little thought. The one she wanted was at the end.

It was impossible to miss. An odd red glow emanated from around the edges, as if there was a bright light inside. Frowning, Lu touched the handle, expecting it to be hot, but it was ice-cold. The door creaked open, and inside—

The room was huge, four times the size of her living room back home. Bookcases lined one wall, full of leather-bound tomes that looked as if they hadn't been touched in decades, and on another hung dozens of old-fashioned weapons and instruments. But to her horror, mounted above them were the heads of hunted animals. Instead of bucks and bears, however, they were horses. Dappled horses, black horses, white horses—and every single one of them boasted a long horn in the middle of its forehead.

Not horses. *Unicorns.*

She should have been shocked, but her surprise felt muted. Somewhere in the back of her mind, her dream-self had been expecting this—looking for it, even. But why? She stepped cautiously into the room. An oddly shaped dinosaur skeleton was posed artfully on a raised platform toward the center, but it was unlike any dinosaur she'd ever seen, with a strangely flat and elongated muzzle and a pair of gigantic wings that stretched nearly halfway across the room. It looked, she thought, like the dragon in Zac's comic.

Nearby, several glass cases rested on tall pedestals, and at first Lu thought there were butterflies pinned inside. When she took a closer look, however, she realized the tiny winged creatures had humanlike bodies attached, and her insides constricted.

Fairies. Unicorns. Dragons. What *was* this place?

She turned around, desperate to leave, but the door had disappeared. In its place stood another pedestal, this one boasting a bird the size of an eagle. It had orange and red feathers and purple plumage nearly as long as Lu was tall, and its wings were spread as if to stop her, but it didn't move. And as Lu stared at the beautiful bird, its lifeless black eyes stared back. It, too, was a trophy.

An intense sadness washed over her, the same kind of sadness she felt whenever she thought about her mother. And before she could say or do anything else, the room dissolved, and she awoke with a start.

It was a dream, she told herself as she took in the shadows of her mother's childhood bedroom. Just a dream. Fairies and unicorns and dragons weren't real, after all, and there was no reason her heart should have been pounding and her body breaking out in a cold sweat underneath the light blanket.

But it was also the most realistic dream she'd ever had, and she was sure that if she went downstairs and found the chained doors, she would also find a room full of senseless murder and death.

The thought chilled her to her bones. It wasn't real, though—how could it be? Animals like that didn't exist. She was exhausted, and her subconscious had simply combined the manor with the drawing Zac had shown her on the plane. Just because her mind was playing tricks on her didn't mean she had to fall for them.

Knock, knock, knock.

The sharp rap of knuckles against the door made her jump, and as Lu bolted upright, she got tangled in the blankets and fell off the edge of the bed. Hitting the floor with a thud, she grunted, sharp pain piercing her elbow and hip. Terrific.

"Are you all right?" said a soft voice, and light flooded the room. Penelope stood in the doorway, her brow knit.

"Yeah," said Lu, more embarrassed than anything as she rubbed her elbow. "What time is it?"

"Just after seven," said Penelope, not appearing entirely convinced. "Dinner's ready, if you're hungry."

In the other bed across the room, Zac sat up and yawned, his dark hair a tangled mess. Lu ran her fingers through her own, hoping it wasn't that bad. She still couldn't shake the disturbingly vivid dream, but her stomach gurgled, and as much as she didn't want to be here, she did have to eat eventually. So, with some reluctance, she got ready for dinner.

As Penelope led them back down the grand staircase to the first level, Lu couldn't help but glance toward the corridor where the chained doors had been in her dream. They couldn't really be there, of course. That was impossible. But she couldn't stop herself from wondering, either.

The dining room turned out to be a long, vaulted gallery with large oil paintings of landscapes and old men hanging on the walls. Lu thought it might have been impressive once upon a time, but while it stretched across the entire width of the manor, with windows on opposite ends, it was almost entirely empty now.

Their footsteps echoed as she and Zac followed their cousin to the far end of the room, where Rowena sat at the head of an old wooden dinner table. Her nose was buried in a newspaper, and she glanced up only long enough to eye them reproachfully. Lu was relieved—she wasn't interested in being yelled at again.

Beside Rowena sat a gangly boy with auburn hair who looked a couple of years older than Lu and Zac. He had headphones on and was tapping his fingers to the beat of the music, and as they all approached, he scowled and slumped in his seat, somehow looking more miserable than Zac ever did.

"This is my brother, Oliver," said Penelope cheerfully. "He doesn't play well with others, so try not to take it too personally."

A nearby door swung open, and Aunt Merle appeared, carrying a large tray filled with platters of food. "Ah, just in time. I hope you're both hungry."

"Zac can't have gluten," said Lu automatically as the smell of grilled chicken and roasted vegetables wafted toward her. "Or fish, or nuts, or dairy. And I don't eat meat."

"Of course you don't," muttered Oliver. He toyed with the frayed edges of his cloth napkin and glowered at her. Lu had no idea what she had done to upset him, but before she could respond, Rowena set her newspaper down.

"We're aware of your brother's dietary restrictions, Tallulah. But I'm afraid if your vegetarianism is merely a choice—"

"We'll make it work," insisted Aunt Merle. "We have plenty of salad and vegetables for you tonight, and I'll be sure to adjust the menu accordingly in the future. I cook everything myself, so if anything seems questionable to you, Zacharias—"

"Zac," he muttered. "Everyone calls me Zac. And everyone calls her Lu."

Oliver let out a barking laugh. "Lu? Who would choose *Lu* over Tallulah?"

"Me," said Lu, her eyes narrowed and her face growing hot. "And since it's my name, not yours, I'm pretty sure no one cares what you think."

"Enough." Rowena slammed her hand down on the table, and the dishes clattered. They all lapsed into silence, and she took a deep breath, reining in her temper. "It's been a long day, and I have no intention of sitting here listening to you bicker. Oliver, hold your tongue. Tallulah, if you prefer Lu, then that's what we'll call you. The same goes for you, Zac."

"Thanks," said Zac quietly, staring at his plate.

For nearly a minute, no one said anything, while Aunt Merle served them one by one. "Where's Conrad?" she said as she put two drumsticks and a thigh on Zac's plate. At least, Lu noted, she didn't offer her any.

"Tending to an emergency with Alcor," said Rowena. "Won't make it back until well after dark."

"What a shame. He's your mother's brother," explained Aunt Merle, focusing on Lu and Zac. "I'm sure he's very excited to meet you both."

"There'll be plenty of time for that," said Rowena, stabbing her potatoes with more force than necessary. "You two—you'll do everything you're told, is that understood? Not a toe out of line. This forest is dangerous, and if you wander off, you'll be putting yourself at risk of serious injury."

"Yeah," said Oliver with a laugh that sounded suspiciously like a taunt. He held up his forearm, which bore three healing slashes. "You don't want to lose an eye. Or worse."

"Are those claw marks?" said Lu, her curiosity overriding her disdain for now. "What kind of animals do you raise?"

"We do not *raise* anything," said Rowena. "And we don't tell gruesome tales of our own incompetence at the table."

Before Oliver lowered his arm, Lu spotted another mark on his palm, strangely pale and half-hidden by his fingers. She couldn't make out the whole pattern, but it looked eerily familiar—like an ornate *W*. "Our mum had a scar like that," she said, confused. "Right beneath her thumb."

"Did she?" said Aunt Merle, and Zac also nodded. "A hazard of being in this family, I suppose. Oliver, do be a dear and hand me the salad."

As they passed the dishes around, Lu turned to Penelope. "If you don't raise animals, then do you have pets, or—"

"We care for the animals on our land," said Rowena shortly. "We do not *raise* them."

"What kind?" pressed Lu eagerly. "Can I help? I take

care of a feral cat colony back in Chicago, so I'm used to working with animals. I could feed them for you, or—"

"We don't take care of a *cat colony*," said Oliver, spitting out the words like they tasted bad. "We deal with animals that could actually kill—"

"No," said Rowena shortly, and though it was quick, Lu didn't miss the look of utter fury she gave Oliver. "We are not talking about this right now. Lu, you and Zac will stay in the shop with Merle, like we've already decided. And," she added loudly, over Lu's protest, "there will be no arguments. Shop. Manor. That's it."

The rest of dinner was a miserable affair, and Lu didn't say much, leaving Zac to answer Aunt Merle's and Penelope's constant barrage of questions. He didn't seem as unhappy as he had before, and she eyed him suspiciously over something the rest of them called "pudding," which was much more like soggy cake than anything found in a plastic cup. He seemed back to his normal brooding self, however, when he asked to use the phone after dinner.

"Who on earth could you be calling?" said Rowena as she stood and pushed in her chair.

"Our dad," he said, and Lu heard a hint of anxiety in his voice. "I want to make sure the plane—" He stopped. "I want to make sure he's okay."

"Of course he is," said Rowena dismissively. "There's no need to waste a call to check."

"It's their first night away from home," said Aunt Merle, wrapping her arm around Zac's shoulders. "If he wants to call, let him."

"It sets a bad precedent," said Rowena as her footsteps echoed throughout the otherwise empty dining hall. "I won't have him calling his father every night for a bedtime story."

Zac's expression crumpled, and for a moment, he looked like he might actually cry. Lu burned with protective fury. Though she'd never once used their mother's death as an excuse for anything—she'd even turned her homework in on time after the funeral—Lu glared at their great-aunt's retreating form.

"Our mum just died," she snarled. "And you're telling us we can't say good night to our dad?"

Rowena stopped and slowly turned, a single eyebrow raised on her weathered face. "He has the number to the house. If he wants to speak to you, he'll call."

As she exited the room, leaving Lu feeling like her entire body was engulfed in a bonfire of rage, Aunt Merle enveloped Zac in a hug. "If he hasn't contacted us by morning, I'll make sure to give him a ring," she murmured. "In the meantime, why don't you both go upstairs and get ready for bed? I'll be up shortly to tuck you in."

"You don't need to tuck us in," said Lu, striding angrily toward the foyer. "We're not babies."

"No, you're not," said Aunt Merle as she and Zac followed. "You'll be thirteen in October, won't you? That must be rather exciting."

Lu shrugged. "Not really." Celebrating their birthday would be pointless if she didn't have any friends left by the time they returned home.

Aunt Merle dropped them off at the bottom of the grand staircase, and as she bustled out of sight, Lu couldn't help but glance yet again down the corridor where the room in her dream had been. "Are you okay getting upstairs on your own?"

Zac gave her a withering look. "If you don't want Aunt Merle to baby us, then stop babying *me*. It's humiliating."

"If you actually remembered to take your medication like you're supposed to, I wouldn't have to," she shot back. "Did you even bring your inhaler to dinner?"

Zac said nothing, and instead he stormed up the steps, leaving her alone in the foyer. She considered going after him, but this might be her only chance to investigate without one of their great-aunts breathing down her neck. And so, taking care not to make any noise, she slipped across the foyer and toward the corridor that had been in her dream.

Though she hadn't seen this part of the manor that afternoon, the wallpaper and the furnishings were exactly what she'd dreamed, all down to a crooked portrait of a man with a handlebar mustache. How was that possible? Maybe her mind was playing tricks on her again, she reasoned as she edged down the hallway. She'd never had jet lag before. Maybe this was part of it.

But as she turned again, she saw them: the double doors with a chain wrapped around the handles. Her mouth fell open, and she looked around the empty corridor, half expecting someone—Oliver, probably—to be hiding nearby and snickering at her stupidity.

No one was there, though. She was completely alone— just her and the doors in her dream.

Tentatively she stepped forward. The chains were heavier than she expected, and when she tugged on the old-fashioned padlock, it didn't give way. Who had the key? And what were they trying to keep hidden?

Lu had a sinking feeling she already knew the answer. But even if she'd been right about the doors, that didn't mean the trophy room really existed. Maybe she'd seen pictures of this place in her mum's photo albums. Maybe she'd watched a movie they'd filmed here. Maybe, maybe, maybe.

But the more she tried to convince herself, the more disoriented she felt. She was exhausted, mentally and physically, and none of this made sense. She needed to sleep—*really* sleep instead of a nap interrupted by unsettling nightmares. Whatever lay beyond the double doors could wait.

On her way back, however, she heard voices floating

down the empty hall. And as she reached the base of the grand staircase once more, the voices grew louder, and she heard her brother's name come from an open door on the other side of the foyer.

". . . far too dangerous for Zacharias." This was Rowena's gruff voice, and she didn't seem to be making any attempt to whisper. "I don't know what their father was thinking, sending them here."

"He wasn't thinking," said another voice—this one unmistakably Aunt Merle's. "He's grieving, and he recognized that he is not fit to care for them in his current state."

"He has a responsibility to those children," sputtered Rowena. "He can't simply impose them upon the nearest unsuspecting relative."

"He did not *impose*. I offered," said Aunt Merle. "He was going to employ a nanny, Rowena. A *nanny*. What could possibly be worse for those children than having another caregiver appear in their lives at such a vulnerable time, only to disappear in six months or so? The poor lambs would be traumatized. They ought to be with family right now, and so they are."

Lu hadn't had a clue their dad was considering a nanny. The thought immediately sent prickles of resentment through her, but still, she would've preferred that over sending them to a foreign country for the summer.

"You can pretend all you want, but we both know the

real reason you invited them," said Rowena darkly. "You've doomed them."

"I've done no such thing," said Aunt Merle, sharper now. "Josie wanted them to visit."

"Josie had her head in the clouds," snapped Rowena. "She always saw good where there was none, and look what's happened because of it."

Aunt Merle tutted. "I understand your fear, love, and that is precisely why this was necessary. We only have so much time before their thirteenth birthday. Perhaps family legend is true, or perhaps it's nothing more than a story to frighten us all into obedience. Either way, as long as they are here, they are safe."

"Safe?" scoffed Rowena. "Is that what you call it? You don't understand, Merle. You couldn't possibly—"

"Don't you dare." Aunt Merle had gone dangerously quiet now—so quiet that Lu crept closer, using the winding banister for cover. "We both want what is best for the children. Out in the world, we have no idea what might happen to them. But here, on our land—"

Suddenly a door behind the staircase burst open, and footsteps thudded against the wooden floor. A man's voice cursed softly, and Lu crouched down, hoping he didn't spot her. "Merle? Rowena?"

"In here, Conrad," called Aunt Merle, and as Lu peeked out from her hiding spot, she saw a thin man with faded red-gold hair step inside the office. From the quick glimpse Lu caught, she thought she spotted a large desk and several chairs.

"Did you know about this?" demanded Rowena.

There was a slight pause, and the man exhaled. "I take it the twins arrived."

"So you did know," she said. "And yet you didn't think I should?"

"Well, Merle and I agreed—"

But at that moment, Lu felt a steel-toed boot dig into her hip, and she yelped. Looming above her, with his headphones hanging around his neck, was Oliver.

"Don't they teach you manners in America?" he said shortly.

Standing, Lu glared at him, her patience drastically dwarfed by all the questions swimming through her mind. "I guess rudeness must be a family trait," she snapped. "Are you going to rat me out?"

Oliver smirked, but there was no mirth behind it. "We'll see. For now, it's much more fun to watch you squirm."

With a huff, Lu dashed up the stairs, taking them two at a time to get away from him as quickly as possible. But as annoying as Oliver was, he was hardly her biggest worry right now.

What family legend was Aunt Merle talking about?

Why were they safe here? And why did Rowena think they were doomed?

She burst into the bedroom she shared with Zac, prepared to tell him all about it. But upon spotting his splotchy, tearstained face, she froze. "Are you okay?"

"I'm fine," said Zac in a choked voice, and he hastily turned toward the wall.

He wasn't fine, but she had no idea how to comfort him. And somehow, despite her eagerness and curiosity, she didn't think tales of legends and doom would help right now. Zac was enough of a mess as it was, and she couldn't bring herself to make it worse. Not until she understood what was going on.

"I'm taking a shower," she mumbled. And with her gaze averted, she grabbed her towel and pajamas and hurried out of the room, closing the door behind her.

7

ZAC

EVEN THOUGH ZAC HAD BARELY SLEPT ON THE journey to England, he spent most of that first night lying awake in bed, crying quietly and struggling against the weight of panic threatening to crush him.

His father was fine, he told himself over and over. Aunt Merle would know if the plane had crashed. It would have been on the news, and as the hours ticked by, he tried to convince himself that someone would have told them by now.

But what if it was something else? What if his father had had a heart attack running through the terminal to catch his flight? What if the plane malfunctioned, and no one knew because it was the small hours of the morning, and Aunt Merle and Rowena were fast asleep, and—

Zac clenched his jaw, his head swimming and his heart pounding. His father was *fine*. He was probably back in Chicago by now, sitting at his computer while eating a microwave dinner. Both of his parents would not die within a month of each other. The odds of that happening were astronomical, and it just—wouldn't.

Everything was fine. Everything was fine. Everything was *fine*.

As he repeated this mantra to himself, over and over again, a strange image appeared in his mind—a flash of a moss-covered forest, with golden light streaming through the branches of huge, ancient trees all around him.

He blinked and shook his head, momentarily startled out of his panic. What *was* that?

But when he closed his eyes, it was there again, sharper this time. He could smell a warm summer day and feel the heat of the sun on his skin, and when he looked down, he saw his sneakers planted firmly in the green underbrush, as if he were really there.

This was new, he thought wryly. Out of all the ways his mind had come up with to protect him from the worst of his anxiety, this was by far the most vivid. And, as he inhaled deeply, savoring the sensation of being outside and not being on the verge of a coughing fit, it was definitely his favorite.

But before he could figure out if this was a dream or a delusion, an all-too-familiar laugh echoed from behind him. His heart skipped a beat, and he spun around.

There, not ten feet away, stood a girl in profile, her head tilted upward as she stared at something in a tree that was three times as wide and far more gnarled than the ones surrounding it. She wore denim overalls with a dark braid hanging down her back, and though she was no more than eighteen years old, Zac would have recognized her anywhere.

It was his mother.

"You have to come down eventually," she called, her voice higher than he remembered. "Sulking won't change anything."

The only response Zac could hear was the faint ruffle of feathers, but she laughed again, and the sound of it filled him with warmth and longing.

"All right," she said. "You have five minutes to get it out of your system. After that, you're coming with me, and we're going to have a nice day together."

Shaking her head the way she had whenever Zac had said something amusing—or, more likely, ridiculous—she turned away from whatever was in the tree, looking straight at him instead. For a fraction of a second, their eyes met, and everything inside of Zac froze.

It was her. It was really her.

He blinked, and suddenly she was gone. The forest melted away, replaced by the shadows of her bedroom, and he stared at the ceiling, too stunned to move. After a moment, however, a sob bubbled up inside him, and he buried his face in his pillow as his body shook with grief.

It was a dream, that was all. Just a dream. It didn't feel like it, though—it had felt as real to him as lying in that bed, surrounded by darkness. But at long last, as his mother's laughter echoed in his mind, he managed to fall asleep.

The next morning Zac awoke to Aunt Merle's soft knock and the creak of the bedroom door opening. "Your father rang shortly before midnight," she announced. "He's back in Chicago, and he sends his love."

Zac pushed himself up onto his elbows. "He's okay?" he said groggily, and Aunt Merle nodded.

"Right as rain. Just busy with work, it seems, and he said he'll be out of contact for a few days, so you shouldn't worry. Now—up, up, both of you! Breakfast will be ready any minute."

Despite Zac's relief at knowing his father had made it home safely, he couldn't dredge up any enthusiasm about the day ahead. His eyes were scratchy, his entire body felt like it was made of lead, and he couldn't shake the dream he'd had the night before. As he and Lu went through their morning routine, he felt as if he were sleepwalking, with every part of him that mattered turned inward, grasping onto the sound of his mother's voice. He could have closed his eyes and stayed in that moment forever. It was all he'd wanted for a month—to see her one last time, to hear her one last time. And somehow, impossibly, he'd gotten his wish.

He had to fall back down to earth eventually, though, and after a breakfast of fruit and eggs that tasted fresher than any he'd ever had before, he and Lu joined Aunt Merle in her shop. Though it stood on the corner of the main road and the drive that led to the manor, Zac wasn't at all surprised he hadn't noticed it the day before. Half-hidden by overgrown wildflowers and forest that threatened to engulf it, the shop looked more like a rickety, abandoned cottage than anything worth visiting. Once they got close enough, however, Zac could make out the faded wooden sign above the door: GENUINE OTHER-WORLDLY ARTIFACTS AND ODDITIES.

It didn't exactly roll off the tongue, he thought, wheezing after the quarter-mile walk up the drive. As Aunt Merle unlocked the door and Lu bent to examine a ladybug sitting on a flower, he dug around in his backpack for his inhaler. His lungs were burning, and he wasn't sure if it was asthma or allergies. Probably an infuriating combination of both. It would be the mud icing on a dirt cake if he spent the entire summer in some tiny English hospital, far away from the nurses and doctors he knew so well.

"All right, dear?" said Aunt Merle as she wiggled her key in the door.

"I'll live," he mumbled after sucking in the medication that forced his lungs to relax. "Just—the walk was long."

"You'll get used to it," said Aunt Merle affectionately. "A bit of exercise will do you good. Get some color in those cheeks."

Yeah, because it was that easy, he thought miserably. But as Aunt Merle pushed open the door, his bitterness dissolved as he got his first glimpse inside the dimly lit shop. The narrow aisles were full of countless trinkets for tourists—colorful key chains, T-shirts and mugs with the shop name printed across the front, and yellowing guidebooks so old that Zac could picture the younger version of his mother flipping through the very same pages. And despite the name of the shop, he didn't see any genuine otherworldly artifacts or oddities.

But past the tourist trinkets and guidebooks, beyond the rows of snacks and hiking supplies, he spotted a large and well-kept display running along the back wall. Heavy velvet curtains framed the glass shelves, deep blue with silver sparkles that looked like the night sky, and it was so completely incongruent with the rest of the shop that as Aunt Merle fiddled with the antique cash register behind the counter, Zac couldn't resist slipping through the narrow aisles to see what was there.

At first glance, the items themselves seemed mostly mundane. A few throw pillows, some bracelets and necklaces made from small stones and shells, and prints of forest landscapes all lined the neat shelves, among other items. But the closer Zac looked, the stranger the eclectic collection became. In one handwoven basket was an assortment of oddly metallic rocks carved into perfect half circles. The colors ranged from midnight blue to iridescent pearl, but as interesting as they were, it was the handwritten label attached to the basket that caught his attention.

Ethically sourced Dragon Scales: £15

Zac blinked several times to make sure he was reading it right. Dragon scales? There was no such thing as dragons, of course, but still. Who would buy something like that?

"Unicorn hair? Are they serious?"

Lu's voice sounded from only inches to his right, and Zac jerked away, nearly colliding with a shelf full of souvenir towels. His sister peered into a basket full of shimmering thread, and he forced his muscles to unclench, relieved he wasn't the only one who thought this was a bunch of ridiculous nonsense.

"Weird, isn't it?" he muttered. "There are dragon scales

here too. And pillows stuffed with yeti fur. Paintings by centaurs. Bracelets made by mermaids—"

"They're rather proud of their art," said Aunt Merle from behind them, and this time Zac and Lu both jumped. "Or I expect they would be, if such creatures were real," she added, tapping the side of her nose.

"Do—do people actually buy this?" said Zac once he found his voice again. "Fake dragon scales and—and fairy flora?" There was a basket full of glass flowers, too, that were no bigger than the tip of his finger.

"Oh, it's what the shop's known for," she said pleasantly. "Genuine otherworldly artifacts and oddities. And as for whether our customers believe in their authenticity—well, I suppose that's up to them, isn't it?" she added with a wink. "Either way, such mythical items are quite rare, so of course we also sell more practical merchandise. We're a one-stop shop for everything a visitor to the Lake District might need."

Zac glanced at his sister, trying to catch her eye, but her expression was strangely distant as she flipped through the paintings. "This stuff—it's *cruel*," she sputtered, glaring at Aunt Merle. "You're making them work for you. It's—it's slave labor."

"What are you talking about?" said Zac, baffled. "None of this is real, Lu. It's all garbage."

She blinked, and for a moment, none of them moved.

"Of course," she finally mumbled, her shoulders sagging. "Sorry. I know it's all fake."

"Even if it wasn't," said Aunt Merle gently, "we would never take from those who were not willing to give. Though I will say quite honestly that I have never met a mythical creature, as much as I would love to. Now," she added, "why don't you two pick out some sweets from the front, and you can explore the rest of the shop?"

As Aunt Merle led them to a rack of candy, Zac watched his sister closely, alarmed by her outburst. Lu might have been a little weird, especially when it came to animals, but she knew none of that stuff was real. Why had she reacted like that?

Choosing a snack took longer than it should have, since none of them were familiar to Zac. He had to read each label for allergens, and by the time he'd finally found something he could eat—a pack of gummies full of odd shapes he couldn't identify—Lu had retreated to a small room in the back. With a mumbled thanks to his great-aunt, Zac hurried down the aisles to join her, relieved to be out of sight of those strange artifacts.

"You okay?" he said. But as he set his backpack down in the stuffy, too-warm room, a cloud of dust exploded in his face, and he sneezed.

"You shouldn't be in here," she said despondently from behind a splintering wooden desk. As if to prove her point, she ran a finger over one of the dozen file boxes stacked on the desk, leaving a trail in her wake. Zac shook his head.

"I'm not staying out there with Aunt Merle all day," he managed before another round of sneezes. His eyes began to water, and reluctantly he decided she was probably right. He was already starting to itch. "Just—wanted to make sure you're okay."

"I'm fine," she insisted. "Jet-lagged, I guess. And your comics and Mum's stories . . ." She shook her head. "I'm tired, that's all." She nodded to an old plastic telephone tucked between two piles of boxes. "I tried calling Sophia. The number doesn't work."

Zac's heart leaped at the sight of the phone, and he took half a step forward as he scratched his forearm. "Did you try—"

"Yeah, I tried Dad, too. It didn't work either." She turned away from him, but Zac could still see her rub her eyes. "Sophia was so mad when I told her we were leaving for the summer. If I don't talk to her, she'll never forgive me. And—besides, I need to know if the raccoon is okay. I took it to the emergency vet, but . . ." She grimaced. "And Rufus. I need to know that he's getting his medication. And the rest of the cat colony—"

Her cheeks flushed at the last part, and Zac remembered how mercilessly Oliver had teased her at dinner the evening before. Taking as deep a breath as he dared in that dusty back room, he said carefully, "You know, if you wanted to, we could sneak off and find the animals. They have to be somewhere, right?"

Lu turned toward him, seeming to forget for a moment that her eyes were rimmed with red. "You heard Rowena. We have to stay in the shop with Aunt Merle. And besides—"

She stopped herself suddenly and bit her lip. Zac frowned. "Besides what?"

"Nothing," she mumbled. "It's not safe."

He sniffed, his nose already stuffed. "We'll keep our distance. I can't get close, anyway. And if we're caught, what's Rowena going to do? Lock us up someplace worse than this?" Zac gestured around them. "This is about as miserable as miserable can get."

"Yeah, but—" Lu hesitated. "You're allergic to practically everything outside."

"I'm allergic to everything in here, too," he argued. "I'll wear a mask. I have my inhaler, I took my pills this morning, *and* I have two EpiPens in my backpack."

She looked him up and down, as if deciding whether or not he could handle it. Zac squared his shoulders, doing his best to look stronger than he'd felt in years, even with his eyes running and his skin red from hives. At last Lu sighed. "Why are you doing this? Is it because you feel sorry for me?"

He shook his head. "If the Wildewoods are real, then I

want to find them. And I can't do that without you."

A frown flickered across her face, and for one horrible moment, he thought she would say no. But instead she stood, brushing the dust off her shorts. "If we get caught, I'm throwing you to the wolves and saving myself."

He exhaled, his relief sharp in his chest. "Probably the smart thing to do," he said with a shrug. "I couldn't outrun them anyway."

A slow smile spread across Lu's face, chasing the shadows away, and he couldn't help but grin back. Their life might be in shambles right now, but at least he felt like his sister was on his side.

"Come on," he said. "Let's go find the Wildewoods."

8

LU

CROUCHED BEHIND A DISPLAY OF UMBRELLAS, LU peeked down the main aisle of the shop.

Aunt Merle was humming to herself as she read a battered paperback novel behind the cash register. She was only a few feet from the door, and if they tried to leave, she would spot them in an instant.

"I could cause a diversion," whispered Zac as he lingered behind Lu. "Pretend to need my inhaler or something."

She shook her head. "They don't understand how serious your asthma is. If you fake an attack now, they'll never believe you again."

"They will when I turn blue," he muttered, but Lu

ignored him. There had to be a way to get out without their great-aunt noticing.

Before she could come up with any brilliant plans that didn't include taking advantage of her brother's illnesses, however, the bell over the door rang, and a stocky man wearing a superhero T-shirt and flip-flops stepped nervously inside. He glanced around the shop, his eyes a bit too wide, and Aunt Merle set her book down, beaming.

"Good morning," she said. "How can I help you today?"

"I, uh . . . I heard you have some—rare items," he said, and to Lu's surprise, he was American. "You know . . ."

"Genuine otherworldly artifacts and oddities?" supplied Aunt Merle, and he nodded, scratching his stubble sheepishly. "You've come to the right place. Everything is just this way, if you'll follow me."

She hopped off her chair and led him up the aisle, heading straight for Lu. Scrambling around the corner, Lu managed to grab Zac's arm and pull him with her at the exact moment Aunt Merle and the customer passed the umbrellas.

"Our selection isn't terribly big," said their aunt as she reached the shelves framed by velvet curtains. "But authenticity is guaranteed."

Lu snorted softly and motioned for Zac to follow her. Together they crawled across the wooden floor, past the sunblock and guidebooks, and managed to reach the row of candy bars.

"Dragon scales?" said the man, his voice rising a few notches. "What are they really made of?"

"I'm afraid that's a trade secret," said Aunt Merle. "But they're impenetrable, and if you buy enough of them, they'll protect you from even the hottest of fires."

They were inches from the front door now, and Lu froze, eyeing the bell. It was attached to a long string, and if they didn't want to disturb it, they would have to be careful.

"Follow my lead," whispered Lu, and she slowly—very, *very* slowly—opened the door. The hinges squeaked softly, but to her relief, the man was in the middle of another question, this time about the so-called unicorn hair.

With her eyes glued to the bell, she managed to crack the door just wide enough to slip through. She held it open for Zac to follow, and once he had escaped, she gently closed it again, exhaling with relief when it quietly clicked shut.

Together they hurried back up the gravel drive, and Lu didn't speak until the shop was well out of sight. "I can't believe someone would actually buy that junk."

"They have to stay in business somehow," said Zac with a shrug. Lu made a face.

"I thought that's what the cheesy hats were for. Do you think she'll notice we're gone?"

"Not for a while. I closed the door to the back room, so she'll probably assume we're in there."

Pleased—and impressed, though she would never admit it—Lu led the way toward the wrought-iron gate, which Aunt Merle had left open. By the time the manor came into view, she could hear Zac's breathing grow labored, and she purposely slowed down. "Where do you think the Wildewoods are?"

"No idea," he said, wheezing faintly. "And stop babying me. I can walk just as fast as you can."

She doubted that, but she returned to her normal pace anyway, weaving between the trees that lined the drive. He managed to keep up, though when they passed the manor and ventured into the dappled emerald forest beyond the unkempt garden, he had to pause and put on a medical mask, the kind that kept out allergens and germs. He didn't wear them often, considering he barely ever stepped outside, and for once, Lu didn't tease him about it.

"You should go back in the house," she said, trying to hide her worry behind feigned annoyance. The trees and pollen couldn't possibly be good for him, despite what Aunt Merle seemed to think. "Go draw in Mum's room or something. They probably keep the animals in the Wildewoods, anyway, and you're undoubtedly allergic to them." And she couldn't stomach the thought of a repeat of the raccoon incident. There were no adults around this time to help if something really went wrong.

Zac scowled. "I thought we were doing this together," he said, his voice only slightly muffled by the mask.

"We are," said Lu. "But what if—"

She stopped suddenly as movement in the trees caught her attention. Pressing her finger to her lips, she crouched behind a large fallen log.

"What?" said Zac, annoyed, but as he twisted around to peer in the same direction, a familiar man with fading red-gold hair emerged from the trees. With a gasp, Zac dropped down beside her. "Who do you think—"

"*Shh.*" Lu craned her neck and watched as he walked into the forest and away from the manor, holding an old-fashioned black bag that looked like something doctors might've carried a hundred years ago. "That's Uncle Conrad, Mum's brother. I saw him talking to Aunt Merle and Rowena last night."

"You didn't tell me that," said Zac, a hint of hurt in his voice.

Lu shrugged. "You were—busy. I'll tell you about it later."

They watched as Conrad moved through the trees with the kind of stride that made it clear he knew where he was going. "Do you think he's headed to the Wildewoods?" said Zac.

"Only one way to find out." Lu rose and followed their uncle, doing her best to walk lightly through the lush late-spring undergrowth. Behind her, Zac wasn't nearly as quiet as she was, but Conrad was so far away that Lu hoped he wouldn't notice.

It wasn't long before she stumbled across a path so worn down by time and boot prints that it was nearly five feet wide. This wasn't the kind of path that was taken only once a week; this was the kind of path that led somewhere important.

"This has to be it," said Lu quietly. By now they'd lost sight of their uncle in the forest, but she didn't doubt for a moment that this was the direction he'd taken. The path headed away from the house, and they followed it as the manor disappeared into the trees completely, leaving Lu with a sense of unease. Zac walked beside her, wheezing audibly, as if he had a whistle buried in his chest. But every time she slowed down, he glared at her, and she swallowed her nerves.

Finally, just as she began to wonder if turning back might be the best thing for both of them, the path bent sharply toward a pair of strange trees. They looked older than the ones surrounding them, with their gnarled branches intertwined, making it impossible to tell where one tree began and the other ended.

"Whoa," said Zac as they approached the odd arch. "Have you ever seen anything like this before? Is this normal tree behavior?"

"I don't think so," said Lu, touching one of the trunks. It was warm from the sunlight streaming through the leaves. "Or at least I haven't seen anything like this in Chicago."

The path cut straight between the pair of ancient trees, and Lu passed underneath the arch, keeping an eye out for any sign of their uncle. As soon as she stepped through, however, the air around her seemed to change. The hairs on the back of her arms stood up, and somewhere above them, a strange, musical birdcall echoed through the forest.

"What *is* that?" said Zac as he ventured forward, squinting up into the canopy.

"I think it's a lark," said Lu distractedly, glancing around the woods. Nothing around them looked different, but a knot formed in her stomach, and every one of her senses was suddenly on high alert. Something wasn't right. She didn't know what, exactly, but she was sure of it.

"Do you think we're close to the Wildewoods?" said Zac from the path ahead of her, his wheezes easing now. But the Wildewoods were the furthest thing from Lu's mind at the moment, and as a breeze rustled the leaves, she shivered.

"We should go back," she said suddenly, looking over her shoulder through the tree arch. "There's nothing here. Maybe Conrad left the path, or maybe the Wildewoods are in another direction—"

"Lu." Zac's urgent tone cut through her, and she snapped her head back around to look at him. Her brother stood twenty feet away, staring at whatever lay beyond the curve in the path.

"What?" she said as she rushed forward to join him. "Did you find—"

She stopped, and her mouth fell open. Around the bend, the forest gave way to a large, sun-soaked meadow full of tall grass that rippled in the gentle wind. In the distance, beside a building that looked like a long yellow stable, was an enclosed pasture with half a dozen grazing horses.

Despite Lu's unease, she gasped in excitement. She'd never seen a horse up close before. Pictures, sure—and she loved books and movies about horses. But she'd never had the chance to touch one. Without a second thought, she darted through the knee-high grass and colorful wildflowers, heading straight for the pasture.

"Lu, wait," called Zac, and she slowed, though she didn't look back.

"I've always wanted to ride a horse," she said eagerly. "Do you think they'll let us? They'll have to, right? If we're stuck here all summer—"

"Lu . . ." Panting, Zac caught up to her and grabbed her elbow. "Those aren't horses."

"What are you talking about?" she said with a laugh. "Of course they're horses. Look—that's a dappled gray, and that one's a bay, and that's a chestnut and—"

But as the horse closest to the fence turned away, allowing her to see its profile, she stopped cold. Just like the hunting trophies in her strange dream the day before, these creatures looked like horses, but with one giant difference.

They too had long spiral horns set in the middle of their foreheads.

"They're not horses," repeated Zac, his grip tightening on her arm. "I think . . . I think they're unicorns."

9

ZAC

ZAC LEANED AGAINST A SPLINTERING RAIL FENCE, staring directly into the brown eyes of a unicorn.

Part of him could hardly believe it. There was no such thing as unicorns, after all, or at least that was what he'd told himself as he and Lu had approached the pasture, clinging to each other as if everything they were seeing might suddenly melt away and reveal itself to be one giant joke.

But now that he'd come face-to-face with a large black stallion with a sharp ebony horn nearly as long as Zac's arm, he couldn't deny it. His mother's family was hiding unicorns in their backyard.

"Maybe the horns aren't real," said Zac, his chest tight.

But it wasn't from an oncoming asthma attack this time. Instead his heart was pounding so hard that he was vaguely amazed he was still standing.

"Are *you* going to try to grab one to find out?" said Lu as she stroked the side of a dappled gray with a horn that seemed to be made of pure silver. "Besides, look at the white one over there—look at its mane."

Zac peered around the black male and spotted the unicorn Lu was talking about. It looked much more like the unicorns he'd drawn in *THE WILDEWOODS SAGA*—white, with a sparkling crystal horn and a mane that shimmered like tinsel in the sunlight.

Like the tinsel Aunt Merle sold in her shop.

"Lu," he said slowly. "If the unicorn hair is real, then . . ."

Their eyes met, and instantly he knew she was thinking exactly the same thing. He dug through his backpack with trembling hands, and once he'd pulled out his unfinished graphic novel, he flipped through the pages.

Unicorns. Dragons. Sea monsters. Fairies. Lu lingered over his shoulder, and for once he didn't mind.

"Do you think they're all real?" she said quietly, and he shook his head.

"I don't know what to think anymore."

Zac slid his sketchbook back into his bag, and the pair of them refocused on the pasture. "I had a nightmare about unicorns yesterday," said Lu suddenly. "Or—I guess it wasn't about unicorns, exactly. I dreamed I was wandering through the manor, and I found a room full of these horrible hunting trophies in the east wing. But instead of normal animals, they looked like . . . unicorns. And dragons. And fairies."

"It was just a dream," said Zac. There was a long, stitched-up laceration running along the black stallion's side, and judging by the lack of swelling, it was nearly healed.

"I went looking for it, though," she admitted. "After dinner last night. I knew the way there, and it was exactly like I'd dreamed. But the doors into the wing were chained shut, and I couldn't get past them. If that part was real . . ."

With a strange, thoughtful expression on her face, Lu headed toward the yellow stable. Muttering a curse, Zac tore himself away from the unicorns and followed her.

"Lu, if those creatures are real—"

"Then Mum was telling the truth," she finished for him. "Then the Wildewoods aren't just a name she borrowed. They're a real place."

"But that's impossible," he said. "If unicorns and dragons were real, wouldn't we know? Wouldn't the whole world know?"

She didn't answer. Instead she reached the stable door and pushed it open—so slowly it didn't even creak.

Zac wasn't sure what he was expecting—the inside of a dark and dusty unused barn, maybe. But it was a wide, clean facility that smelled like a mixture of hay and hospital, with bright lights overhead and a long row of stalls running across the length of the building.

His eyes began to water. "What—what is this—" he tried to say, but he finished with a loud sneeze.

"Shh!" Lu ducked down, as if she expected Uncle Conrad to pop around the corner at any moment. But there was no movement other than the impatient stamping of hooves somewhere deep within the building.

After a beat, however, another sneeze echoed from the opposite end of the stable. It was much softer and more high-pitched than Zac's, and he frowned, curious. Wiping his runny nose, he readjusted his mask and started down the aisle. "Come on," he said. "I want to see what's back here."

"Are you crazy?" hissed Lu. "You're already sneezing—"

"It's just hay," he said, and as if on cue, he sneezed again. "And I'm not wheezing anymore. Are you coming, or are you going to keep hiding?"

Lu straightened, her expression stony. "Since when have you ever wanted to do anything interesting or fun?" she muttered, but she followed him anyway, and he didn't bother responding. It was a valid question—he wasn't exactly brave most days. But the stories their mother had told them had kept him going during the worst of his attacks, during the hospital stays and endless doctor appointments and tests. During the days when Lu disappeared from dawn until dusk, playing outside with her friends while he was stuck at home, too sick to risk another attack. To discover that the Wildewoods were real—that their mother hadn't been making them up after all—was like getting a piece of her back. He felt closer to her here, knowing she must have walked down that wide path a million times, that she had been inside this stable. And he wanted to see as much of it as possible before they were caught.

Zac checked each stall as they passed, having to stand on his tiptoes to get a good look inside. Though most were empty, presumably homes for the unicorns in the pasture, when he peeked into a stall toward the end, he immediately staggered backward, stunned.

"What?" said Lu, and she too peeked into the stall. Rather than jumping back, however, she froze, clinging to the wooden half door.

"Has anyone ever told you it is rude to stare?" said a low, gruff voice. Lu didn't move. Zac crept back toward the stall, his hands shaking as he peered over the edge once more.

There, lying on a pile of fresh hay, was a man with thick red hair that continued to sprout all the way down his spine. His face was angular and his dark eyes narrowed as he glared at them, but that wasn't the part that scared Zac.

Past the man's torso, instead of having the lower half of a human, he had the body of a chestnut horse.

"You're—you're a centaur," gasped Zac.

"And you are a human," said the centaur. "A new one, from the looks of it."

"I—" Zac opened and shut his mouth, not knowing what to say. It was then that he noticed one of the centaur's back legs was wrapped in a splint. "Are—are you okay? Do you need help?"

That seemed to bring the centaur up short, and he shook his head, his hair—his mane?—falling limply into his eyes. "Conrad takes good care of me. It should not be long before I am back with my herd."

"Your herd?" squeaked Lu. "You mean there's more of you?"

"Ten score," said the centaur, raising his head proudly. "We are all that remains of what was once the most power-ful herd in Europe."

Zac had no idea how many ten score was, but it sounded like a lot. "And you just . . . hang out in Aunt Merle's back-yard?" he said weakly.

The centaur tilted his head. "You are kin to Merle and Rowena?"

"They're our great-aunts," Lu said. "I'm Lu, and this is my twin brother, Zac. We're from Chicago."

"I have heard of this place," said the centaur. "The humans have spoken of it in the past. It is where Josie, daughter of Alastair, migrated."

Zac felt as if a lightning bolt had struck him, and goose bumps appeared on his arms. "Josie was—she was our mum."

The centaur bowed his head. "I was sorry to hear of her passing. She was always a friend to our herd."

Zac had no idea what to say to that, but Lu managed a quiet, "Thanks." And after another beat, the centaur sighed.

"I am Alcor, son of Mizar," he said reluctantly, as if he were revealing information he was supposed to keep to himself. "When I am healed, should you be in need of a guide, it would be an honor to show you the Wildewoods."

"Really?" said Zac. "It's more than just this?"

"Much more," said Alcor with a hint of amusement. A hundred questions ran through Zac's mind—how big were the Wildewoods? How did they keep it hidden? Were there other species? Where did Alcor's herd live?

But before he could say a word, there was another sneeze at the end of the aisle, and Zac glanced around, trying to find the source. "What else is down there?" he asked the centaur.

"Only the nursery," said Alcor, stifling a yawn. "The others are all well enough to graze."

"We should probably let you rest," said Lu, releasing the half door. "It was nice to meet you, Alcor."

"It was an honor to meet you both, Lu and Zac of Chicago," he said with a bow of his head. And as the centaur settled down once more on his pile of hay, Zac waved goodbye and followed Lu toward the source of the sneezes, feeling faintly dizzy. Centaurs. Unicorns. What would they run into next?

That question answered itself as he turned the corner and nearly ran straight into a metal gate unlike anything else in the stable. Confused, he peered over the top into a large open area. Instead of hay and wood, however, it was full of rocks and sand, and within seconds, Zac understood why.

Scattered throughout the enclosure were reptiles the size of iguanas. Unlike iguanas, however, or any other lizards Zac had ever seen, these creatures were covered in tiny gemlike scales that glittered in the sunlight streaming through glass panels in the ceiling. And to Zac's astonishment, they each sported a pair of delicate membrane wings sprouting from their spines.

"Are those . . . ?" said Lu softly from beside him, and Zac could only nod.

Baby dragons.

A violet hatchling near the gate wriggled toward them, so small it didn't seem to know how to walk yet. Zac stared, sure this had to be another dream, when the little creature sneezed, and a spray of sparks exploded from its nostrils.

"Guess we know why this part isn't made of wood," said Lu faintly. The others seemed to notice their arrival too, and they stumbled over to join the violet one. There were maybe twenty in all, and a few shared the same coloring—siblings, Zac assumed—while the remaining dragons formed the rest of the rainbow. Some were ruby red, while others were emerald green, sky blue, or irides-cent white, and there was even a pair so black they would have been nothing more than shadows in the moonlight.

"Hey, little guy," said Zac, and he leaned over the gate, reaching out for the first violet hatchling. "You're cute."

"Don't do that!" cried Lu as the dragon sniffed his hand. "They could be venomous. Or bite your fingers off. You can't just pet a wild animal, Zac."

He stepped back reluctantly. "You do it all the time."

"No, I don't," she said. "I never try to pet the feral cats unless they approach me first. And I'm careful around other animals, because I know what they could do to me if I'm not. You've spent practically your whole life indoors, Zac. Listen to me when it comes to this stuff, all right?"

He scowled. "You can't keep bossing me around. You're not Mum."

"No, I'm not," she snapped, her voice colder now. "And I'd love to get to explore this place without worrying about you all the time, but I don't really have a choice, do I? Since you have absolutely no common sense."

"I do too," he said, his frown deepening. "Just because you got to play outside and hang out with cats doesn't make you—"

"Who's there?"

A voice echoed from the opposite end of the stable, startling them both into silence. Zac and Lu exchanged a panicked look, and after a moment, Zac dared to peek around the corner.

Near the entrance, holding his black bag, was Uncle Conrad.

10

LU

LU STOOD FROZEN BESIDE HER BROTHER, BARELY daring to breathe. There was no exit on this side of the stable, not without going through the dragon pit. And as cute as they were, she wasn't willing to take that chance.

"I heard you," called Conrad. "There's no use trying to hide. Penny? Oliver? You know you're not allowed in here without me."

Lu glanced at Zac, who stared back as if he expected her to tell him what to do next. But other than risk it with the dragons, there was only one way out: the truth. Maybe Rowena would lock them in their room for the rest of the summer, but she couldn't make them forget that unicorns and dragons and centaurs really existed.

As Lu stepped forward, prepared to reveal herself, however, another voice called out. "It is only me, Conrad," said Alcor the centaur, sounding more tired than he had before. "If you could spare a moment, the pain in my leg is quite intolerable. I believe the splint may be too tight."

"Oh." Their uncle shuffled across the hay-strewn floor, and Lu heard the squeak of hinges. "Let me take a look."

Lu peeked around the corner. Conrad was inside Alcor's stall now, and with the door closed, the path was clear. Gesturing for Zac to follow her, she crept up the aisle, ducking down so she wasn't visible.

The centaur grumbled something unintelligible as they passed his stall, and through the thin slats, Lu spotted Conrad crouched beside Alcor's injured leg, carefully removing the splint. After checking to make sure Zac was right behind her, she hurried as fast as she dared, her sneakers not making a sound on the concrete floor. Six stalls to go. Five, four, three—

"Achoo!"

Zac's thunderous sneeze echoed through the stable, and Lu froze.

"Who's there?" said Conrad immediately, and Lu didn't waste a second. Grabbing her brother's elbow, she pulled him toward the door, keeping him upright as he stumbled. As soon as they were outside, she tore across the meadow, heading for the forest. Somehow, miraculously, Zac managed to keep up with her, and they darted into the trees until she could no longer see the stable.

"That was close," she said, tucking her hair behind her ears. But though she had barely worked up a sweat, Zac dropped his backpack and eased down onto the mossy forest floor, his wheezes growing louder by the second. She hastily dug into his bag for his inhaler, and suddenly the run wasn't the only reason her heart was pounding.

But as soon as he tore off his medical mask and breathed in a couple of puffs, he began to relax. "That," he wheezed, "was *amazing*. Dragons! Baby dragons! Can you believe it?"

"No, I can't," said Lu as relief spread through her. She looked around. "We need to get you back to the manor. Aunt Merle will be looking for us soon, and—"

"I want to see more," said Zac instantly, and he struggled to his feet. "I'm okay. I promise I'm okay."

"You're not okay. We've been out here too long already, and we need to go back," she argued. "Look, you have hives from the dust and hay and who knows what else."

Zac checked his bare arms, looking surprised to see bright red rashes blossoming on his skin. "They'll go away," he insisted, still breathing heavier than Lu would've liked. "Come on, you know you want to see more—"

"Later," she promised, and it took an enormous

amount of willpower not to give in. Of course she wanted to see more. This place was *incredible*, but Zac was sick, and she was responsible for him. She was always responsible for him. "Do you think you can walk back now, or do you want to wait until it's easier to breathe? Do you need an EpiPen?"

As she searched his backpack for the EpiPens he'd supposedly brought, Zac didn't respond. Annoyed, she glared at him. But he wasn't paying attention to her anymore. Instead he stared at something beyond her, his mouth slack and his eyes wide.

"What?" she said as she spun around. "What do you—"

Her entire body went cold. Staring at them through the trees, no more than twenty feet away, was a violet dragon, exactly the same shade as the baby they'd seen in the nursery. Except this one was as tall as a house, with sharp spines lining its back and white smoke billowing from its nostrils with each breath. Somehow, Lu imagined more than sparks would appear if it had to sneeze.

"Don't say anything," she whispered, her heart in her throat as she slowly reached for her brother's hand. "Walk backward with me, one step at a time. No sudden movements, all right?"

Out of the corner of her eye, she saw Zac nod, and with enormous care, she moved her foot back. One step. Two steps.

But with the third step, her foot landed on a twig, and a loud *snap* echoed through the trees. The violet dragon snorted, lighting a small bush on fire, and it lumbered forward, flattening the fallen logs and underbrush in its path. Lu squeezed Zac's hand, and the two of them stood as still as statues, waiting for the dragon to move.

It stretched its neck out until its snout was only inches away from their faces. Zac began to tremble, his palm growing damp in hers, but Lu forced herself to stay as calm as possible. Maybe it could smell fear. Maybe it wouldn't attack if they didn't move.

The dragon sniffed the air suddenly, inhaling an enormous amount, as if it had stuck its nose in an exotic bouquet. Its emerald eyes went black, and a low growl emanated from its throat.

Lu swallowed.

The dragon raised its head toward the sky and roared, thunderous and loud enough to rattle her bones. Its black eyes focused on her and Zac again, and in an instant, Lu knew what was about to happen.

"No!" she shouted, shoving Zac out of the way. The two of them fell into a heap on the soft dirt as a plume of fire exploded from the dragon's snout, missing them by inches.

With her mind reeling, Lu tried to crawl away and drag her brother with her. It was their only chance at escape—

stay low to the ground and find a tree to hide behind, and hope like crazy the dragon lost interest. Why had they run into the forest? Why hadn't she led him back to the tree arch?

Why were their aunts keeping *dragons* in their backyard?

Zac felt like a wet sack of cement, and though she put all her strength into it, Lu could move him only a few inches. Had he been burned? She raised her head just enough to check him over, and she realized he was curled up in a ball. That wouldn't save him. They had to get out of there.

At that moment, however, a bright flash of gold lit up the sky, so vivid that it nearly blinded her. But as quickly as it had appeared, it vanished, and beside her, Zac cried out, hiding his face in the dirt.

Nearby, the dragon looked puzzled, as if it, too, had seen the golden flash. But instead of running away, as Lu had hoped it would, it seemed to shake off its confusion and refocus on them. And before Lu could shove Zac behind a large oak tree, the dragon opened its mouth again, and another plume of fire shot straight for them.

In that split second, Lu turned away, squeezing her eyes shut and throwing herself over her brother as if she could shield him from the flames. She didn't have time to wonder if it would hurt, or if she would see her mother again when it was over. She was frozen in time, her entire body braced for the sensation of being barbecued by a massive violet dragon.

But then, behind them, she heard a grunt and the muffled sound of fire hitting something solid. "Oh, no you don't, Surrey," said a rough voice. "Back with you now, girl—*back*."

Though trees and underbrush were burning and the smell of smoke saturated the air, Lu realized with vague shock that she hadn't been hurt at all. The soles of her sneakers seemed a little softer than usual, maybe, but otherwise, she was completely unharmed.

"Zac?" she said urgently, scrambling off him. "Are you—"

"I'm okay," he said, sitting up and rubbing the dirt from his cheek. "But I don't think Rowena is."

Lu whirled around. Their great-aunt's back was turned toward them as she drove the dragon into the trees with a massive shield. She was limping as she moved forward, however, and the protective leather that covered her shins was burned black and crisp.

"Rowena!" yelled a male voice—Conrad. *"Rowena!"*

"I'm over here," she called, calm as could be despite her legs being scorched by a gigantic dragon. "Surrey's trying to visit her hatchling again, and she found the twins instead."

"The twins?" Conrad burst from the trees, breathless and disheveled. "But—"

His face fell as soon as he caught sight of them, and at once Lu felt a rush of guilt. Usually when she got into trouble at home, it wasn't completely her fault. Sometimes she accidentally stayed out too late while taking care of Rufus, or occasionally her dad forgot she'd told him where she was going, and he panicked when he finally realized she wasn't home.

But this was entirely her and Zac's fault.

"I'm sorry," she squeaked. "We didn't know—we thought maybe you had horses, or—or sheep, or—"

"Enough," said Rowena sharply. "Surrey, go home."

Reluctantly, the dragon spread its enormous wings and rose into the sky, causing a gust of wind so strong that Lu nearly fell over. Amazed, she watched as the dragon flew away, until it had disappeared over the tops of the trees and into the blue sky.

"Are you children all right?" said Conrad, kneeling beside them and checking both Lu and Zac for injuries.

"I'm fine," insisted Lu, her voice still shaking. Now that Rowena and Conrad knew they were here, there was no point in delaying the inevitable. "Why are there dragons on your land? And unicorns? How do they even exist? And what about the centaur—"

"Rowena." Conrad's sharp voice interrupted her. He'd noticed Zac's rash, or so Lu thought. But as Rowena limped toward them, Lu spotted what Conrad had found—a white marking on the palm of her brother's hand, so bright it almost seemed like it was glowing.

"Were you burned?" said Lu, panic rising in her voice. If Zac was seriously injured or got an infection, their father would never forgive her.

"No," said Zac, frowning. "Look—it's exactly like Mum's scar. And you've got one too."

Startled, Lu turned up her palms. Just below her left thumb was a glowing *W*—the same *W* that her mum had had. And the same *W* she had noticed on Oliver at dinner the night before.

As Conrad reached for her, she saw the exact same white mark on his hand, and she snatched hers away. "What's going on?" she said. "How—"

Rowena grabbed her wrist none too gently and examined the marking. "Exactly what I told Merle would happen," she muttered. "You were doomed from the moment you set foot on these lands and triggered the curse. If you children had followed the rules—"

"Doomed?" said Zac, his voice cracking. "No one said anything about us being doomed. And what curse?"

"Curses aren't real, Zac," snapped Lu, even though the line between real and imaginary had just been blown to pieces.

"Curses are very real, and you had better accept that, because you've managed to stumble face-first into one," said Rowena, her voice rising with fury. "And nothing and no one—not even I or your father—can get you out of it."

"Rowena, what's done is done, and scaring them won't change anything," said Conrad, climbing to his feet. "Those burns on your legs look painful. Let's get you back to the house and treat them, and then we'll figure out what to do next."

"What do you *think* we have to do next?" Muttering to herself, Rowena limped into the trees. "Both of you, come with us. And try not to mess up the rest of your lives more than you already have."

Bewildered, Lu trailed after her. "We're sorry," she repeated. "We were just curious—"

"When I give you an order, I expect you to follow it," barked Rowena. "Now that you've proven yourselves incapable of behaving, you'll spend the rest of your holiday confined to the manor."

"What?" said Lu, hurrying to catch up to her. Despite her injuries, Rowena was moving astonishingly fast. "You can't—"

"I can do whatever I please, especially in my own home," she said. "The same can't be said for you two. Now pipe down and follow me, before you manage to get into a fight with another dragon. The next one might not be as nice as Surrey, and if you get yourselves fried to a crisp, I'm the one who will have to explain it to your father."

Stunned, Lu looked to her brother, but he was staring at the palm of his hand as they walked, oblivious to the rest of the world and the fate they now faced.

An entire summer locked in a dusty manor together, all while knowing dragons and unicorns were only a quarter of a mile away. Lu couldn't think of anything worse.

11

ZAC

ZAC NORMALLY DIDN'T BELIEVE IN CURSES. WHO did? Curses were for fairy tales, and they usually had to do with princesses and knights and evil witches.

And dragons. Which sort of made sense, all things considered.

But now that they knew dragons were real—and unicorns, and centaurs, and whatever else the Wildewoods were hiding—it didn't seem like such a huge leap to believe in curses, too, after he'd had a little time to process it all. And as he and his sister sat on opposite sides of their mother's old bedroom, he sketched the familiar symbol that had appeared on their palms, trying to make sense of it.

Inside the Wildewoods, it had been so white it had seemed to glow. But as soon as they had stepped through the strange tree arch on their way back to the manor, it had faded into something less supernatural and more like a pale scar. It was identical to their mother's, the same cursive *W* in the exact spot beneath his thumb, and he had no idea what it meant, or why it had appeared.

"Have you ever heard of anything like this happening before?" he said. Across the room, Lu shook her head, seemingly too baffled by everything that had happened that day to even pretend to be annoyed.

"Last night I overheard Aunt Merle and Rowena talking about a family legend," she admitted. "I didn't understand it, and I still don't, but—it had something to do with our thirteenth birthday. And . . . something about us being doomed."

There was that word again. Zac shivered. "We're not doomed. Dad would not have sent us to a place where anything bad could happen. Aunt Merle wouldn't have invited us if we were in danger."

Something strange flickered across Lu's face, but whatever it was, she didn't explain. "What kind of curse do you think Rowena was talking about?"

"I don't know. Whatever curse gave us these marks, I guess."

"Is there anything in your comic?" she pressed. "I mean, if the Wildewoods are real—"

"There's nothing in it about a curse," said Zac with a sigh. "I helped write it, remember? I'd know if there was."

"You should read it again," she insisted. "Or I can. Maybe there's something you missed."

"Trust me—Mum never mentioned a curse. Or that any of this was real. Or that her scar was contagious."

Lu said nothing for a long moment, and when she did speak, she sounded distant. "Can I read it anyway?"

Zac opened his mouth to refuse, but no sound came out. He hadn't shown anyone the graphic novel except his mother. He didn't have any friends in Chicago—how could he, when he was one wrong move away from an emergency-room visit at all times? And the thought of showing his sister had never occurred to him. Before, he'd been positive she would make fun of it, and he'd been working on the project for so long that he wasn't sure he could take it if she did.

On the other hand, the Wildewoods were real, and they were in this together. And they both needed as much information as they could possibly get.

"Just make sure you don't mess it up," he mumbled, and he fished through his backpack and pulled it out. She crossed the room, and Zac tried not to wince when she took it from him.

"I won't," she promised, opening to the first page. Her eyes scanned the drawings and text, and Zac had to look away, unable to take the tension. What if she hated it? What if she thought it was stupid?

A soft knock on the door startled both of them. It wasn't locked—they still had to use the bathroom, after all—but they'd been forbidden from joining the rest of the family for dinner, and Zac had a feeling that Rowena was the kind of person who didn't care if they went hungry. Still, with Lu distracted by the graphic novel, he hauled himself to his feet and went to open the door.

Penelope stood on the other side, holding a large covered tray that smelled delicious. She smiled at him tentatively, as if she wasn't sure whether he was mad at her. "I heard about what happened," she said quietly, almost in a whisper. "I thought you might be hungry."

At that exact moment, Zac's stomach let out a loud growl, and Penelope giggled. His face grew warm, and he stepped aside to give her enough room to enter. "Thanks," he said. "Lu gets cranky when she hasn't eaten."

"Me?" scoffed his sister, but her protest was halfhearted. And as Penelope set the tray down on the dresser and revealed two plates underneath the cover—one with pasta and a creamy tomato sauce, the other a medley of vegetables and beef in gravy—someone else slipped into the room.

Oliver.

"Well done on ruining the rest of your lives," he said, shutting the door behind him and leaning against it. "And on your first full day here, too. I'd be impressed if it wasn't all so idiotic."

"Oliver, stop it," snapped Penelope. Turning her attention back to Zac, she handed him his plate and added, "Aunt Merle made it all. Yours doesn't have any gluten, dairy, nuts, or . . ."

"Fish," finished Zac, though his appetite had suddenly vanished at Oliver's words. "What do you mean, ruined the rest of our lives?"

"You didn't ruin anything," said Penelope, glaring at her brother now. "It was going to happen no matter what. It just—happened early. Like it did for me."

"What happened early?" said Lu, eyeing Oliver warily from across the room. "We have no idea what's going on, so if you'd like to enlighten us, that would be great."

Oliver snorted, and though Penelope gave him a look that could have melted steel, he started in without hesitation. "I can't believe Aunt Josie never told you about the family curse."

"It isn't a curse," said Penelope as she brought Lu her plate. "It's a responsibility."

"Maybe for you," spat Oliver. "You didn't have a life back home. *I* did."

"Back home?" said Zac as he perched on the edge of his bed, his plate balanced on his lap. "I thought this was your home."

"We lived here until I was five and Oliver was seven, and our parents divorced," said Penelope, before her brother could grumble out a response. "Our mum moved to London and took us with her. We visited for holidays, of course, but we mostly grew up there."

"And I had friends there," muttered Oliver. "There were things to do, and we weren't stuck in the middle of nowhere."

Zac frowned, his dinner untouched. "Why did you have to move back? Did your mum lose custody?"

"Our mum's brilliant," said Oliver with a sneer. "Loads better than our dad, who's always out on the land and never sees us."

"What Oliver's trying to say is that none of us really had a choice," said Penelope, far more gently than her brother. "Our family's—special. We're caretakers of the Wildewoods."

Zac's mouth went dry, and he stared at his beef and vegetables. From the other side of the room, Lu said, "Our mum told us stories about this place growing up. We never knew they were real."

"Of course you didn't," said Penelope with a shrug. "Even if she'd told you they were, would you have believed her?"

Zac shook his head. He'd seen the dragon with his own eyes, and he still couldn't believe it. "What do you mean, we're caretakers?"

"That's what this means," said Oliver, thrusting his palm out toward both of them so they could see his matching mark. Penelope opened her hand too, revealing the same. "We don't get to choose anything about our lives. From the moment we turn thirteen, we're branded, and we have to—"

Penelope shushed him, and to Zac's surprise, he lapsed into silence. She hesitated. "It's all a secret, you know, so you can't tell anyone. If you do, Rowena will kill me. And you, too, probably."

"Even if we did tell someone, they wouldn't believe us," said Zac wryly, echoing Penelope. "But we won't."

"Promise," said Lu firmly. "We just want to know what's going on."

Penelope took a deep breath, as if preparing herself. "Whenever a member of our family turns thirteen, the *W* appears, marking them as a caretaker of the Wildewoods and all the creatures it protects."

Zac looked at his palm again. "The creatures that aren't supposed to exist?"

"They exist," muttered Oliver from his spot against the door. "They all bloody exist, and they're a nightmare."

"They are not a nightmare," said Penelope, scowling at her brother. "They need us. Our father studied to be a vet so he could help them," she added to Zac and Lu. "I want to do the same, once I take my exams."

"Yeah, we all know you love them," said Oliver, venom dripping from his voice. "Never mind the fact that—"

"If you're going to insist on interrupting me, then you can leave," said Penelope furiously. "This is hard enough as it is. They don't need your bitterness on top of everything."

They stared at each other for the better part of twenty tense seconds, but at last, Oliver turned on his heel and left, all but slamming the door behind him. Zac jumped, his plate nearly spilling out of his lap, and Penelope winced.

"I'm sorry about him," she said. "He didn't want to leave London. I don't really blame him, of course—we knew it was coming, but I think he believed that if he ignored it, things would be different for him. That he wouldn't have to go."

"Have to go?" said Lu, her brow knit with confusion. "What do you mean?"

Penelope shook her head, not quite meeting their eyes. "Our family has to take care of them. Otherwise, no one else will. They're the last living mythical creatures in the world, and the Wildewoods are their sanctuary. It's huge, of course, but it still isn't big enough to give them the space they would have in the natural world that would keep them safe from predators. Our job is mostly to do what we can to protect them from each other, and to keep the different species as separated as we can. The phoenix does most of the hard work, but we do day-to-day things. Everything we can, really, to help."

"Phoenixes?" said Zac. "They exist too?"

She pursed her lips. "Phoenix. Singular. He's the last one left in the entire world," she admitted. "His magic created the Wildewoods hundreds of years ago, when mythical creatures were being hunted to extinction."

"They were being hunted?" said Zac, and he glanced at his sister. She had gone pale. "Why? Who would do that?"

Penelope frowned. "Not many people even knew they really existed, but those who did . . . well, several of the creatures have magical properties. Dragon scales, for instance, are impenetrable, and phoenix blood can cure nearly anything. That's why he created the Wildewoods— to protect the remaining creatures from the outside world. Only those with a mark can enter, usually through the tree arch," she added. "There's another entrance at the north end of the Wildewoods, but it's in a dangerous area, and we never use it."

"We saw the tree arch," said Lu. "I mean, obviously, since we found the Wildewoods. But how do you keep it hidden?"

"The phoenix is the one who does it," said Penelope with a shrug. "His magic hides it somehow. I mean, it's there, of course, but it's also . . . not. You could walk around the tree arch and never end up inside the Wildewoods, even though it takes up the same space. And if someone without the mark walked through it, they still wouldn't be able to enter. No one outside of the family bloodline can visit the Wildewoods. I think that's why my mum divorced my dad. She thought we were all mad, since she couldn't see it for herself."

"Mad?" said Lu.

"Crazy," translated Zac. "Mum used to say you were mad sometimes, like when you started feeding those feral cats."

Lu threw one of her pillows at him, but it barely reached his feet. Zac started to throw it back, but a floorboard outside the room squeaked, and they all froze. A few seconds later, a nearby door opened and shut on creaky hinges, and Penelope sighed with relief.

"It's just Oliver," she whispered. "He hates it here, in case that wasn't already obvious. When he turned thirteen and the mark showed up, he threw a fit and tried to run away. But he knew he had to do it—we've both known since we were little. And instead of being separated for a couple of years, until I turned thirteen, I decided to go with him. That's why I got mine early—because I chose to enter the Wildewoods, just like you did."

Zac traced the mark on his palm. "I'm sorry about your parents," he said, and Lu nodded in agreement.

Penelope shrugged. "Most people who marry into the family leave eventually. It must drive *them* mad, living with a bunch of people who take care of mythical creatures every day. Aunt Merle's the only one who's stayed in the last few generations," she added. "But that's because she's happy in the shop."

"She never goes into the Wildewoods?" said Zac, taken aback.

"She can't," said Penelope. "She's not part of the bloodline—she's married to Aunt Rowena."

"Oh. Dad acted like she was—you know, a blood relative."

"She's been in the family for so long she might as well be," said Penelope. "She knows as much about the Wildewoods as Rowena. She just can't go inside."

Zac frowned. He couldn't imagine knowing all those creatures were real, and yet never getting to see one for himself. No wonder Aunt Merle loved the shop so much. Those bits and pieces of the Wildewoods were the only parts she ever got to experience.

"What about our grandparents?" said Lu. "I mean— what happened to them?"

Penelope went quiet for a long moment. "Grandpa Alastair was Aunt Rowena's brother," she said at last. "He had an accident in the mountains when I was eight. No one ever told me what happened."

Goose bumps appeared on Zac's arms. It was all too easy to imagine what could have happened to their grandfather. "And our grandma?"

"She left too," said Penelope. "When your mum and my dad were kids. Like I said, most people who marry into the family do. Sometimes they visit," she added. "I usually see my mum for Christmases and birthdays. But mostly when they're gone, they're gone."

"Except Aunt Merle," said Zac, and Penelope nodded.

"Sometimes it works out. I'd hate to see what Rowena would be like without her."

So would Zac. He finally took a bite of his dinner, his appetite only partially returned. "I bet the phoenix is the bird we heard when we entered the Wildewoods," he said to his sister. "The one you thought was a lark."

Penelope looked puzzled. "I'm not saying you're wrong, but . . . the phoenix hasn't been spotted by anyone in our family in almost twenty years," she said. "Aunt Josie was the last person who had any contact with it."

The dream Zac had had the night before flashed through his mind, and he thought of the unseen creature his mother had been speaking to. "They were friends, weren't they?"

Penelope blinked, startled. "How did you know that?"

Zac's cheeks grew warm. "Our mum told us," he lied. "I mean—in her stories. It sounded like they were friendly."

"I don't remember her mentioning a phoenix," said

Lu, glancing at his graphic novel again. Zac hastily tried to change the subject.

"Do you think Rowena will change her mind and let us go back?"

"I don't know," admitted Penelope. "She's stubborn, but it's silly not to let you return with supervision. I mean, Oliver and I work in the Wildewoods almost every day. We even—"

Before she could finish, there was another series of creaks in the hallway, and this time another door opened. Penelope paled.

"I need to go," she whispered. "I'll bring you breakfast tomorrow, all right?"

"But—" protested Zac, before another, much louder squeak sounded directly outside their room. And as all three of them stared, the door creaked open, revealing Aunt Merle on the other side.

"Rowena's on her way up, and she's in a foul mood," she warned. Penelope shot Zac and Lu an apologetic look before hurrying to join Aunt Merle, and they disappeared into the hallway. Zac heard several more creaking footsteps and protesting hinges, but at last the noise quieted.

"Can you believe this?" said Lu. "I mean—can you *really* believe this?"

Zac shook his head. "Why didn't Mum ever tell us about this place?"

"She wanted to," said Lu. "Or at least that's what Aunt Merle said yesterday. I guess she was saving it for when we turned thirteen. Maybe she thought we'd know how to scare off dragons by then."

Zac fell silent, focusing on his dinner. As cool as it was, knowing that all those creatures existed, he couldn't ignore the fact that they'd nearly died that morning. If Rowena hadn't been there . . .

He swallowed hard and set down his fork. Lu had thrown herself in front of the dragon to try to protect him. She would do it again, he realized, if they went back. Even if they were careful, eventually their luck would run out, and no matter how cool dragons and unicorns were, he couldn't lose his sister.

"Maybe it isn't such a bad thing we're stuck in the manor for the rest of the summer," said Zac with all the nonchalance he could muster. "At least we won't run into any dragons out here."

"Maybe," echoed Lu distantly. But she set her plate aside, and for the rest of the evening, she hungrily pored through his graphic novel, searching for clues he knew weren't there.

Whatever happened—no matter how dangerous the Wildewoods were—they were marked now. And no one, not even Rowena, could change that.

12

LU

LU AWOKE SUDDENLY TO THE LOUD RAP OF KNUCKLES against their door. She'd been in the middle of a dream— the same one she'd had their first day in the manor. This time, however, even though she knew what she would find in that abandoned wing, every door she opened led straight to the trophy room.

The knock sounded again. On the other side of the room, Zac mumbled something unintelligible, and without waiting for permission, Oliver burst inside, fully dressed in protective leather gear much like the kind Rowena had worn the day before.

"Get up," he announced, turning on the light. "Rowena wants to talk to you."

It was still so early that the sun had barely peeked over the horizon, and Lu groaned. "I promise we won't leave the manor," she mumbled into her pillow. "Just let us sleep."

"Not an option." He marched over and tugged her blanket off. Yelping, Lu sat straight up, and Oliver repeated the process with Zac. "You have five minutes."

As Oliver left, Lu seriously considered going back to sleep, but their cousin had taken the blankets with him. Muttering a few nasty words under her breath, she dressed and brushed her teeth, and together she and Zac trudged down to the foyer, where Rowena sat in a moth-eaten velvet chair, her legs wrapped in thick white bandages.

"The damage is done," announced Rowena without greeting. "You're marked, and there's nothing we can do about it now. So you might as well be put to work."

"Work?" said Zac uneasily, while Lu immediately perked up.

"We get to go back?"

"You do," said Aunt Merle, who bustled into the foyer with a bundle of clothing in her arms. "I've found some overalls in your size, and some wellies that ought to fit."

As Aunt Merle dropped two pairs of rubber boots in front of them, Oliver leaned against the wall with his hands in his pockets, wearing a sizable smirk.

"Since I'm unable to handle my duties in the mountains today, Oliver will take over for me," said Rowena with a sniff, clearly not happy about acknowledging the extent of her burns. "And you two will take over for Oliver."

Lu eyed the khaki overalls, her stomach sinking. There was only one reason Oliver would look so smug about it, and that was—

"Poo," he said, grinning from ear to ear. "You get to clean up poo."

Mucking stalls was much more difficult than Lu had imagined. Not that she'd ever really thought about it, but now that she had managed to clean out two stalls and fill them with fresh hay, her muscles ached, and she desperately needed something to drink.

When she neared the exit, where she'd stashed a refillable water bottle, she noticed Zac lingering in the doorway, his mask in his hand as he stuck his head outside. Tears streamed down his cheeks, and his skin was so red that it hurt Lu just to look at it.

"Zac really can't be in here," she called to Conrad, who was in a stall nearby, tending to the black unicorn with a gash in its side. "He's allergic to hay, and to dust, and—"

"Yes, yes, I can see that," said Conrad, frowning. He exited the stall nearest the door and stepped over to examine Zac.

"I took a Benadryl already," said Zac with a giant sniff. "It's not much better out here."

"There is quite a bit of pollen outside today," admitted Conrad, and he sighed. "Well, Rowena might grumble about dodged duties, but we could send you back to the manor—"

"No!" Zac shook his head and wiped his nose on his shirt. "I can stay. Please."

Conrad didn't seem convinced, and the lines around his eyes deepened as he squinted. "You wouldn't happen to be allergic to dragons, would you? The little tykes love a bit of attention."

"I—I don't know," said Zac honestly. "Other than yesterday, I've never really run into one."

Conrad chuckled. "No, I suppose you wouldn't have, would you?"

Lu set aside her rake and joined them. "Little tykes?" she said. "You mean the babies?"

"Indeed," said Conrad. "I usually try to play with them when I can, but it's been busy here lately, and I'm afraid the poor things have felt rather neglected."

"Why are they here, anyway?" said Lu. "Don't they have parents?"

"They do," said Conrad. "Surrey, the dragon you, er, met yesterday—she's mother to one of the hatchlings. She and her mate, Devon, spend a great deal of time lurking nearby, hoping for a glimpse of their baby. They're hiding near the pasture now, if you take a look."

Lu peered outside, and though it took her a moment, she finally spotted two violet dragons hidden among the cluster of trees beyond the unicorns. Despite the fact that Surrey had tried to burn them to ash the day before, Lu couldn't help but feel sorry for her and her mate.

"Whoa," said Zac quietly. Apparently he'd found them too.

"Why can't their hatchling stay with them?" said Lu, turning back to their uncle.

"The mountains are dangerous, with so many dragon breeds living in such close proximity," explained Conrad. "Before the Wildewoods were created, they had the entire world to roam and make their own, but here . . . well, long-term survival for the hatchlings is much more difficult. Their numbers were dwindling, and when I returned after university, I decided to set up the nursery for them. They remain here for the first six months or so, until they're able to fly on their own and defend themselves, which is when they return to their parents. That's part of what Rowena does in the mountains," he added. "She looks for eggs and hatchlings."

Zac sneezed so loudly that the black unicorn stamped his hooves nervously. "I'd like to play with them," he said with a sniffle. "I'll be careful."

"Of course," said Conrad. "So long as you're not allergic to them, too, I think that would do you both some good. Come with me—I've got protective gear so you won't get burned."

As Zac followed their uncle eagerly through the stable, Lu trailed after them, wondering if it was even possible to be allergic to dragons. Animal dander she could understand, but she was sure Zac had never been around reptiles before. And as Conrad dressed Zac in long gloves covered in what looked like real dragon scales, as well as an apron made of the same material, Lu dug through his backpack for an EpiPen, just in case.

"Your mum loved the hatchlings too," said Conrad, a bit misty-eyed. "It always horrified her, what the babies went through to survive. She used to come to me when we were younger, crying her eyes out, and nothing anyone said or did could comfort her. She's the real reason I built this place, you know. And we've been saving the hatchlings' lives ever since." He hesitated, tying the apron string securely around Zac's waist. "I'm very sorry I couldn't make it for the funeral. I miss her every day."

"She would've wanted you to stay here and take care of the animals," said Lu, absolutely sure of that. "You did the right thing."

Conrad wiped his eyes, and with a quick sniff, he seemed to collect himself again. "Yes, well. One must always try. Now, Zac, I can't promise your clothing won't smolder a bit, but fingers crossed you won't get burned."

"Burned?" Horrified, Lu turned to her brother. "Zac—"

"Can't stop me, Lu," he said firmly, and slipping away from Conrad, he darted into the enclosure.

Lu rushed forward to watch. Zac waded into the center as the hatchlings scampered toward him, a kaleidoscope of colors. At first Lu held her breath, certain Zac was about to get bitten or catch fire or any number of terrible things she was sure could happen when baby dragons were involved. But though the hatchlings swarmed him, some even climbing his overalls, they were far more like eager puppies than dangerous fire-breathing creatures. In fact, a violet dragon much like the pair outside perched on Zac's shoulder, nuzzling his cheek and purring.

"See? Nothing to worry about. He's perfectly all right," said Conrad. "I'll be tending to Zeus if you need anything. When your brother's ready to come out, have him throw a handful of the treats stored in the apron, and the hatchlings will scatter."

Lu nodded, her eyes glued to her brother. Conrad returned to the stalls, and as soon as his footsteps faded, she pulled on another set of protective gear and slipped through the gate, keeping to the edge of the nursery. Unlike her brother, *she* had a healthy respect for wild animals, especially ones that could breathe fire. But her cautiousness didn't seem to deter them, and as soon as the hatchlings spotted another person in their enclosure, several of them broke away from the crowd and came to join her.

"This is awesome," said Zac with a laugh, petting an emerald-green baby that had replaced the violet hatchling on his shoulder. Several of the dragons began to climb Lu's leg, and she winced as their claws dug through her thick overalls, just shy of cutting into her skin.

"Yeah, it is," she agreed with a widening grin as an iridescent white one leaped from her hips to her shoulder. It too began to purr as it headbutted her cheek like a kitten. A scaly, reptilian kitten with wings and very sharp teeth.

"Is Conrad still around?" said Zac, and she shook her head, trying to reposition a shimmering blue baby so its talons weren't digging into her arm. The little creature clung on for dear life, but eventually she managed to loosen its grip and set it beside the white one.

"He's with the unicorn," she said. "Whose name is Zeus, by the way."

"That's the coolest name I've ever heard." Zac untangled a little red dragon from his apron strings, and when he looked back up at her, he froze. "Uh, Lu—where's that dragon going?"

"What dragon?" she said, but as she twisted around, horror washed over her. The violet hatchling was balancing on the edge of the gate only a few inches away, peering out into the open stable.

Moving slowly, so she wouldn't startle it, she dug into her apron pocket for a handful of brown pellets. The other hatchlings immediately began to swarm her, excitedly exhaling sparks from their tiny snouts, but as she tossed them toward the center of the pen, the violet hatchling didn't even seem to notice. Instead, after a cursory glance at the others, it took a giant leap off the barrier and landed on the concrete floor.

With a muttered curse, Lu tried to open the gate, but several more hatchlings had reattached themselves to her overalls, no doubt expecting more treats. And as she watched, the little violet dragon scurried around the corner, toward the stalls and the open stable door.

Terrific.

"Throw all your treats to the other side of the pen," said Lu urgently to her brother, who was staring at her with wide, watering eyes. "It'll give us time to escape."

Zac hesitated for only a moment, and together they threw the entire contents of their aprons into the opposite corner. Every single hatchling made a beeline for the unexpected feast, and as they climbed over each other, hissing and sparking, Lu opened the gate, waiting for Zac to slip through before she followed and shut it firmly behind her.

"Come on," she called as she darted around the corner and down the aisle. The violet hatchling was nearly at the door already, its claws skittering on the floor as it scrambled for freedom.

"What's going on?" said Conrad, sticking his head out of Zeus's stall.

"Uh—nothing," she said frantically. "Just, you know—getting some fresh air."

She sprinted past him and reached the door in time to see the violet hatchling disappear into the meadow. "There," she said as her brother caught up to her, breathing heavily. "It's headed for the forest."

"I'll go the other way and try to catch it," he wheezed, clutching the strap of his backpack. He couldn't run very quickly, though, and Lu knew that if they were going to save the hatchling, it would be up to her.

She raced through the wildflowers, her eyes trained on the knee-high grass for any sign of the dragon. Each time she saw a flash of violet scales, she leaped toward the baby, only to miss it by inches. It was playing with her.

But they had nearly reached the trees now, she realized. Just a few more yards, and—

"Watch out!"

Zac appeared out of nowhere, launching himself directly at the hatchling. Lu skidded out of the way, narrowly avoiding a direct collision, and in those few precious seconds, the dragon froze, allowing Zac to scoop it up with his thick gloves.

"Gotcha!" he cried triumphantly, grasping the baby dragon gently in his hands. It squirmed and huffed tiny clouds of smoke, clearly agitated to have lost the game.

Lu let out a sigh of relief. That had been terrifyingly close. "Let's get it back to the nursery before it escapes again," she said. "Do you think you can hold on to it, or do you want me to—"

She stopped suddenly, cold dread washing over her. Zac was staring at something over her shoulder, all the color drained from his face as a low growl echoed behind her. And though every nerve in her body screamed at her to run, she turned slowly, knowing all too well what she would find.

There, her head hovering only a few inches from Lu's face, was Surrey.

13

ZAC

ZAC'S LUNGS BURNED AS HE HELD HIS BREATH, NOT daring to move a muscle.

As Surrey hovered near his sister, a second violet dragon appeared at the edge of the forest, somehow even bigger than the first, with red scales placed above its narrowed eyes like eyebrows. As it took in the sight of the hatchling clutched in Zac's hands, it too growled, sounding like an entire pack of wolves.

"You must be Devon," said Zac shakily, and he released his grip on the hatchling. Immediately it scrambled up his arm and onto his shoulder. "I'm Zac. This is Lu. And—and I think this is your hatchling."

Time seemed to stand still as Zac waited for the dragons to do something—anything, even if it meant flame-broiling both him and Lu. Devon's hot breath singed the hair on his bare arms, and he shut his eyes, his heart pounding.

He'd been close to death several times in his life. Sometimes it was a bad asthma attack. Other times, like last summer, he'd been stung by a wasp and had gone into anaphylactic shock. And then there was the time he'd accidentally taken a bite of a fish stick and his throat had closed up on him before he could even swallow it.

But death by dragon was new. At least it was a better story than an asthma attack.

At long last, the hatchling on his shoulder sneezed, and sparks flew from its snout, burning a small hole in Zac's shirt. Devon whuffed in response, and the hatchling made a strange chirping sound. To Zac's amazement, the baby dragon scrambled to the ground and leaped onto its sire's enormous talons, wriggling eagerly in greeting.

As Surrey and Devon dipped their heads to nuzzle their hatchling, Zac shot his sister a shaky grin, though his chest was painfully tight. "Still alive," he said weakly, reaching into his backpack for his inhaler.

"Barely," she said, sounding as breathless as he felt. "I can't believe I didn't realize I was standing so close to the nursery barrier."

"It's not your fault," said Zac. "You didn't mean for it to happen."

But the stricken look on Lu's face made it clear that she wouldn't be consoled, not about this. "What are we supposed to do now?" she said uncertainly. "Leave it here?"

"Well, that wouldn't be ideal," said another voice.

Zac whirled around. Their uncle stood ten feet away, holding a bucket of something that looked disturbingly like fresh meat. "We can explain," Zac said hastily.

"No need. This isn't the first time a hatchling's escaped," said Conrad, and he moved slowly toward them. Surrey froze in place, her nostrils flaring as she corralled her baby underneath her protectively, while Devon spread his impressive wings and thick white smoke began to pour out of his snout.

"It's all right," said Conrad in a strangely soothing voice. "You know who I am. You know why your little darling can't stay here with you."

Slowly the smoke began to dissipate, and Devon snorted, folding his wings once more. Zac took a nervous step back, but Conrad gestured for them to stay put.

"No sudden movements," he said. "They're friendly, but when they believe their hatchling is being threatened, all bets are off."

"This is what you call friendly?" said Lu through clenched teeth. Zac just gulped.

"Here you are, little one," said Conrad, and he dropped a few of the brown pellets at his feet. The hatchling immediately peeked out from behind its mother's talons, and though Surrey let out a rumble in protest, the baby dragon scrambled toward the snacks.

"Do you want me to grab it?" said Zac, and without breaking eye contact with Surrey, Conrad shook his head.

"Devon and Surrey haven't had their treats yet." Reaching into the bucket, he tossed a rack of raw meat between the adult dragons, and then another. Devon turned away first, sniffing the offering before gobbling it up in single gut-wrenching crunch. Conrad threw a few more slabs, and finally Surrey twisted around as well.

"Now," said Conrad quietly, and Zac grabbed the happy hatchling, making sure to scoop up a few extra treats. With Surrey and Devon still munching on their meal, Conrad hastily shepherded the twins back across the meadow, and for once, Zac didn't have to be told to walk faster.

"Surrey and Devon won't eat us alive next time they see us, will they?" he said nervously. "For taking the hatchling away again."

"There's no need to worry," said Conrad. "If they truly wanted to, they could tear the roof off the nursery in seconds. But dragons are far more intelligent than you might think, and they understand what the nursery is for. They will be reunited in the autumn, once their hatchling can join them in flight."

Somehow Zac didn't find that terribly comforting, but he nodded anyway. "We don't have to tell Rowena about this, do we?"

Conrad chuckled. "I'd rather keep my head, if it's all the same to you."

As they approached the pasture, Zac spotted Oliver leaning against the railing, feeding the unicorns apples. "Did they let hatchlings out?" said their cousin, sounding mildly amused.

"I recall the same thing happening to you more than once," said Conrad. "You're back earlier than I expected."

Oliver rolled his eyes. "One of the centaurs said there's an emergency at the pond. They insisted I come and get you."

"Very well," said Conrad with a heavy sigh. "We'll be along shortly."

Once Zac returned the violet hatchling to the nursery, where it quickly started a play-fight over a few crumbs of remaining pellets, Conrad helped him and Lu out of their protective gear, which Zac was all too happy to shed. And after Conrad grabbed his black medical bag from Zeus's stall, he led them out of the stable and back to the pasture.

"Zac and Lu will be coming with us," said their uncle,

as Oliver hopped off the fence. "It would be good for them to see more of the Wildewoods."

"How big is this place, anyway?" said Zac, scratching a hive on his arm. At least they were starting to go down a little.

"Big enough," muttered Oliver. "Dad, you know this is probably just another hangnail, right?"

"If it is, I'll bandage her up and we'll be on our way back soon enough," said Conrad, leading them down a wide path. "And if it isn't, then we'll be glad we made the trip, won't we?"

"What's at the pond?" said Lu, perking up at the prospect of meeting another kind of creature.

Their uncle chuckled. "You'll see," he said as they headed into the forest. Lu didn't exactly seem satisfied with the response, but she didn't press, either. Considering Conrad hadn't immediately sent them back to the manor after the hatchling incident, Zac couldn't blame her for not wanting to push their luck.

But as they hiked through the woods, Zac began to fall behind, his lungs laboring despite the dose he'd taken from his inhaler not half an hour earlier. His body wasn't used to this kind of physical activity. Most days he spent holed up in his room, and a single flight of stairs could easily wind him. Eventually, panting, he stopped and leaned against a tree, trying to catch his breath.

"Hold on," called Lu to the others, and she jogged to his side. "Do you need your inhaler?"

He shook his head. "Already used it," he managed. "I just need—to rest a minute."

Conrad hurried to join them, and he insisted on listening to Zac's lungs, as if that would somehow help. Oliver lingered farther up the trail, his hands shoved into his pockets and his expression sour.

"Maybe I should go ahead," he called. "Let you know if it's worth the trip."

"Even if it's just a scratch, you know they'll want me there," said Conrad with a sigh. "Perhaps you could escort Zac back to the manor—"

"No," said Zac with as much force as he could muster. "I'm okay. Just—go slower, all right?"

Conrad seemed dubious, but he wrapped his arm around Zac's shoulders and let him set the pace. Lu walked only a few yards ahead of them, and she glanced back anxiously every twenty feet or so. Finally, after her umpteenth worried look, he couldn't take it anymore.

"Will you stop acting like I'm about to pass out?" he said, exasperated.

"Excuse me for caring," she muttered, though she faced forward once more, much to Zac's relief. While he still struggled to catch his breath, moving at a slower pace really did make the hike easier.

"It's not much farther now," said their uncle, nodding ahead. "We'll cross the stream just around that bend, and the pond is only a quarter of a mile or so beyond."

Quarter of a mile probably seemed easy to Conrad, but it might as well have been a marathon to Zac. He nodded anyway and soldiered on, part of him wishing he'd stayed behind. He'd never hiked this far in his life—the most he'd ever walked was the distance between the parking lot and his doctor's office, and even that had been a struggle sometimes.

At last they came to the other side of the bend, and to Zac's surprise, the trees abruptly stopped, revealing a bright blue sky and vast hilly grasslands that stretched out before them, with mountain ranges on either side. The trees picked up several miles away, and in the distance, Zac thought he could see what looked like a herd of wild horses. Unicorns? Or some other creature they'd never seen before?

"Wow," said Lu, her mouth hanging open. "These are all the Wildewoods?"

"This and beyond," said Conrad proudly. "Beautiful, isn't it?"

Stunned, Zac gaped at the view. "I thought it was—you know. All woods," he admitted.

"An easy assumption to make," said their uncle kindly. "The forest surrounds this entire expanse of land, and the

Wildewoods stretch for miles in every direction, completely protected from the outside world. There's no place like it, and we're incredibly lucky to call it our own."

Oliver's scowl made it clear he didn't consider them lucky at all. "They'll see this view a million times, Dad. Can we get going now?"

"No time is ever as lovely as the first," said Conrad, though he reluctantly gestured for Lu and Zac to follow him. Not far from the edge of the forest was a stream, and while it wasn't very deep, Zac still shivered as they splashed through the shallow water in their rubber boots.

"You must never cross the stream without one of us," warned Conrad as they reached the other side. "With Surrey and Devon still sniffing about, I couldn't possibly leave you at the stable right now, but Rowena would be furious if she knew you were out here."

"Why?" said Lu immediately, before Zac could ask the question.

"Because that side"—Oliver pointed back toward the forest—"is safe for us. Most of the time, anyway. On this side, you'll die if you don't know what you're doing."

"Oh, you mean the dragons won't kill us after all?" said Zac innocently, and Oliver snorted.

"Sure, if that's what you want to think."

They continued to trek across the sloping grassland, and it was even more of a struggle for Zac than the forest had been. But at last, as they crested another hill, a shimmering blue lagoon came into view, easily the size of a small lake and surrounded by a rainbow of wildflowers. Several boulders seemed to have been strategically placed along the edges, creating shadows and places for the inhabitants to hide.

"*This* is what you call a pond?" said Lu, astonished.

"It's a nickname," muttered Oliver. "You know, like 'Lu.'"

Though she said nothing, her hands tightened into fists, and for a moment Zac thought she actually might punch Oliver. But to his mild disappointment, she strode away, skipping down the hill toward the lagoon instead.

It really was beautiful, and as the hot midday sun beat down on them, Zac couldn't help but imagine how cool the water must be. But as they approached, he spotted something on the shore, lying in the flowers. No, not something—*someone.*

A girl with black hair streaked with gold lay on the edge of the lagoon, her eyes closed. The sunlight reflected off the water, causing Zac to squint, but in the shadows of the boulder, he could have sworn he saw other people crowded around, staring at the girl.

"Who *is* that?" he said, but Conrad swore and took off at a run, leaving him behind.

"Not who," said Oliver, hands in his pockets as he

continued to stroll at a leisurely pace. "*What.* And look closer. You'll figure it out."

Zac edged down the slope, and only when Conrad knelt beside the girl did he realize what he was seeing. He'd thought her legs had been submerged in the water, but she didn't have legs at all. Instead, from the waist down she sported a blue tail with shimmering fish scales that blended in with the shoreline.

"Is that—?" began Lu, appearing at his side.

"Yeah," said Zac, amazed. "She's a mermaid."

14

LU

LU TROTTED DOWN TO THE EDGE OF THE LAGOON, barely able to contain her excitement. Mermaids existed. Actual *mermaids*. They had always been her favorite part of her mother's stories, and now she would have the chance to meet the last remaining mermaids in the world.

But her excitement faded when she reached her uncle, who was crouched beside the mermaid lying on the shore. Near the spot where the girl's torso met her tail, where her hip would've been if she were human, was a deep set of puncture wounds set in a half circle. A bite mark.

"Whoa," said Zac as he joined them. "That looks nasty."

"Yes, it is," said Conrad, kneeling beside the mermaid and gently inspecting the injury. "Did any of you see anything?"

At first Lu thought he was talking to her, but the water near the rock formation rippled, and a mermaid with silver hair and the greenest eyes Lu had ever seen emerged from the shade. "It was a hideous beast," she said in a heavy accent Lu couldn't place. "The body of a lion, the tail of a scorpion—"

"And a human face?" finished Conrad, his own draining of color. "Oliver—"

"Yeah, I heard," he said, all his smugness gone now as he grabbed the flashlight hanging from his utility belt. "I'll check the perimeter and see if I can track it."

"Be careful," said Conrad firmly. "And whatever you do—"

"I know, Dad," said Oliver. "Avoid the tail."

He headed off into the grasslands, his eyes on the ground as he presumably searched for any sign of whatever it was that had bitten the mermaid. Lu moved toward the edge of the lagoon, trying to get a better look at the others. The ones who hadn't ventured out were all clustered beside the rocks, clinging to each other as their eyes glowed eerily in the shadows.

"Do you know what animal did this?" she said to her uncle, kneeling next to the lagoon and touching the water.

It was surprisingly warm. The mermaid with silver hair hissed, however, and Lu snatched her hand back.

"Stay away from the shore," warned Conrad, his gaze not wavering from the injured mermaid. "And I know exactly what did this. A manticore."

"A what?" said Lu, scooting back to the safety of the grass.

"They live in the Scorchlands—a forest on the other side of the mountain range with the other more . . . threatening creatures," said Conrad grimly. "Usually the dragons and centaurs keep them from crossing into the grasslands, but every now and then, something makes it over. Most often it's a chimera or a harpy, especially during breeding season, when they're looking for a safe place to keep their young. I can't remember a time it's ever been a manticore."

"Why is the tail so bad?" said Zac, who inched toward the lagoon a few yards behind them. The silver-haired mermaid didn't hiss at him, though—instead she swam closer, her green eyes even brighter now.

"Manticores are venomous," said Conrad, his head down as he worked to clean and disinfect the dark-haired mermaid's wound. Lu watched what he was doing, filing the information away for when she returned to Chicago. "The sting from their tail is deadly. It's a brutal, painful death, especially for humans. We can't harm any of the creatures in the Wildewoods," he added. "It's part of the magic that holds this place together. Oliver won't be able to defend himself."

Lu paled. "Was she stung?" she said nervously, leaning toward the unconscious mermaid.

"I don't see any other injuries," said Conrad. "Just a bite mark. This far away from its usual terrain, the manticore will undoubtedly be hungry. Unicorns and centaurs can outrun it, but mermaids . . ."

Mermaids couldn't run, and they were trapped in the lagoon with no way out. Lu's stomach churned. "Do you think it'll come back?"

"Impossible to say. Mermaids aren't helpless," he added, glancing into the shade of the rocks. "They must have chased it off. But if it gets hungry enough . . ."

"Will it wander across the stream?" said Lu nervously.

"That's always a possibility, but I'm sure Oliver will track it down and lure it back over the mountains. Of course, I'd rather he and Penelope both stayed far away from anything that lives in the Scorchlands, but he's got a knack when it comes to dealing with the dangerous ones." Conrad sighed and pulled several cloth bandages from his bag. "We'll keep an eye out. We always do, though, and there's really nothing to worry—*Zac, no!*"

Lu snapped her head around to look at her brother, her heart pounding. He'd stuck his feet in the water. Zac stared back, confused. "What?" he said, as Conrad scrambled down the shore toward him. "I'm not doing any—"

All at once, his body flew forward as something underneath the surface pulled him into the lagoon. "Zac!" screamed Lu, darting toward the water. *"Zac!"*

Conrad was already there, wading into the lagoon and groping around. "Let him go," he ordered, but his voice trembled. "You know better—all of you know better. *Let him go.*"

A few mermaids surfaced, giggling like small children, but Zac wasn't with them. Lu didn't think. Yanking off her rubber boots, she threw them into the wildflowers and sprinted across the shore. The giggles turned to hisses, but she didn't care. With a running leap, she dove into the warm water, ignoring her uncle's protests.

Instantly the world grew quiet. Though the salt water stung her eyes, it was surprisingly clear, and she realized the lagoon was far deeper than she'd imagined. Silhouettes of several mermaids quickly surrounded her, and in the distance, she spotted another shape being dragged into the darkness below. Zac.

"Let him go!" she shouted into the water, her voice muffled and muted. Before she could swim any closer, however, thin fingers with long, talonlike nails gripped her limbs, pulling her back toward the light. Lu fought as best she could, lashing out with her legs and fists, but there were too many of them, and they were much stronger than they looked.

She surfaced abruptly, and with a coordinated swing, the hissing mermaids flung her onto the shore. Lu landed with a bone-bruising thud, but as soon as she righted herself, she scrambled toward the lagoon once more, determined to reach her brother. They could throw her out as many times as they wanted. She wouldn't be intimidated by a bunch of fish princesses.

But the moment she touched the water, one of the mermaids launched a small rock at her, hitting her right in the middle of her forehead. Lu stumbled backward as her vision exploded in a shower of stars, and the mermaids screeched with laughter before diving back into the lagoon.

"Lu—Lu, don't," said Conrad, and he grabbed her arm, preventing her from trying to jump in again. "They'll kill you, too."

"You have to do something," she sobbed. "Zac—*Zac! Bring him back! Bring my brother back!* He can't breathe—he can't—"

But the dark waters were still now, and there wasn't a mermaid in sight. Tears streamed down her face as desperation clawed at her, demanding she save him. There was nothing, though. The mermaids had him, and they weren't letting him go. Zac couldn't hold his breath for more than twenty seconds, and it had to have been at least a minute by now. Even if the mermaids released him, even if he managed to swim to the surface, his lungs would be severely damaged. And they were so far away from the manor, let alone the nearest hospital. By the time they reached one . . .

"Please," sobbed Lu, going limp in Conrad's iron grip. *"Please."*

Suddenly a strange sound echoed above them—the same melancholy call she and her brother had heard the moment they'd stepped into the Wildewoods. And as Lu stared into the water, a bright golden light flashed across the grasslands, momentarily blinding her.

The cry grew louder, and Conrad's hold on her relaxed as he gazed into the sky with a slack jaw. Lu didn't care what was up there. Her brother was down in the deep recesses of the lagoon, and he was dying, if he wasn't dead already. Nothing else mattered.

But then, to her astonishment, the mermaids began to surface. One by one, they appeared, their hair different colors and decorated with small shells and glass beads. And finally, *finally*, the one with silver hair and green eyes appeared, and Zac's unconscious form bobbed to the surface beside her.

"Zac!" shrieked Lu, jerking away from her uncle before trying yet again to dive into the water. Conrad was quicker, though, and he caught her before she could touch the gentle waves. Though several of the nearby mermaids hissed, the others swam toward the shore, pulling her brother along with them.

As soon as Zac was close enough, Conrad grabbed the

straps of his waterlogged overalls and dragged him to the shore. His face was sickly pale, and his eyes were closed. Worst of all, he wasn't breathing.

"I know CPR," said Lu immediately, dropping to her knees beside her brother, but Conrad had already begun chest compressions. One, two, three, four—each one a steady push against Zac's chest as he tried to force the water out of his lungs.

Again, again, again, again. Lu could barely breathe, and she clung to Zac's hand, her eyes full of tears. He had to be okay. He had to be.

Again, again, again, again.

Again, again, again, again.

"Come on," she whispered. "Come on. You've got this."

Again, again, again—

An enormous amount of water spilled from Zac's mouth like a fountain, and at last he began to cough violently. Lu crumpled, her shoulders shaking as she cried, though this time they were tears of relief.

"Deep breaths," said Conrad gently, rolling Zac onto his side so he could expel the rest of the salt water. "You're all right. You're safe now."

Zac didn't seem to be paying attention to either of them, though. Even as he coughed, his eyes were trained upward and wide with wonder. "Whoa," he managed to choke out. "What—what's that?"

"What's what?" said Lu, baffled, and at last she looked up, squinting into the sky.

There, hovering no more than thirty feet above them, with golden light radiating from his fiery feathers and outstretched wings, was the phoenix.

15

ZAC

STILL WEARING HIS DAMP SHIRT AND BOXERS, ZAC sat at the base of the nearest hill, his wet overalls spread out on the grass nearby as they slowly dried in the warm summer sun.

Lu hovered beside him anxiously, as she watched him breathe. It was unnerving, and she'd been that way—asking him over and over if he needed anything—for the past half hour.

"I'm fine," he insisted. "I'm alive. I'm not going to die."

"Didn't seem like it for a minute there," she mumbled, but she sat down next to him and stared at a spot several yards away—the same spot Zac was focused on too.

The phoenix stood on the sloping grassland, watching them with shining black eyes. His impressive wings were folded against his body, and while he hadn't flown away, he also hadn't gotten too close.

"Madness—utter madness," their uncle had mumbled when the phoenix had first landed nearby, though he didn't approach the fiery bird either. As Conrad continued to tend to the injured mermaid, however, he glanced up several times a minute, as if he couldn't believe his eyes.

Zac was sure the phoenix had saved his life, but he didn't know how or why. Right place, right time, maybe? The Wildewoods were huge, though, and he was also sure the phoenix had saved their lives the day before, when Surrey had attacked them. He'd seen that same golden light then, too, and he'd felt the same thunder in his bones, as if the phoenix's presence was enough to awaken a part of him that had been asleep for a long time.

"Penelope said he hasn't been seen since Mum left," said Zac quietly to his sister, not taking his eyes off the bird. "Why is he here now, then?"

Lu shrugged, also watching the phoenix warily. She seemed nervous, though—apprehensive about something Zac didn't understand. "What if he's dangerous?"

"He isn't," said Zac, absolutely certain. "He saved me. He saved both of us."

Lu seemed to understand, though she didn't say anything

in return. In the quiet that followed, Zac slowly began to inch closer to the bird. His lungs burned no matter how shallowly he breathed, and his limbs felt like they were made of lead, but he couldn't let an opportunity like this pass by.

"Zac . . ." said Lu in a warning voice, but he ignored her. The phoenix wouldn't hurt him.

"Hi," he said quietly, only a few feet away now. The bird froze, his gaze focused on Zac. But the phoenix didn't flinch, and he didn't spread his wings to take off, either. "I'm Zac."

Silence filled the space between them, and Zac remained still. In the sunlight, the phoenix's red and orange and golden feathers sparkled, and his long plumage was a deep cerulean, the same color as the water in the lagoon. Zac had never seen anything like it in Chicago, not even in books or movies.

"Thank you," he added after a beat. "For—you know. Saving me. And for saving us from Surrey. We appreciate it."

The phoenix tilted his head, as if he understood him, and a low trill sounded from his throat. Zac grinned.

"We owe you one. Or two," he said, and with the kind of bravery that came from almost dying half an hour earlier, he slowly reached out his hand. The phoenix grew still once more, but rather than shying away, as Zac expected, he craned his neck toward him, gently headbutting his palm.

Instantly a series of images flashed through Zac's mind, each more vivid than the last. His mother, young again, feeding an injured dragon on the mountains as the phoenix perched on a nearby rock, cautious and protective.

His mother even younger than before, sitting cross-legged beneath the gnarled tree as she spoke in a low voice to the phoenix, the quiet between them broken by her familiar laugh.

A man with dark hair dressed in clothes that hadn't been in style in decades, helping a little girl who couldn't have been more than six pet a unicorn foal in the pasture. His mother, Zac realized. And his grandfather—Alastair. Nearby, a teenage Conrad tended to a grumpy centaur, laughing at his little sister's antics.

And finally, he saw himself and Lu as they walked into the Wildewoods the day before. He heard the phoenix's cry—he was sure it had been the phoenix now—and could see himself looking around for the source. The phoenix had been perched only a few trees away. How hadn't they seen him?

When the flashes ended, Zac gasped, as if his lungs had completely forgotten how to work on their own. Without a word, he stared at the phoenix as everything clicked into place.

The strange images he had been seeing ever since arriving at the manor—they'd been from the phoenix. Was he trying to get to know Zac? Were they some kind of gift?

Zac didn't know, but as he gazed at the bird, his eyes grew watery, and he blinked hard.

"Are you okay?" said Lu, moving toward him carefully, presumably so she didn't startle the phoenix. "We need to get you back to the manor. If there was something in the water, your lungs could get infected—"

"I'm fine," he managed, hastily rubbing his eyes. "It's just the pollen."

"You should be wearing a mask," she said immediately. "I can't believe you've been out here this long without one."

She was right, but Zac didn't feel sick, not when he was touching the phoenix. Somehow the bird's presence washed all the familiar tightness and wheezing and itchiness away. "I'm okay," he repeated, calmer this time as he stroked the phoenix's feathered head. "He knew Mum. They were friends."

"How do you know that?" said Lu, sounding both hopeful and suspicious all at once.

"I don't know. He just—showed me," said Zac, and he lowered his voice so Conrad couldn't hear. "Try it. Pet him."

Dubious, Lu held out her hand the same way Zac had. The phoenix froze once more, but after an encouraging smile from Lu, he gently headbutted her palm too. Lu's grin grew, and she ran her fingers down the phoenix's neck and wing.

"Did you see them?" said Zac eagerly. "The memories?"

"Memories?" said Lu, her attention still on the bird. "No. You saw memories?"

"Images—like movie clips, almost all of them about Mum," he said, his cheeks growing warm. Had he imagined them? No. They'd been too strong, too specific. "You're sure you didn't see anything? Maybe you should keep petting him."

"Or maybe there was something in the water that's making you hallucinate," said Lu, sounding genuinely concerned. "We should really get back."

Zac brushed his fingers against the phoenix's soft feathers once more. He wasn't crazy, and he wasn't hallucinating. He'd seen the memories just then, the same way he'd seen them in his dreams. They were real.

"Ingrid will be all right," said Conrad from his spot on the shore. He helped the now-conscious mermaid back into the water, where she swam gingerly toward her friends in the shade. "How about you, Zac? Feeling any better?"

He nodded. "Just tired, that's all."

"I'm sure you are." With his task done, Conrad walked slowly toward the phoenix, openly staring at the magnificent bird now. "I haven't seen him in years."

"Penelope said he disappeared when Mum left," said Zac. The phoenix turned his attention to Conrad, ruffling his feathers.

"Yes," agreed their uncle, and he crouched down a few feet away. "The rest of us never saw him, not unless he was with her. The phoenix chose your mother very early on, and he was rather attached to her. No wonder—your mother had an affinity for animals. It was a dark day for the creatures of the Wildewoods when she left to marry your father."

"Mum liked animals?" said Lu, stunned.

"Of course," said Conrad with a gentle chuckle. "It'd be hard not to, wouldn't it? Growing up in a place like this."

"But—I always thought she hated them," said Lu. "I mean, she acted like they were diseased or something. I never even saw her pet a dog."

"Probably because I'm allergic," said Zac guiltily. How different would their lives be if he wasn't so sick all the time?

"I'm certain your mother made many difficult sacrifices in order to do what was best for the both of you," said Conrad, reaching for the phoenix as if he were about to touch him. "She loved you both very, very mu—"

All of a sudden, the phoenix cried out, his trill echoing throughout the hilly grasslands. With a flash of golden light, he spread his wings and took off into the sky, flying so quickly that he was nothing more than an orange streak on a cloudless day. Zac watched, both astonished at the spectacle and disappointed he'd left so soon. But the fact that he'd been there at all—that was special.

"What a remarkable creature," said Conrad with a sigh, sounding as dismayed as Zac felt. "Now let's get you home. Rowena's going to have a fit when she hears what happened."

"Do we have to tell her?" said Zac, accepting Conrad's help in standing. His legs trembled beneath him, and with his lungs still burning, he wasn't entirely sure he could manage the walk back, but he didn't have much of a choice.

"I'm afraid so," said Conrad, picking up his bag. "Spotting the phoenix for the first time in nearly two decades is certainly something she needs to hear about, and we can't leave the mermaids out of the story."

Lu wrapped her arm around Zac, allowing him to lean on her if he needed it, and for once, he didn't protest. All he could think about as they started the long trek back was how this would be yet another reason for Rowena to banish them from the Wildewoods. The thought of never returning made him ache, and he steeled himself for the fight he knew was coming.

But Rowena's opinion didn't matter. The only things that did were the phoenix and the memories Zac had seen, the pieces of his mother he hadn't had before, and he wasn't about to give them up so easily.

16

LU

"YOU MUST BE JOKING."

While Rowena stared at Conrad in disbelief, Lu sat in a chair across from her, trying not to squirm. She and Zac were in the shadowy, old-fashioned office Lu had glimpsed on their first night in the manor, and their great-aunt sat behind a massive oak desk that looked like it had been carved from a single gigantic tree. Lu had tried to distract herself by studying the dozen or more maps of the Wildewoods that were hung on the wall behind Rowena, but her aunt's sharp voice demanded her full attention.

"It's the truth," said her uncle. "I saw the phoenix myself. He saved Zac's life—"

"Why on earth would he save the boy? The twins have only been here for a couple of days."

"Perhaps he can sense Josie on them," said Conrad uncertainly. "Or perhaps it's something else entirely. Perhaps he saw them come into the Wildewoods, and he grew curious."

Rowena shook her head. "That bloody bird's connection to them is no stronger than the connection he has to the rest of us. There's simply no logic." She turned to face the twins once more. "Did anything odd happen? Anything at all?"

Zac pressed his lips together, his gaze averted, and Lu squared her shoulders. Somehow, even though she wasn't convinced they were real, she knew it was in their best interest to keep his visions a secret. At least for now. "A bunch of mermaids tried to drown my brother, and a phoenix saved him," she said tartly. "What part of that *isn't* weird?"

Rowena drummed her fingers against the desk. "I should never have let you go back," she said at last. "You've been in mortal peril twice already, and you aren't trained to protect yourselves."

"We'll learn," insisted Lu. "Conrad's teaching us—"

"Conrad has his own duties to attend to," said Rowena. "Besides, I've made my decision. You can stay in the manor, or you can stay with Merle in her shop. Those are your two choices for the rest of the summer."

"But—that's not fair!" cried Lu. Beside her, Zac also protested, though with considerably less energy. "You said we could visit if we did chores—"

"Chores Zac cannot do," said Rowena. "And chores you did not finish."

"Then get me a flashlight, and I'll go do them right now," said Lu stubbornly. "I'll clean the entire stable if I have to. You have to let us go back—we're part of this family too."

Rowena had already opened her mouth, but at Lu's mention of family, she exhaled, as if all her arguments had suddenly escaped her. Her expression settled into one of annoyance, and she looked to Conrad. "I don't suppose you'd like to say anything."

"She has a point," said Conrad with a slight shrug. "They're both marked."

What that had to do with it, Lu had no idea, but Rowena muttered a curse to herself and leaned back in her chair. "You'll muck out the stalls daily, and since your brother can't manage, you'll do his work for him. Is that what you want?"

"Yes," said Lu defiantly. "That's exactly what I want."

"And," continued Rowena, "you have to scrub the nursery clean once a week."

Lu sniffed. "Fine."

"And—" This time, Rowena's piercing gaze fell on Zac.

"You cannot have any further contact with the phoenix."

"Come on," groaned Zac, his head falling back. "He's not the one who tried to kill us."

"He saved our lives," agreed Lu, glaring at their great-aunt. "Twice. Just because you don't like the phoenix doesn't mean—"

"This has nothing to do with my feelings for the phoenix and everything to do with the danger you're putting yourselves in around that creature," she snapped. "You've been here for all of forty-eight hours, and you've already decided you know better than the generations' worth of knowledge that was passed down to me—knowledge you missed, because your mother decided to run away instead of remaining here with her family."

Rowena might as well have slapped them. Lu stared at her, stunned. "You think Mum ran away?"

"Of course she did," said Rowena bitterly. "And it was a massive mistake, as we all could have told her."

"Rowena," said Conrad gently, but it didn't matter. Lu had already heard everything she wasn't saying.

Their mother had run away to marry their father, and if that was a mistake, then so were Zac and Lu. Swallowing hard, she stood, pushing her chair back noisily. "If I had to live here and listen to your stupid rules and the way you order everyone around, I'd run away too," she said. "The only mistake Mum made was telling Dad about her family.

If she hadn't, then maybe we wouldn't be stuck here with you. Come on, Zac," she muttered, helping her brother up. And as their great-aunt watched in stony silence, Lu led her brother out of the office and toward the staircase.

"Do you really think she'll stop us from seeing the phoenix again?" said Zac. Lu shook her head.

"How can she? The phoenix doesn't like her. He likes you, though, and if he wants to see you, she can't stop him," she pointed out. "The most she can do is yell at the phoenix and wave her shield around."

"She'd probably scare him away," mumbled Zac.

"She can barely walk right now," said Lu. "It'll take her days—maybe weeks—to heal. You'll have plenty of time to find the phoenix again, if you want."

Together she and Zac ascended the stairs, and once they were in their shared room, Lu made sure Zac was tucked in with his sketchbook and nebulizer before going to shower. After the tension of the day, her muscles ached, and all she wanted to do was sleep.

But when she returned to the bedroom, her hair damp and teeth brushed, Zac was drawing in his sketchbook furiously, with more energy than he should have had after nearly drowning.

"You should sleep," she said as she climbed into her own bed. Someone had washed her sheets during the day, and she buried her face into her pillow, inhaling.

"Can't," said Zac, continuing to draw. "I want to get them down before I forget."

"Get what down?" said Lu. "You'll see the phoenix again."

"No, not him," said Zac distractedly, his pencil flying over the page. "The images. The memories."

Intrigued, Lu stood again and padded over to his side of the room. "You're drawing them?" she said, not sure whether to be impressed or worried that he really had hallucinated.

"Yeah—I mean, no one's showing us pictures here, right?" said Zac. "I want you to see what she looked like too."

Lu peered at his sketchbook apprehensively. There, in shockingly lifelike detail, was a drawing of a teenage girl with a long braid down her back. She was almost twenty years younger than she had been the last time Lu had seen her, but her smile, her chin, her eyes—she was unmistakably their mother.

"How many of these do you have?" she said quietly, clasping her hands together to stop herself from trying to touch the delicate pencil lines. Zac flipped back several pages to show her.

Again and again, he'd drawn their mother. In most of the pictures, she was around the same age as the first, but in a few, she was younger. And in one, she was only five or six years old, and she stood next to a roughly sketched unicorn foal as she gently touched its nose.

"This is really her?" said Lu, her words catching as she spoke. She cleared her throat. "You're sure it wasn't just—your life flashing before your eyes or something? You did almost die today."

"I'm sure," said Zac, turning back to the newest portrait and continuing to shade it in. "I only saw it all afterward, when I was petting the phoenix."

Lu bit her lip. Maybe he was telling the truth. She saw that trophy room every time she fell asleep, after all, and it wasn't so far-fetched that those nightmares were coming from the phoenix. If they were, she desperately wished for a good dream too. Or at least something new. Because no matter how many times she visited the real doors that led into the east wing, they were always chained shut.

"I'm sorry you have to do all the chores in the stable," said Zac suddenly, his pencil pausing mid-stroke. "Maybe if I put on a mask—"

"No," said Lu, tearing herself away from the drawing and returning to her side of the room. "I can do it. You can't. It's okay."

"But I want to help," he said, frowning. "There has to be something—"

"If there is, we'll talk about it then," she said. "If there isn't, you can draw all day or something. I don't mind. I just want to be there, and I don't want anything to happen to you, all right?"

Zac took a deep breath and let it out slowly. "Okay," he finally agreed. And after a beat, he added, "I don't want anything to happen to you, either, you know."

"What do you mean?" she said as she settled back into bed.

"You shouldn't have jumped in after me today," he mumbled. "I mean—thank you, but—you could have died."

"You could have too," she said. "And you're my brother. Even if you're annoying most of the time, I'm always going to jump in after you."

And though he said nothing in return, just as she rolled over to try to get some rest, she thought she saw a flash of unease cross his face before he finally refocused on his drawings.

17

ZAC

AT BREAKFAST THE NEXT MORNING, ZAC COULD feel Rowena's stare, a silent warning to obey her orders regardless of the way their conversation the night before had ended. But instead of meeting her eye, Zac focused on his plate of eggs and fruit, wolfing down his food and tuning out the buzz of conversation between the other members of their family. He mumbled a few times when asked a direct question, but his mind was focused solely on the phoenix.

Zac didn't know why he was drawn to the strange creature, or why the phoenix was drawn to him, and honestly, he didn't care. All Zac wanted was to see him again, and when Conrad and the others were finally ready to head out, Zac happily tagged along before Rowena could suggest he spend the day in Aunt Merle's shop instead.

While Lu trudged toward the stable to get started on her chores, Zac lingered near the pasture, watching Penelope tend to the unicorns. She spoke to them in a gentle voice and fed them treats of apples and carrots, and when she caught Zac watching, she waved him over.

"Dad said you can't go into the stable," she said. "Do you want to help me?"

"I—" Zac hesitated. He wanted to find the phoenix again, but with Penelope so close, he couldn't wander off without her noticing. "Yeah, okay. What do you do with them, anyway?"

"Most of this group is recovering from injuries," she said, stroking the muzzle of a roan unicorn. "But there are a few that were rejected from their herds, and I've been try-ing to tame them."

"Aren't they already tame?" The dappled gray unicorn with a silver horn nudged his shoulder, and Zac rubbed its nose.

"No, not at all," said Penelope, sounding amused, but at least she was polite enough not to laugh. "Horses, for the most part, have been domesticated and bred to carry riders. Unicorns haven't. Here, feed him this. Palm up and open, or else he'll chew your fingers."

She passed Zac a carrot, and he did as instructed, offering it to the unicorn. It whinnied at him happily before eating the carrot directly from his hand, and Zac grinned.

"Is it weird that I'm allergic to horses, but unicorns don't make me sneeze?" he said as the unicorn nudged him for another treat.

"Not really," said Penelope. "They're different species, even if they do share common ancestors. Do you want to try to ride him?"

Zac blinked. "Wait—what?"

"Ride," she said with a smirk. "That unicorn. With me."

"But—I've never ridden a unicorn before. Or a horse," he added quickly. "I'll probably fall off."

She shrugged. "Maybe. But at least then you'll be able to say you've ridden one. Besides, Hermes is saddle-trained. So is Athena." She patted the roan's muzzle. "We'll go slow, I promise."

Zac didn't have much of a choice, not when he didn't have any chores to do, and he watched nervously as Penelope saddled the unicorns and led Hermes over to a large wooden block with steps on one side.

"I've been teaching them to kneel so they can help their riders climb up, but Hermes isn't quite there yet," said Penelope apologetically. "But he will be by the end of the summer, I think."

Taking a nervous breath, Zac climbed the steps and

hooked his boot into the stirrup, pulling himself awkwardly into the saddle. As he settled over Hermes, gripping the horn for dear life, he watched as Penelope effortlessly hopped up onto her roan unicorn without using the block.

"This is what you do? You ride unicorns all day?" said Zac as Hermes pranced impatiently beneath him, making him feel like his insides were being slammed against his rib cage. One sudden movement, and he was sure he'd fall straight into the mud below. How did anyone keep their balance this high up?

"Something like that," said Penelope with a grin. "I also follow the herds and look for the sick or injured. Contact the centaurs and see if they need any help. Check in on the mermaids, the fairies, the pixies and satyrs—you know, the usual rounds."

"The usual rounds," echoed Zac with a straight face. "Completely normal. Do you go to school?"

"Of course," she said, and she nudged Athena with her heels. The unicorn began to walk, and even though Zac didn't do anything, Hermes followed. "Oliver and I both go to school only a few miles from the manor. It's a lot smaller than our school in London, but I like it here. He doesn't, though," she added. "He wants to move back in with our mum. But—" She hesitated.

"But what?" said Zac, most of his attention focused on not falling out of the saddle.

Penelope was quiet for a beat. "But we can't abandon Rowena and Aunt Merle and Dad. Besides, someone will have to take care of the animals when they're gone."

Zac had never heard anyone talk about death so easily before, as if it were inevitable. He knew it was, of course—if anything, the past month had shown him the terrifying and stark reality that death could happen at any time, to anyone, even those he loved most. But before finding his mother in the kitchen, it wasn't something he'd ever thought about. Now, the only thing that could successfully distract him from those horrible, oppressive thoughts were the Wildewoods.

"What happens if there's no one in the family left?" said Zac. "Do the Wildewoods still exist?"

Penelope nodded. "The phoenix holds this place together, not us. We're just the caretakers."

A shiver ran through Zac. "Then what happens when the phoenix dies?" he said.

"That won't happen. Phoenixes are immortal. Or—he's immortal, I guess," she corrected herself. "Whenever his body gets too old or feeble, he bursts into flame and is reborn from the ashes."

Zac frowned. "But if phoenixes are immortal, then why is he the only one left?"

Her expression grew pinched at that, and she urged Athena into a brisk walk. To Zac's dismay, Hermes followed her lead, and once again he felt like his teeth might rattle out of his head.

"He can't die from sickness or trauma, not like other animals," said Penelope. "But there are—other ways. Horrific, inhumane ways. Thankfully, the details have been lost over time."

Zac said nothing for a long moment as the unicorns trotted along the forest floor. "But the Wildewoods are safe as long as the phoenix is here, right?"

"Yeah, the Wildewoods are safe," she said, and he could hear the smile in her voice. "Oliver may not like this place, but I do. I think you and Lu might too, once you've had time to adjust."

"We already do," promised Zac. "If I had a choice—"

But before he could finish, Hermes neighed loudly, and without warning, the unicorn shot forward. With a cry, Zac grabbed onto the saddle horn with both hands, his legs tightening around the unicorn's body as he struggled to keep himself upright.

"Hermes—no!" shouted Penelope, but she already sounded far away. Zac risked a glance over his shoulder. He could see her and Athena through the trees, but Hermes outran them, galloping between thick trunks and around low-hanging branches.

As Zac clung to the saddle for dear life, panic crashed through him and his palms grew sweaty on the leather.

Ducking his head, he begged the unicorn to stop, but Hermes kept running, faster and faster, until the forest around Zac was a blur. He squeezed his eyes shut and wrapped his arms around Hermes's neck. It would be okay. It had to be okay. Unicorns couldn't run forever—or at least he didn't think they could.

Minutes passed, though it felt like hours to Zac. At last Hermes slowed to a stop, and he dipped his head, forcing Zac to sit back up. Blinking, Zac looked around, his hair a mess and his pulse still racing. Where were they?

"We need to go back," he said urgently. "I don't know where we are." But no matter what Zac said or did, Hermes seemed perfectly content to graze near the base of a large, gnarled tree.

Not *a* gnarled tree—*the* gnarled tree, Zac realized, startled out of his worry.

It was the same tree that he'd seen in his first dream of his mother, he was sure of it. But why had the unicorn taken him here? Was it a coincidence?

The rustle of wings caught his attention, and Zac craned his neck, gazing up at the dense canopy of leaves blocking the morning sunlight. There, only a few feet above his head and tucked into one of the lower branches, was the phoenix.

"It's you," said Zac, shocked. "What are you—"

Hermes began to prance, jolting Zac up and down, and

it wasn't until the unicorn reared onto his hind legs that Zac realized he was attempting to unseat him. Though he miraculously managed to hang on, the moment Hermes returned his front hooves to the ground, Zac hastily swung out of the saddle. As he tried to climb down gracefully, however, his foot got tangled in the stirrup, and he wound up sprawled on the ground, the contents of his backpack spilling out onto the dirt.

Zac sat up. His backpack must have been open for the whole wild ride. Cold horror washed over him, and he began to search his things. His graphic novel—where was it?

At last he found it, tucked between two drawing pads. Relieved, he hugged it to his chest. Some of his charcoal pencils were missing, and he couldn't find his inhaler, but those he could replace. "Did you tell Hermes to bring me here?" he said, looking up at the phoenix. "Is this some kind of trick? Because I really do need to get back."

Suddenly, the unicorn whinnied and started to trot off, leaving Zac on the ground clutching his sketchbook. "Wait!" he cried, scrambling to his feet, but Hermes broke into a run, kicking up dirt and clumps of grass before disappearing into the forest once more.

Sighing, Zac sat back down and leaned against the tree. At least he had some water and a banana for lunch. "You could have just asked me to meet you somewhere," he said.

"Next time, send me a dream or something. I know you can do it."

The phoenix trilled, and it was a strangely musical sound. With a few flaps of his golden wings, he flew down and settled on the grass beside Zac, only a foot away now. Zac held out his hand the way he had at the lagoon, and the phoenix didn't hesitate to headbutt his palm.

Instantly Zac could see his mother again, and a lump formed in his throat. This time, she was maybe twelve, the same age he was. She walked along the stream that separated the forest from the grasslands, and the phoenix flew above her, his wings outstretched as he lazily glided on the wind.

"I miss her," admitted Zac as he stroked the bird's feathers, trying not to feel ridiculous for talking to an animal about his grief. The phoenix trilled again, however, and the memory faded, replaced by another one. But Zac wasn't in the Wildewoods anymore. Instead he was inside his bedroom in Chicago.

A knock sounded on the door, and though he was aware he wasn't actually there, he couldn't control himself as he called, "Come in."

His mother stepped inside, holding a plate. "I brought you lunch," she said, her voice warm. "How's the title page coming along?"

Zac glanced down. He had only just started his graphic

novel, he realized. This must have been from a year ago. "I'm not drawing the dragon right."

"It looks right to me," she said, sitting on the bed beside him. "The tail's a bit short, perhaps, but you've got the wings drawn perfectly."

Zac immediately took an eraser to the tail. "How do you know what a dragon looks like, anyway?"

He knew he hadn't noticed it then, when the memory had really taken place. But now, helpless to change anything about it, he saw an odd flash of emotion cross his mum's face. "Everyone knows what a dragon looks like," she said in an amused voice, but Zac thought he could hear pain behind it too. "And you're nearly there, my love. Nearly there."

She kissed his hair, and the memory dissolved as another one took its place. Him, his mother, Lu, and their dad, all at the dinner table, laughing over a joke Zac had long forgotten.

Another one—his mother sitting beside him during one of his hospital visits, telling him one of her many stories about the Wildewoods.

Yet another—this one of Zac crying when he was younger, only five or so. Lu's first day of school, he realized, as he watched her run off toward the bus without a thought for him. He felt his mother's arms around him, though, and as miserable as he was, he knew it would be okay.

One last memory flashed through his mind, and as soon

as he saw the green striped socks he was wearing as he padded down the hallway, his stomach dropped. He didn't want to see this. He'd tried so hard to avoid remembering, but the scene had already begun.

The house was immaculate—nothing like the dusty corridors and peeling walls of the manor. His mother had always been good at taking care of him and making sure nothing entered their home that would make him sick. He hadn't appreciated it then. He'd never thanked her.

He wanted to close his eyes as he rounded the corner toward the kitchen, knowing what he would find, but he couldn't change anything. He could only relive it again and again, over and over in his memory, unable to ever forget.

Her feet came into view first, her toenails painted deep violet. And then her jeans, and the hem of her shirt—and there, at last, she lay on the floor, her eyes closed and her chest still.

"Please," he whispered brokenly to the phoenix. "I don't want to see this. I don't want to remember."

The phoenix trilled mournfully, and at last the image dissolved, returning Zac to his spot beneath the gnarled tree. His eyes were overflowing with tears, and he blinked hard, letting them drip down his face.

"Why did you want to see that?" he said, his throat tight. "Did you think she wasn't dead?"

The phoenix dropped his head, and a sense of overwhelming sadness washed over Zac. It wasn't his own, though—instinctively, he knew it was the phoenix's. He'd lost a friend, too. Maybe this was his way of grieving. Of finding closure. Zac knew that if he hadn't seen her for himself, he would never have believed his mother was really gone. How could he? She'd been there every moment of his life. It seemed impossible that one minute she was there, and the next she simply wasn't.

He rested his head against the tree, hollow and miserable as he cried himself out. The phoenix didn't move from his side, and he set his head in Zac's lap, as if trying to offer him comfort. Nothing in the world could make this any better, though. It was something they both had to live with.

"I like seeing your memories of her," Zac finally said after several minutes had passed. "It makes me feel like she's still here somehow."

The phoenix nudged his knee, and Zac brushed his fingertips against the bird's feathers once more. Sunshine streaked through the trees, turning ordinary fallen logs and patches of moss into things of ethereal beauty, and a strange sense of peace washed over him. No wonder his mother had loved this place so much.

"Is this what you did with my mum?" he said. "Just sat here and talked and—walked around? Like friends?"

The phoenix lifted his head, his dark eyes focused on Zac's. And suddenly, without explanation, Zac could sense just how important his mother had been to the phoenix. His only friend, he thought—the only one left in the world who really cared.

"I'll be your friend," he offered. "We can spend the whole day together, as long as Rowena doesn't find out."

The phoenix perked up, his feathered crown rising. Zac managed a grin.

"I'll take that as a yes. I mean, you'll have to tell Hermes not to ditch me again, but . . ." He trailed off, eyeing the phoenix. "You know, don't you? You know what Rowena told me last night. That's why you had Hermes bring me here."

The phoenix ruffled his feathers, neither confirming nor denying, and Zac smirked.

"Can I draw you?" he said. He'd brought his fancy colored pencils with him just in case, and as he pulled them out of his backpack, the phoenix waddled a few feet away, not nearly as graceful as he was in the sky. Zac's heart sank, but rather than leaving, as Zac assumed he would, the phoenix stopped and faced him in a perfect pose.

"You're a natural," said Zac with a laugh, and grabbing his drawing pad and favorite sketching pencil, he got to work.

The hours slipped by as he drew the phoenix, focusing on every detail. The feathers were the hardest part, and they took longer than he anticipated, but the phoenix didn't seem to mind. And as the drawing took shape, Zac was sure it was the best one he'd ever done.

Sometime in the midafternoon, however, the phoenix tensed, his eyes on something in the distance. Zac twisted around. "Is Hermes back?" he said. "Because it's getting late."

The unicorn didn't appear, though. Instead Zac heard voices in the distance—indistinct at first, but as they grew closer, he realized they were calling his name.

"Zac! Where are you? *Zac!*"

He climbed to his feet, his muscles stiff. "I'm over here!" he yelled, waving his arms. "Penelope? I'm right here!"

But it wasn't his cousin who burst through the trees. It was his sister, her face red and cheeks tearstained.

"Zac!" cried Lu, and she threw her arms around him so tightly he could hardly breathe. "Penelope said—she said the unicorn took off—and we couldn't find you—we've been looking—your inhaler was on the ground—and the manticore—I thought—I thought—"

She burst into tears, still clinging to him. Alarmed, Zac hugged her back, not sure what to say. "I'm fine," he promised. "I think the phoenix told Hermes to bring me here."

"The phoenix?" she said with a sniff, raising her head. "Where?"

"Right—" Zac looked around, but the phoenix was gone. He frowned. "It's just you. Why would he disappear?"

His question was answered a moment later as Oliver crashed through the underbrush. "Finally," he said with a huff. "Come on, it's a long walk to the tree arch, and I still have to finish my chores."

"Good to know you were worried," said Zac, eyebrow raised. Lu released him, and he hastily closed his drawing pad before Oliver could see it.

"The only thing I'm worried about is how cold dinner will be by the time I get back to the manor," said their cousin. "Now let's *go*, before the manticore finds us."

As Oliver began to retrace his steps, Lu hugged Zac once more. "You're really okay?" she said, her eyes still watering. Zac nodded, studying her uncertainly. She looked the way he felt whenever he worried about their father.

"I'm really okay," he promised. "I've been drawing."

"You could have died without your inhaler," said Lu. "And if the manticore had found you—"

"Then the phoenix would have protected me," said Zac.

Lu fell silent, and once he'd grabbed his backpack, she looped her arm in his and helped him across the uneven ground. He was sure he'd been safe the whole time, but Lu hadn't known that. And he couldn't blame her for being scared.

"I'm sorry," he said at last. "I really didn't have any way back."

"I know," she mumbled, her eyes focused on the ground. After a beat, she added, "Maybe everyone's right. Maybe you shouldn't be hanging around the phoenix. He's just an animal. He doesn't understand that you need your inhaler, or that you can't walk long distances on your own. And if he's going to—to play tricks like this every time he wants to see you—"

"He's lonely," insisted Zac. "He wants a friend."

"And he could have killed you in the process," said Lu, her voice catching. "I'm just saying that if you're going to hang around him, then make sure he knows you have to stay close. Otherwise you're going to force me to agree with Rowena, and no one wants that."

"I'm pretty sure the world would explode," said Zac, and Lu forced a smile. But as they walked, he could feel the phoenix's eyes on them, unseen from the highest branches of the trees, and he knew that no matter what Lu said, this was only the beginning of their friendship.

18

LU

AFTER SPENDING MOST OF THE MORNING AND afternoon in a panic over finding her brother, Lu was completely drained.

Ever since they'd arrived in England, she'd been tense, waiting for the next moment she'd have to jump into action to help Zac breathe, or save him from mermaids, or find him in a massive forest with dragons and a manticore on the loose. It was *exhausting*, and she had no idea how their mother had done it. How had she spent all day, every day, watching over Zac and not worrying herself to death?

As soon as Lu thought it, her blood ran cold. An aneurysm had killed their mother, not Zac. Not all that worry. Lu hadn't known what an aneurysm was—she'd never even heard of it—and the thought that something she didn't even know existed could steal someone she loved . . .

"Do you want to see my drawings?" said Zac from the other side of the bedroom. It was past dinnertime now, and Rowena had been purple with rage at the news of what had happened. Their great-aunt couldn't blame Zac for this one, though—not when it had been the unicorn who'd run into the forest and then abandoned him. But Penelope had gotten a stern talking-to, and Zac and Lu had been sent to their room with a dinner tray and strict orders not to bother the adults.

"Show me," said Lu wearily, and Zac held up his sketchbook. He'd drawn the phoenix in half a dozen different poses, and several of them he'd even colored in.

"I like this one best," he said, pointing to the only finished picture. In it, the phoenix was looking over his wing, his blue-and-orange plumage on full display.

"I can't believe he stood so still for you," said Lu, shaking her head. "Did you see anything else? Any—visions?"

Zac hesitated and lowered his sketchbook into his lap. "Nothing important," he mumbled.

"You're sure?" she said, and he nodded. Lu didn't

believe him—or at the very least, she was sure he was hiding something—but before she could press, a floorboard creaked outside their room.

"Don't you dare," came a harsh whisper, barely audible from Lu's spot on her bed. There was a thump as something hit the wall, and with a scowl, she got up and crept over to the door.

"Let me go, Oliver," said another low voice—Penelope. "They have a right to know."

"Rowena said not to," he hissed. "If you do this—"

"They're our cousins," she insisted. "Wouldn't you want to know?"

"I already do, and it ruined my life," said Oliver. "You're just going to make them miserable."

"And hiding it won't? Stay out of it if you want, but I'm telling them."

Lu heard another thump, and suddenly there was a knock on the door only inches from her ear. Scrambling backward, she barely made it to her bed before Penelope stuck her head inside the room.

"Do you have a minute?" she said, far more somber than usual.

"Uh—yeah," said Lu, stretching like she was only just sitting up. On the other side of the room, she saw Zac roll his eyes. "What's going on?"

Penelope slipped inside and closed the door with a firm

click. "The adults are talking about you downstairs," she said. "They're scared, I think. Of what could have happened to Zac."

"I was fine," he insisted, pencil in hand as he worked on his drawings. "The phoenix—"

"Was with you the whole time. I know," said Penelope. "That's why everyone's so scared."

Lu frowned. "Why? He saved Zac's life."

"Yes, but . . ." Penelope bit her lip, and Lu patted the space on the bed beside her. Reluctantly Penelope perched on the edge of the mattress like a bird about to take flight. "The phoenix is dangerous."

"Everyone keeps saying that, and no one's bothered to explain," said Zac, annoyed. "So what if he created the Wildewoods? So what if he has magic? What's so bad about that?"

Penelope lowered her gaze to the small mark on her own palm, and she traced the *W*. "Aren't you upset you have this?"

"Upset?" said Lu, glancing at her own. "I mean—yeah, it's not going to be easy to explain to Dad. But it's just a mark."

Penelope shook her head. "It's not just a mark. It's a brand—the phoenix's brand. It's a punishment."

"A punishment?" said Lu. "Why? We didn't do any-thing."

"No, but . . ." Penelope pressed her palms together, interlocking her fingers so Lu couldn't see the mark anymore. "Our ancestors did."

"Ancestors?" Lu blinked. "What do they have to do with anything?"

Penelope said nothing for a long moment—long enough that Lu thought she wouldn't answer at all. But at last she said, "Centuries ago, our ancestor, Thomas Wilde, was the greatest hunter in the world. And I don't mean bears or wolves," she added. "I mean mythical creatures. Magical creatures. The creatures that most people believe never really existed in the first place."

"The animals the Wildewoods protect," said Lu slowly, and Penelope nodded.

"He was famous for it. He had buyers all over the world for things like dragon armor and powdered fairy wings and—and phoenix blood."

Lu stared at her, not knowing what to say. Zac, on the other hand, looked up from his drawing, his expression dark.

"We're related to someone who killed phoenixes?" he said, disgusted. "That's *horrible*."

"It was all horrible," agreed Penelope. "Every part of it. But kings wanted unicorn skulls because they thought the horns gave them divine powers. Sailors thought tying mermaid bones to their ships would protect them from other sea creatures. And they all paid good money. Money that built this house," she muttered, glancing around the room as if it personally offended her.

Lu shivered. In her mind, she could see the trophy room she dreamed about, and suddenly everything made sense. "But how did the family go from hunters to—to caretakers?" she said.

"Thomas Wilde was the only person in the world who knew how to hunt a phoenix and kill it," said Penelope grimly. "They're usually immortal, and the magic that lets them regenerate is in their blood. Thomas Wilde discovered a way to—to trap them and exsanguinate the poor creatures."

Zac paled. "Exsanguinate? You mean . . ."

"Drain their blood," she clarified. "There's a special technique to keep the healing magic stable. No one knows it anymore—those secrets died with Thomas Wilde. Even if they hadn't, no one in our family would ever try it. We protect the animals in the Wildewoods. We don't murder them for money," she said fiercely. "But before he died, he hunted phoenixes almost to extinction, selling their blood to the highest bidder until only one mated pair remained."

"My phoenix?" said Zac.

"And his mate," she said with a nod. "When Thomas Wilde realized what he'd done, he stopped hunting them.

He had enough money to last him generations, after all, so what was the point? But then his daughter got sick. The kind of sick that can't be cured."

"And he went after the last pair of phoenixes?" said Lu softly.

Penelope pressed her lips together, once again staring at her hands. "He caught the female. And he murdered her for her blood. For a long time, some members of the family justified it, saying he had to—his daughter was sick, and he had no choice."

"But he did have a choice," argued Zac.

"He did," said Penelope. "And he made it a long time before his daughter was even born. The phoenix—your phoenix—went mad, according to family legend. In his grief, he created a sanctuary, and he summoned all the remaining magical creatures. That's when the entrances appeared on the land surrounding the Wilde family estate," she added. "And the phoenix called to Thomas Wilde's daughter, too. The moment she stepped through the tree arch, this mark appeared on her palm."

Lu was quiet for a long moment, too shocked to speak as she traced her own *W*. "It wasn't her fault, though," she finally managed. "It was Thomas Wilde's. Did anything happen to him?"

"The phoenix cursed him, too," said Penelope in a hushed voice. "For the rest of his life—twenty years, at least—he felt like he was being burned alive. Day and night, he was in constant agony. Legend has it that all he did was lie in bed and scream."

"He deserved worse," said Zac darkly. "He should've had his blood drained."

"Zac!" admonished Lu. "That's horrible."

"What he did was horrible," said her brother, his eyes flashing with fury. "You know it was."

"Of course, but that doesn't mean—"

Penelope cleared her throat. "Everyone in the family knows what he did was horrible," she said. "No one makes excuses for it, and we all think it's barbaric and disgusting. We love the animals. It's part of who we are—it's in our blood. Literally," she added. "Thomas Wilde's daughter is our great-great . . . er, I'm not quite sure how many greats, but probably close to twenty, great-grandmother. After she recovered from her illness, she married and had seven children. And those children helped her care for the Wilde-woods for their entire lives. And their children after them, and theirs after them."

"All the way to us," said Lu, touching her palm again. "Every single one of them stayed?"

"They were marked on their thirteenth birthdays," said Penelope, not daring to meet Lu's eye. "They had no choice."

All the air seemed to leave the room, and for a moment,

the silence between them was profound. "What?" said Lu at last, her voice breaking. "What do you mean, they had no choice?"

Suddenly, from the center of the house near the stairwell, Conrad's voice rang out. "Penelope?"

Anguished, she stood. "If they find out I said anything—"

"*What do you mean*, they had no choice?" demanded Lu. "You can't just say something like that and not—"

"I'm sorry," said Penelope, her expression crumpling as she hurried toward the door. "That's why no one wanted to tell you about the Wildewoods. That's why—that's why you were supposed to stay with Aunt Merle. We're all marked when we turn thirteen, whether we want to be or not. But Rowena thought . . . she thought that since Aunt Josie left, if you didn't enter, you wouldn't be marked at all. But you are, and now—"

"And now what?" said Lu, fear running through her and seizing her senses. "*Now what*, Penelope?"

Their cousin gripped the doorknob, finally looking up at her and Zac. "The mark—it doesn't just mean you can enter the Wildewoods. It means you're bound to them. And if you leave . . ." She wiped her cheek. "I'm sorry."

"What?" said Lu, frantic now. "What's going to happen when we fly home at the end of the summer?"

"Penelope?" called Conrad again, much closer now. She cracked open the door and glanced into the hallway.

"You can't go," she whispered. "Not anymore. You're tied to the sanctuary. And if you try . . ." She took a deep, shuddering breath. "I'm sorry. If you try to leave for good—if any of us tries to leave for good . . . we'll die."

And before Lu could absorb what she'd said, she was gone.

19

ZAC

ZAC STARED AT THE DOOR THAT PENELOPE HAD disappeared through, his heart pounding and the room suddenly spinning. "What did she mean, we'll die?" he blurted to his sister. "We'll just—leave England and—and—"

"I don't know, Zac. Okay? I don't—" Lu's voice broke, and her breaths were coming in gasps. "We have to go home. We can't—we can't stay here anymore. I need to see Sophia. I need to see Rufus. I need—"

She buried her face in her pillow, her entire body trembling. Immediately he stood, but what was he supposed to do? Tell her it was all right? It wasn't all right. He might not have had friends back in Chicago like Lu did, or cats he looked after, or school or any of the anchors she had, but it was still their home. And the thought of staying in England forever—far from their father and everything they'd ever known—sent a chill down his spine.

Slowly he approached her bed and sat down beside her. Before arriving in the Wildewoods, they'd barely had anything to do with each other, and he didn't know how to comfort her. But he knew what his mother would've done, and he wrapped his arm around Lu's shoulders.

"Mum left the Wildewoods," he reminded her quietly. "And that means Penelope's wrong. There has to be something we're missing—something they don't know about."

Lu looked up, her face red and already stained with tears. "Don't you get it? This is what Rowena meant when she said we were doomed. We can never go home, Zac. We can never see Chicago again. And if we try—if we try to leave—"

She dissolved into tears again, and Zac hugged her fiercely. "We'll find a way out of this," he said. "I promise. I'll figure it out, okay?"

But no matter what he said, Lu continued to sob. He stayed with her, his mind whirling as she cried herself out. And once she'd fallen into a fitful sleep, he returned to his bed, and he began to plan.

They weren't doomed. They couldn't be. There was

a way out of this curse—their mother had proven that. But how had she done it, and why hadn't her entire family escaped with her? What had she done that had been different from the others?

The solution came to him quicker than he'd expected, and once he'd settled on it, he relaxed. It was obvious, after all. The one thing everyone else seemed to be afraid of. The one thing she'd befriended.

Somehow, some way, the phoenix had the answer.

The next morning, Zac awoke before the sun and got dressed without making a sound. After sneaking into the kitchen to pack a few pieces of fruit and other things he could eat, he slipped out the back door and into the forest. This was the stupidest thing he'd ever done, and he knew it, but he couldn't stand listening to his sister cry. He couldn't stand knowing that his suggestion—that they go out and find the Wildewoods—had changed their lives irreversibly. And he couldn't stand knowing that there was a solution out there, and that he alone could find it.

The sun was just starting to rise as he stepped through the tree arch and into the Wildewoods. The morning mist gave him an eerie sense of foreboding, and as he approached the stable, he heard the unicorns inside stamping their hooves and snorting as they waited for their breakfast.

As he'd lain awake the night before, he'd imagined

what he would say to the phoenix. He'd repeated his speech over and over until it felt as convincing as it could possibly be—that it was his fault he and Lu had gone searching for the Wildewoods, that his sister didn't deserve this, and that he would stay for as long as the phoenix wanted, if only Lu could leave. The thought of never returning to Chicago made a knot form in his throat, but if that was what it took to make Lu happy, then he would do it.

Yet despite his determination, he still wasn't sure how to find the phoenix in the first place. It was the only kink in his plan, and as he stood in the meadow, he scanned the treetops for any sign of the phoenix. Of course he wasn't here. There was no way this would be that easy.

"Hey!" he called out, feeling like an idiot. "I really need to talk to you. I know you can hear me. Just—come out, all right? I just want to talk."

Nothing. Somewhere in the stable, a unicorn whinnied, and Zac considered his options. He could try to find the gnarled tree again—the phoenix seemed to like that place. But he didn't have a clue where to start. His only other choices, however, were to either wander around aimlessly or to stick near the stable and hope the phoenix showed up eventually. And while the latter had its advantages, it wouldn't be long before the others joined him and started asking questions.

He turned toward the forest and sighed. Fine. If the

phoenix wanted to hide, Zac would just have to find him.

He and Penelope had gone west the day before, and Zac made his way slowly down a faint path he found at the edge of the meadow. He'd given himself a breathing treatment in the bathroom that morning, and he'd made sure to pack his inhaler and EpiPens, as well as a few spare medical masks in case he needed to put one on. If he took his time, he would be okay.

As he went along, he peered up into the treetops, hoping to spot a flash of orange and gold, but all he could see was green. Eventually the mist began to lift and the morning grew warmer, and Zac kept an eye out for the gnarled tree. He had to be close by now, but he had no idea how large the Wildewoods were.

"Are you there?" he said. "Please. I just want to—"

Behind him, he heard something rustle, and he spun around. But there was no sign of the phoenix, and Zac frowned. Where was the gnarled tree? Was he even going in the right direction?

He started forward again, managing another fifty feet before he heard a twig snap nearby. Fear crept through him as he searched for anyone—or anything—among the trees. Maybe it was Hermes. According to Penelope, he was still missing.

"Hello?" he called. "Is anyone there?"

Nothing. The leaves rippled in the breeze, and his

mouth went dry. What if it wasn't Hermes? What if Surrey or Devon had wandered away from the stable?

This was stupid. He shouldn't have been out here alone, with nothing to protect him and no way to really find the phoenix. If something happened to him, Rowena would kill him, and then Lu would resurrect his body in order to kill him again.

But the thought of his sister made him steel himself against his fears. She'd been devastated last night, and she deserved answers. He'd already come this far—he'd walk another twenty minutes or so, he decided, and if he couldn't find the gnarled tree or the phoenix by then, he'd double back.

He pushed onward for a few hundred feet more before a loud crack echoed through the forest, much closer this time. Apprehension prickled inside him as he picked up a fallen branch, gripping it like a weapon. It wouldn't be much help against anything that breathed fire, but at least he'd be able to get in a few good whacks before whatever was out there ate him.

"I have a weapon," he warned, as if that would make any difference. "If you come near me, I'll—"

"Zac?"

A faint call cut through the quiet around him, and he straightened, lowering the branch. "Lu?"

"Zac? Zac!"

"Lu! I'm over here!"

His sister appeared in the distance, and she crashed through the underbrush at breakneck speed, pink-faced and sweating. "You *idiot*," she shouted. "Yesterday wasn't enough? You wanted to scare me today, too?"

"I wasn't—" He sighed. He should've seen this coming. "I wasn't trying to scare you. I'm trying to find the phoenix."

"Why?" she demanded as she closed the distance between them. "You really think talking to him is going to change anything?"

"I don't know," he admitted. "But I have to try. Listen, do you remember where you found me yesterday? I think the phoenix likes that tree, and—"

"That's a mile north of here." Penelope appeared from behind a thicket, kicking the bramble with her rubber boots. She wasn't dressed in her usual khaki overalls, though—instead she wore a T-shirt and sweatpants, and her hair was in a messy braid. Zac glanced at his sister. She, too, was still in her pajamas from the night before.

"I'm sorry," he said, his voice cracking. "I didn't mean to scare you. I was trying to find the phoenix. I thought maybe if I asked him to release us—"

"You think the phoenix will let you go?" said Penelope, baffled.

Zac shrugged, suddenly embarrassed. "I figured it was

worth a shot. I mean, our mum didn't live here anymore. Maybe—"

Suddenly a low growl cut through the forest, and Zac froze. Once again, Lu put herself between him and whatever was making that sound, while Penelope grabbed the back of his shirt and tugged him toward the thicket.

"Get down," she said quietly. "You too, Lu."

Together they all crouched behind the thorny tangle of brush. To his left, Penelope remained perfectly still, while Lu knelt on his other side, gripping his sleeve.

"Don't move," whispered Penelope, her words barely more than a breath, while Zac's heart thudded so loudly that he was sure any creature within a hundred feet could hear it, too. Gritting his teeth, he turned to make sure Lu was all right, but as he did so, something sliced into his cheek.

A thorn.

With a hiss of pain, he touched his face, and his fingertip came back smeared with blood. Penelope's eyes widened, and she stared at him in horror. Zac didn't understand—it was just a cut. But then the growl turned into a ferocious roar, and every muscle in his body froze solid.

Whatever creature was hunting them, it was attracted to blood.

"Run!" cried Penelope. And as Zac watched, stunned, she leaped into the space in front of the thicket, pulling a large hunting knife from her boot.

She was taking the creature on by herself. She was trying to buy them time to get away.

Lu tugged on his elbow. "Come on," she said urgently. "We need to get out of here."

"But Penelope—" he began, fumbling his stick.

"She knows what she's doing. Let's *go*."

As Zac stood, however, he glanced at Penelope, who was now facing the creature. He wasn't sure what he'd been expecting—another dragon, maybe, or a dire wolf or saber-toothed tiger.

The reality was worse than he could've imagined. It was unlike anything he'd ever seen before—a scorpion's tail stuck out of a massive lion's body, creating something unnatural, but it was the head that made his stomach churn. It looked human, with a man's brow and nose and mouth.

"The manticore," he whispered. It was the same creature that had attacked the mermaids—the one Conrad said would be hungry and looking for food.

And Penelope was directly in its path.

"Zac—there's nothing we can do—come *on!*" Lu tugged on his elbow again, pulling so hard that he stumbled backward, but he couldn't leave Penelope. He was the reason she and Lu were out here in the first place.

With all his strength, he wrenched his arm from his sister's grip and darted forward, racing around the trees until he was behind the manticore. "Hey!" he shouted, waving his stick. "Over here, you ugly mutant!"

The manticore twisted around, turning its cold stare on him. From this close, Zac could see a trail of drool dangling from its rows of pointed teeth. He gulped.

"What are you doing?" cried Penelope. The manticore refocused on her, and Zac clenched his jaw.

"The phoenix won't let anything happen to me," he called, realizing how crazy that must sound, but he didn't care. He hit the nearest tree trunk with his stick. "I'm over here, you giant—"

The manticore roared, and Zac's entire body seemed to reverberate from the inside out. He shuddered, gripping his stick even tighter. But the manticore had zeroed in on Penelope again, and it took a step toward her, its deadly tail swishing.

Zac swore. The phoenix likely wouldn't do anything to protect Penelope, not when he'd spent years hiding from her and the rest of the family. Zac wasn't entirely sure the phoenix would protect him, either, but if the manticore had to attack one of them, he was the safer bet. Besides, Penelope could run. He couldn't—not fast enough to escape, anyway.

As the manticore advanced on his cousin, Zac did the only thing he could think of: he hurled his stick straight for its hindquarters. And as it made contact with a loud *thwack*, the monster roared again and whirled around, launching itself directly toward Zac instead.

Defenseless now, he squeezed his eyes shut and held up his arms, as if that would be enough to ward off the massive creature. It had to work. The phoenix had saved him from the mermaids and the dragon. It had to save him from this, too—it had to save all of them.

That single second seemed to last a lifetime as he waited for the phoenix's cry. It never came, though—instead an inhuman scream cut through the forest, so loud and blood-curdling that Zac fell backward onto the soft ground, hitting his elbow on a tree trunk.

"Penelope!" shouted Lu, and Zac finally opened his eyes. Only feet away, the manticore reared on its hind legs, and he realized that Penelope was on its back, riding it like she'd ridden Athena the day before. Her knife was pressed up against the manticore's throat, but though it looked sharp enough to easily cut through fur and skin, there was no sign of blood.

None of the animals could be hurt by humans in the Wildewoods, Zac remembered, distraught. It didn't matter how sharp Penelope's knife was—she was defenseless.

The manticore thrashed and bucked, its scorpion tail writhing, and Zac scrambled backward, trying to avoid the stinger. Penelope held on, clutching its stunted mane and continuing to press the knife into the manticore's flesh, but it was too strong. Her grip began to slip, and Zac looked around, frantic. He couldn't hurt it, but maybe he could distract it long enough for Penelope to—

Suddenly a deep bellow echoed from the trees, and to Zac's shock, Oliver came barreling through the forest. Brandishing a shield nearly as tall as he was, he cracked a long leather whip with a furious cry. Though the tip didn't reach the creature's hide, the manticore skittered backward at the unexpected sound, its eyes narrowed in fear. As the bucking stopped, Penelope fell to the ground, and Oliver cracked the whip again as the manticore hissed.

"Get out of here!" he shouted. *"Go!"*

The manticore gave one last deafening roar before finally darting back into the trees. Though its footsteps faded, Zac's chest tightened, and he struggled to breathe as his head spun and adrenaline surged through his veins.

"Zac!" Lu hurried forward and fell to her knees beside him. "Are you okay? Did it hurt you?"

He shook his head, looking past her. Oliver bent over Penelope, who was still prone on the ground.

"Is she okay?" said Zac hoarsely as he struggled to his feet. "Penelope—"

But as soon as he saw her face, another wave of dizziness washed over him. She was unconscious and deathly pale. Oliver gently rolled her over, exposing a rip in the back of her shirt and an angry red puncture mark on her skin.

The manticore had stung her.

20

LU

THERE WAS NO CURE FOR MANTICORE VENOM.

That was the only thing Lu had been able to think about as they'd carried Penelope to the stable on a stretcher made of branches and two sweaters tied together. It was the only thing she'd been able to think about as Conrad had taken the stretcher from her and rushed back to the manor with Oliver, desperate to save his daughter. And it was the only thing she could think about as she and Zac gathered Conrad's discarded tools and checked to make sure the animals in the stalls were all right before they, too, returned to the manor.

Zac hadn't said a single word since their cousin had been

stung, and it wasn't until they'd slipped unnoticed into their bedroom, directly across the hallway from the commotion of Penelope's room, that Lu realized he was silently falling to pieces. His eyes were glassy, his face was red, and a sob escaped him as he collapsed onto his bed, his backpack discarded on the floor.

Lu edged toward him like he was a skittish cat. "It isn't your fault," she said softly. "You know that, right?"

"Of—of course it's my fault," he managed, his breath coming in great gasps. "I went out there. I was just—I was just trying to find the phoenix. I wanted to talk to him. I wanted—I wanted—"

He was wheezing heavily now, having worked himself into an attack. She knelt beside his backpack and searched the front pocket until she found his inhaler. "Here," she said. Zac made no move for it, though, and her agitation grew. Taking his hand, she wrapped his fingers around the yellow plastic and brought it to his lips. "Use it, Zac."

For a moment, she thought he wouldn't. He had a look about him that she recognized—the same stupid stubbornness she had at times too. But she glared at him and waited, and at last he took a couple of puffs.

When his breathing finally eased, she sat beside him, her fingers laced tightly in her lap. "It isn't your fault," she repeated. "Penelope made a choice, all right? And what happened—it's no one's fault."

"They won't see it that way," he said, wiping his eyes. "You know they won't."

He was right, but she didn't say so. Instead she wrapped her arm around his shoulders. "That's how *I* see it," she said. "What you did, trying to protect her—that was the bravest thing I think you've ever done. The stupidest, too," she added. "But mostly the bravest."

Zac shook his head minutely. "I shouldn't have gone out there."

"Probably not," she said. "But you didn't summon the manticore. You had no way of knowing it would be there, or that it had crossed the stream. None of that's your fault."

"You can say it as much as you'd like," he mumbled. "But I'm never going to believe it."

A soft knock sounded on their door, and Lu looked up as Aunt Merle poked her head inside, carrying a breakfast tray. "Are you children all right?"

Lu nodded. "Is Penelope . . . ?"

Aunt Merle's expression grew pinched. "Conrad is doing what he can," she said as she set the tray down on the dresser. "Beyond that . . . it's in the hands of Mother Nature now."

"There has to be something, right?" said Zac, his voice rising with panic. "I mean—she can't just—she can't just—"

"It's possible a strain of antivenom already in existence might ease the effects," said Aunt Merle, but she didn't sound optimistic. "No human has been stung by a manticore in centuries, and our knowledge about their venom is . . . limited. Oliver and Rowena are both researching options now."

"Can we see her?" asked Lu, her chest growing tight. Zac was right—there had to be something.

"I'm afraid not," said Aunt Merle gently. "Penelope is unconscious and likely to remain that way until . . . until the venom is out of her system. It's a small blessing," she added. "Otherwise she would be in a great deal of pain."

That wasn't at all reassuring, and out of the corner of her eye, Lu saw her brother's expression crumple.

"Isn't there anything we can do?" said Lu desperately. "We could help them research. Or—or—"

"The best thing you can do is stay here and keep yourselves out of trouble," said Aunt Merle. "Give us one less thing to worry about right now."

She kissed their foreheads before leaving, closing the door softly behind her. Lu hugged her brother, and for once, he didn't seem to mind. And as their food grew cold, they sat huddled together, both consumed by the knowledge of what would happen if a cure wasn't found.

Eventually, after the adrenaline of the morning wore off, they both fell asleep curled together on Zac's bed, closer than they'd been since before Lu had gone off to kindergarten and he had been forced to stay home. And yet again, as Lu slept, she found herself inside a vivid dream she couldn't escape.

It was the same one as before—the same dusty wing of the manor, the same room full of twisted cruelties. But this time, as she moved through the disturbing trophies, she spotted Oliver in the corner, crouched beside the bookshelves as he frantically flipped through one of the ancient leather-bound volumes.

"Oliver?" she said, surprised. What was he doing here? How did he even know about this place?

But he didn't respond. Instead he grew still, staring at a single page now. She moved toward him as quickly as she dared, not wanting to startle him.

"Oliver," she said, louder this time. "Is Penelope okay? Why are you here?"

She hovered over him now, but he ignored her completely. He couldn't see her, she realized—she was a ghost to him. Maybe not even that.

Frowning, she peeked over his shoulder, trying to read the page he was fixated on. The words seemed to blur together and change, like they were hiding from her somehow, and she squinted, leaning even closer.

As soon as a single word came into focus in the otherwise undecipherable jumble, the dream dissolved, and she awoke with a start. It was early afternoon now, and she lay at the foot of Zac's bed. He nestled beside her, still fast asleep, and she gingerly untangled herself from him so she could stand.

Her dream had been as vivid as all the others, and her insides churned as she stumbled across the room to her own bed. What was Oliver doing there? And what had he been reading?

Trap. That was the word she'd focused on—the only word on the page that she could read. But what did it mean? Why was it so important that the phoenix decided she had to dream about it?

The phoenix. She swallowed bitterly. He could have made the manticore leave them alone, and instead he had let that monster find them. Zac had been so sure the phoenix would protect him, but the stupid bird hadn't even shown himself. If Oliver hadn't appeared when he had—if they couldn't find a cure for the manticore's venom . . .

Hearing footsteps in the hallway, she doubled back toward the door and cracked it open. She hadn't forgotten Aunt Merle's warning, but she had to know how Penelope was doing.

The door across from theirs stood open, and Rowena leaned against the doorframe, her back to Lu.

". . . fever's up," said Conrad's voice from deeper inside the room. He sounded like he'd aged a decade since that morning. "Not even fairy nectar is helping."

"None of the antivenom the doctor brought is a match?"

said Rowena. Conrad must have shaken his head, because she sighed. "Why didn't she carry a torch with her, or something loud enough to drive it away? She *knows* how to scare off a manticore."

"Other than the knife, she had no equipment at all," said Conrad. "She certainly wasn't dressed for the Wildewoods."

"Those bloody twins," muttered Rowena. "After all the trouble Josie caused in this family, now her children have somehow managed to make it even worse."

Lu shrank back behind the door. The anger in her great-aunt's voice was hot and sharp, and though she wanted to explain, she knew it wouldn't change anything. It didn't matter why Zac had gone out there, or why she and Penelope had chased after him. It didn't matter that Zac had tried to protect her. Penelope had still been stung. And now she was dying.

After a moment, Rowena muttered, "I should call their father."

"And do what?" said Conrad. "Have him take them back to Chicago? There's no need to compound this tragedy with another."

At first Lu didn't understand what he meant, but then she remembered what Penelope had said the night before— the reason Zac had gone after the phoenix in the first place. They couldn't leave the Wildewoods. Not when they were cursed.

She stared at the *W* on her palm and tried angrily to rub it away. Before, it had been a reminder of their mother and all the things she had loved. But now, knowing what it meant—knowing that they were stuck here forever, knowing they were related to someone who had hunted these creatures for money—it sickened her.

"She would've stood a chance if she could've fought back," said Rowena after a long moment. "It's that bloody phoenix—expecting us to sacrifice our lives for what? My brother died on those mountains, and he wasn't the first. If we could protect ourselves at the very least—"

"The phoenix has a long memory," said Conrad with a sigh. "He doesn't understand time the way we do."

"Perhaps he'll understand if we stop helping," said Rowena sharply. "The curse only dictates that we enter the Wildewoods regularly. Anything else we choose to do is above and beyond."

Conrad was quiet for a long moment. "You know I won't be able to sit back and not help. Those creatures are innocent."

"So is Penelope," said Rowena. "And she's your daughter."

"I'm aware," he snapped. "I'm doing everything I can to help her. That needs to be our priority right now—not reigniting old grudges or rebelling against things we cannot change."

The ensuing silence crackled with tension, and at last

Rowena's shoulders sagged. "You're right. I'm sorry," she said simply. "I'll continue to scour the records for anything useful."

"Thank you," said Conrad softly. "When you see Oliver, will you please send him to me as well?"

Rowena nodded. "He's searching the old journals as we speak. Nature always provides a cure for its own poison, though it may come from an unexpected source. If there's anything more we can do . . ."

Conrad's response was nonverbal. Rowena cleared her throat, and as she turned around, Lu ducked back behind the door. If her great-aunt noticed that it wasn't completely closed, she didn't say anything as she limped back down the hallway, leaning on her walking stick.

"Lu?" mumbled Zac from his bed, and he sat up, rubbing his eyes. "What's going on?"

"Nothing," lied Lu. "I need to do something really quick. Are you okay on your own?"

Zac's nod wasn't a surprise. He hated being babysat, and Lu knew it. But his earlier asthma attack seemed to have resolved, and if he did have trouble, Conrad was right across the hall.

Slipping out of their room, she glanced briefly into Penelope's and immediately wished she hadn't. Her cousin lay unconscious on her bed, with a pale blue quilt tucked in around her still body. Penelope's skin was tinged with gray, and her chest rose and fell at a rapid, shallow pace. Conrad was hunched over her, listening to her heart with a stethoscope, and even though Lu could see only half of his face, the worry and tension he carried were obvious.

Taking a deep breath, she hurried down the corridor on silent feet. When she reached the grand staircase, the smell of lunch cooking wafted up from the kitchen, and her stomach rumbled, reminding her that she hadn't had anything to eat yet. It didn't matter. This was far more important.

She descended the stairs to the first floor, making sure to skip the step that squeaked. Instead of turning right toward the kitchen, however, Lu went left—toward the double doors that had been chained together every time she'd checked. But as she turned the corner, she stopped dead in her tracks. The chain dangled from only one of the handles now, and the padlock had been carelessly discarded in a corner.

Hesitating only for a moment, Lu crept forward and gave the doors an experimental tug. Though they opened with ease, the hinges protested loudly enough to echo into the foyer.

"Oliver?" called Rowena from her office nearby. "Is that you?"

Lu darted through the double doors and shut them quietly behind her. She was dizzy from tension now, and as she turned around, she thought her heart might actually stop.

She was here—the long, musty corridor that looked as if it hadn't been touched in a century. It was exactly like she'd dreamed, with sunlight streaming in through holes in the heavy curtains over the windows, illuminating the dust that lingered in the air. The doors along the opposite wall were all closed, and she ignored them as she moved slowly down the hall.

There, finally, was the door she was looking for. Like in her dream, she was drawn to it, and flickering light spilled out from the crack underneath. Feeling vaguely ill, she turned the knob and nudged it open, her throat tight and her hands sweating.

She saw the dragon skeleton first, somehow even more gigantic in real life. It was so tall it nearly reached the high ceiling, and it cast a shadow over the other hunting trophies in the room. Unicorns, fairies, curling horns she didn't recognize, shimmering fins that could only have come from mermaids—everything in her dream and more.

She wasn't surprised it was real, not after everything they'd seen in the Wildewoods, but the disgust that rose within her was as visceral as ever. As she stepped inside, the bookcases came into view, and there, crouched beside them exactly the way he'd been in her latest dream, was Oliver.

A stack of leather-bound books was balanced pre-cariously beside him, most of them discarded haphazardly despite their obvious age. Oliver pored through another, flipping pages faster than he could possibly be reading. He was looking for something.

He was looking for a cure.

She crept through the room, ducking behind pedestals and platforms, trying to get close enough to—what? She wasn't sure. Rowena had said that nature always provided a cure for its own poison. Did she and Oliver think these books would hold the answer?

Lu hid behind the dragon skeleton as her cousin discarded that book and started on another. He did the same thing three times in what couldn't have been more than ten minutes, but it felt like forever to Lu.

Her foot started to fall asleep, and she shifted, trying not to make any noise. Maybe this was a stupid idea. Rowena would have another fit if she knew Lu had found this place. This wasn't the kind of room someone left open for unsuspecting guests to wander into, after all, and the chained doors spoke for themselves. Besides, as disturbing as the trophy room had been in her dreams, actually being here chilled her to the bone, and she was itching to get back to the safety of her mum's bedroom.

Just as she was about to sneak back out, however, Oliver stopped flipping pages. Lu peered at him from her vantage point, watching as his eyes narrowed. "Yes," he said quietly, though his voice crackled with victory and relief. *"Yes."*

He traced his finger over the page, his lips moving as he read to himself. And then, with far more care than he'd shown the other books, he placed it reverently back on the shelf, left the discarded pile on the floor, and hurried out of the room.

Lu stared after him, astonished. He must've found it—a cure. A way to save Penelope. Relief washed over her, a cool sensation that spread from her fingers to her toes, and feeling a hundred times lighter, she started toward the door as well, eager to tell Zac the news. But before she reached it, she stopped, her curiosity overriding her fear. After crossing the room to the tall shelves, she picked up the book Oliver had studied.

The leather felt oddly brittle in her grip, as if one wrong move might make the whole book fall apart. Her hands shook as she let the spine fall open, and she touched the fragile page, avoiding the faded ink.

It was a journal, she realized, and a very old one at that. Everything was handwritten. And not in the neat, blocky letters she was used to—this was cursive, the kind of cursive that was completely undecipherable to her. The letters were long and looped and so crammed together that they looked more like pretty, uneven designs than words, and many of them were smudged.

She turned the pages. Occasionally small drawings and diagrams took the place of words she couldn't read, though none of those made sense to her either. Frustrated, she looked at the cover, but it was blank.

At last she turned to the very first page, hoping for a title or dates at the very least. Instead there was a single line of loopy handwriting—larger than the rest, and somehow clearer, too. This had been written with intent. It wasn't the sloppy scribbles of someone trying to jot down their thoughts before they disappeared. It was a name.

Thomas Wilde.

21

ZAC

THAT MORNING, ZAC WOULD HAVE THOUGHT IT was impossible to feel any worse about what had happened to Penelope than he already did. But now, as he peeked through the opening of his bedroom door and into the room across the hall, he was all but drowning in guilt.

While his view was narrow, he could see his cousin's legs as she lay in bed, completely still. Conrad moved over her, taking her pulse and blood pressure every few minutes, and in between he flipped through a stack of medical textbooks sitting on her nightstand.

It was Zac's fault. He shouldn't have gone into the Wildewoods alone. He should have fought harder against the manticore. If he had, maybe everything would be okay. Maybe Penelope wouldn't be dying.

The guilt wasn't a new feeling. It was the same impossible weight he'd been carrying since he'd found his mother in the kitchen. Ever since that day, he'd asked himself why he hadn't checked on her sooner. She had spent her life watching over him. Why couldn't he have done the same?

No one outwardly blamed him for his mother dying, though. Everyone—even Lu—had told him it wasn't his fault. This, though . . . it was his fault. It was every bit his fault.

"Conrad, could you join me for a moment?" Aunt Merle's voice floated up from the staircase, and Zac hastily hid behind the doorway as his uncle sighed heavily.

"I'll only be a few minutes," he said quietly, presumably to Penelope, and Zac listened as his footsteps creaked out of the bedroom and down the corridor.

He peered through the doorway again. Penelope was still lying in bed, oblivious to her father's departure. And while Zac knew he shouldn't go anywhere near her, not after everything he'd done, he couldn't stand the thought of her being alone right now.

He tiptoed across the hallway and stepped inside her bedroom uncertainly, watching her. He expected stillness—the kind of stillness that had been in his kitchen over a month ago. But her chest rose and fell in shallow gasps as she struggled to hold on, and something inside him broke.

"I'm sorry," he whispered jaggedly, his vision blurred and his face growing hot as he approached her bedside. "I'm so sorry, Penelope. I didn't—I didn't mean—"

He took her hand in his, squeezing her limp fingers. Her skin was warm, he realized. It wasn't cold like his mother's had been, and he took a shaky breath, trying to steady himself. Penelope wasn't gone yet, and the last thing she needed right now was for him to give up hope.

She still had time. She still had a chance.

"The phoenix would know how to cure you," he managed thickly. "But I don't know how to find him. I couldn't today. Maybe he knew I wanted something. Maybe that's the trick of it—he'll only show up if you don't want anything from him." And now Zac wanted something from the phoenix so desperately that he nearly choked on it.

Penelope continued to breathe rapidly, like she was running a marathon in her dreams. Zac pressed his lips together. "I don't know what to do. If I go back in on my own, Lu will come looking for me, and—and the manticore might attack her, too. Or a dragon. But if I tell her I'm going, she'll want to come with me. And if she does . . ." After everything that had happened, both to their mother and to Penelope, he couldn't stand the thought of risking Lu's life too.

Heavy footsteps reverberated from the corridor, and

he tensed. Conrad was back, and from the sounds of it, already halfway down the hall. Zac had no time to slip away without being seen, and that meant coming face-to-face with his uncle's anger and grief.

As panic seized him, he did the only thing he could think of—he ducked underneath the bed, hiding between shoe-boxes and discarded socks, and he listened as the footsteps approached. They paused at the entrance to the bedroom, and for a moment he wondered if he was hiding for noth-ing. Maybe Lu was looking for him, and he'd have to come crawling out and make up a story about dropping a pencil or something.

As embarrassing as that would be, he hoped it was her. But as he peeked around a pile of books about animal care, he spotted a pair of black combat boots unlike anything Lu—or Conrad, or his aunts—ever wore.

Oliver.

His cousin stepped into the room, approaching an arm-chair beside Penelope's bed. The springs squeaked as he sat down, and Zac inhaled sharply, trying to hold his breath. But at that moment, his nose began to itch and his eyes began to water, and he suddenly had the horrible urge to sneeze.

Dust, he realized. There was probably a mountain of it underneath the bed, and he had no way out.

"I'm sorry I wasn't there," said Oliver quietly. "I shouldn't have split us up. I shouldn't have let you go with that idiot. The twins don't know anything about the Wildewoods, and I was stupid to think that being with her would protect you. Of course it didn't. That bird—that—awful—that *monster*—"

His voice caught, and Zac closed his eyes, trying desperately to hold in his sneeze. He pressed his finger to his nose, willing himself to keep silent.

Oliver cleared his throat. "It doesn't matter. I found a cure," he said, and Zac's heart leaped, the sneeze momentarily forgotten. "In the old journals—I know how to fix all of this. But I have to go back out for a little while. I won't be gone long, I promise, and you have to hold on. All right? You have to."

Zac buried his nose in the crook of his elbow. He couldn't hold it in much longer. What excuse could he possibly make for hiding under the bed and eavesdropping on Oliver's private conversation with Penelope? There was none. None that sounded sane, anyway.

His cousin's voice dropped to a whisper. "When I get back, you'll never have to set foot in the Wildewoods again. Neither of us will. We'll be able to live with Mum and actually have a life. We won't be trapped here anymore, and—and—" His voice broke, and Zac was sure he was crying now. "When you wake up, everything will be better," he managed with a sniff. "And I won't let anything happen to you ever again. I promise."

Oliver stood, and the itching in Zac's nose grew to a crescendo. He'd never held in a sneeze this long before. At this rate, his skull would implode with the effort it took, and he grew dizzy from holding his breath.

But at last Oliver's boots thudded against the floorboards once more as he hastily exited the room and darted down the hall. And finally, barely a second after his cousin's footsteps faded completely, Zac sneezed. And he sneezed again. And again. And again.

"Zac?" A different pair of shoes appeared—pale green sneakers he instantly recognized as Lu's. "What are you doing down there?"

Sheepishly Zac crawled out from underneath Penelope's bed, and he sneezed again. His shirt was covered in dust. "I was visiting Penelope, and Oliver came by," he mumbled. "Didn't want him to find me here."

"So you figured you'd crawl under the bed?" She offered him her hand, and he took it, letting her haul him to his feet. "Look at you—you've already got a rash."

"It's—*achoo!*—it's dusty down there," said Zac, wiping his runny nose with the back of his hand. His arms were covered in red, itchy hives. "Oliver said he found a cure."

Instead of looking shocked, like he expected, Lu glanced at a leather-bound book she was holding. "Did he say what it was?"

"No, but I think he's headed into the Wildewoods to get it. And he said something weird, too," Zac added. "He promised Penelope that when she's better, they'll never have to go back there again."

Lu raised her eyebrows. "He found a way to break the curse?"

"I guess," he said, his thoughts swirling unpleasantly around a twisted idea he didn't want to touch. "Conrad will be back any minute. He doesn't know I'm in here."

"He won't mind," said Lu, but she crossed the hallway anyway and returned to their bedroom. "I'll get you a Bena-dryl."

Zac followed her, and while she rummaged through his medications, he eyed the book she had set on the dresser. "What's that?"

"It's a journal, I think. Thomas Wilde's journal," she said. "Oliver was looking through it in—in the other wing. He read one of the pages and got really excited, and he took off. But I can't read the writing. I was hoping you could. Mum made you learn cursive, right?"

"Yeah. She said it would help my art." Zac picked it up gingerly. The pages were delicate and worn, as if they'd been handled countless times over the centuries, and the handwriting was cramped, but Zac could mostly make out the words. "Any idea what we're looking for?"

"None," said Lu, finding the right package and tearing

it open. She offered him a pill, and he swallowed it without taking his eyes off the journal.

"They're instructions," said Zac, absently scratching his arm. "This is about how to extract basilisk venom."

"Basilisks?" said Lu, alarmed. "Those giant snakes?"

He nodded. Once again, that twisted thought surfaced in his mind, and he flipped the page, searching for—what, he didn't know for sure. But he knew he'd recognize it when he found it. *If* he found it. Maybe he was wrong. Maybe Oliver had found another way. "This is how to break out of a fairy's enchantment. And this one—" He made a face. "How to create dragon-hide armor. I guess that explains why Rowena's shield can repel dragon fire."

Lu peeked over his shoulder. "Keep reading," she insisted. "There has to be something about how to save Penelope."

He continued to search, turning the pages with less and less care as he went. Lists of magical ingredients with the highest values. Songs to sing to distract mermaids. The best places to find dragon eggs in the mountains. All horrifying and fascinating, but nothing Oliver could use to heal his sister.

At last, however, Zac turned to a page toward the end of the book. There, in letters so clear even Lu had to be able to read them, were the words he had been dreading.

How to Hunt a Phoenix.

22

LU

LU FROWNED AS SHE SKIMMED THE JOURNAL PAGE over her brother's shoulder. Most of the handwriting was so fancy that there was no way she could read it, but the title of one entry stood out.

"Wait," she said, confused "Does that really say—"

"Yeah," said her brother, sounding like he'd swallowed his own tongue. "It's—it's a list of instructions on how to hunt a phoenix and harvest its blood. Oliver only needs a drop to save Penelope—"

"But you said he wanted to end the curse, too." Her mouth went dry, and suddenly she felt light-headed. "He's going to kill the phoenix, isn't he?"

"I—I think so." Zac flipped the page. "But the process is complicated. Oliver has to trap him first, and that isn't easy. Even if he manages somehow, there's still—ice and tubes and—and other things."

"Penelope wouldn't want him to hurt the phoenix," said Lu, clenching her fists. "He must know that."

"I don't think Oliver cares." Zac grimaced. "The phoenix's magic created the Wildewoods. If Oliver goes through with it, the entire sanctuary will disappear, and the animals could be thrown into our world instead. Can you imagine what would happen to the dragons? Or what some people would do in order to get a unicorn horn for themselves?"

His words settled over her, heavy and impossible not to imagine. If the phoenix died, the Wildewoods would disappear, and the consequences would be devastating for both the creatures and the real world. Their family would be free—*they* would be free—but at what price?

"We have to tell Conrad and Rowena," she said. "If they can find Oliver—"

"Conrad won't leave Penelope's side, and Rowena can barely walk right now," said Zac. "Besides, they won't help us. They'll do everything they can to help Oliver instead. I know they want to save Penelope—I do too," he added. "But the phoenix doesn't have to die in the process."

Lu gritted her teeth. "So what are we supposed to do? Warn him?"

"We can protect him," he said with a hint of ferocity she didn't expect. "If we can get to the phoenix first—"

"You want to go back into the Wildewoods?" said Lu, her heart sinking, and he nodded.

"What other choice do we have?"

Lu closed her eyes and took a deep, steadying breath. "You know Mum always thought *I* was the reckless one, right?"

"Mum would agree with me, and you know it. She loved the phoenix. He was her friend."

Zac was right. Their mother would have agreed with him—more to the point, she wouldn't have wasted time debating whether to go. She would've already been on her way to the Wildewoods by now. "Okay," said Lu at last. "But if we're going to do this, you have to listen to me and not run off whenever you feel like it. We're a team."

"We're a team," echoed Zac, and when she opened her eyes, he was scratching a hive on his neck and grinning. "Let's go save the Wildewoods."

It was surprisingly easy to sneak out of their bedroom unnoticed. Rowena and Aunt Merle were somewhere downstairs, while Conrad was engrossed in a thick textbook at Penelope's bedside. With their backpacks slung over their shoulders, Lu and Zac crept down the hallway, avoiding the squeakiest floorboards, and slowly descended the grand staircase, ready to bolt at any sign of movement from above or below.

Distantly Lu heard their aunts' voices coming from the dining room, and as they passed Rowena's office, she hesitated. "We need a map," she whispered. "I'm going to grab one. If anyone comes by, pretend you're having an asthma attack, all right?"

"Got it," said Zac, and with that, she ducked inside. The office was still dim and dusty, but without Rowena sitting behind the massive desk, it wasn't nearly as intimidating as it had been the evening before. Edging around the mismatched chairs, Lu tiptoed to the back wall, where a dozen or more maps of the Wildewoods hung in shadows.

"Lu," whispered Zac from the doorway. "I hear footsteps."

Without bothering to inspect it, she untaped the nearest map—a medium-size one that was torn around the edges. She couldn't tell if it had any details on it, but it would have to do.

As she hastily folded it up, she hurried out of the room and followed her brother to the back door. Rowena's uneven gait echoed from the dining hall, and Lu held her breath as Zac fumbled with the lock.

"Got it," whispered Zac triumphantly, and he pushed the door open wide enough for both of them to slip outside. With exaggerated care, he closed it, and as soon as the latch clicked into place, he and Lu darted through the back garden.

At last they reached the trees, and Zac paused to catch his breath. Lu watched him anxiously, but he caught her eye and grinned.

"I'm fine," he promised. "Just winded."

Lu wasn't so sure she believed him. He would say anything to get to the Wildewoods now, even if he were in the middle of the worst asthma attack of his life. But as the seconds passed, his breathing seemed to ease, and soon enough they trudged onward.

"How are we supposed to find the phoenix, anyway?" said Lu as the tree arch came into view. And when she glanced at her brother, she could tell by the look on his face that he was worried about the same thing.

"The phoenix finds us," he pointed out. "But maybe we can start at the gnarled tree. I think he likes it there. In almost every memory he shows me of him and Mum, that's where they are."

A wave of jealousy washed over Lu at the mention of memories, but she pushed it aside. Now wasn't the time. "The sun sets in seven hours," she said. "We don't want to be caught out there at night. We'll be eaten for sure."

"Maybe then the phoenix will show himself," muttered Zac, though Lu wasn't convinced. He hadn't come to their rescue that morning, which meant they couldn't count on his protection. They were on their own this time.

As they stepped through the tree arch, Lu felt the now-familiar shiver wash over her as the air around them seemed to change. There was no denying that the Wildewoods were made of pure magic, and the thought of it all disappearing because of Oliver—no, because of *them*—made part of her shrivel up in dread.

"Do you think the tree's marked on that map?" said Zac as they stopped in the middle of the meadow.

"Doubt it," said Lu, though she unfolded the yellowing piece of paper anyway. As soon as she got a good look at it, however, her heart sank. While the edges were mostly intact, the majority of the map was faded and distorted, as if someone had spilled water on it.

"You're joking," said Zac. "The ink's almost all gone."

"I'm sorry," said Lu miserably. "It was dark in the office, all right? I grabbed the first one I could reach."

Much to her surprise, Zac shook his head. "It's not your fault." But he sounded so utterly crushed and dismayed that Lu couldn't help but feel guilty.

"We know it's in that direction, right?" she said, pointing to the west. "We'll head that way, and we'll hope the manticore isn't there anymore."

Zac stiffened. "I forgot about the manticore."

"Of course you did," said Lu, exasperated. "I overheard Rowena and Conrad talking about how to scare it off. A whip isn't the only thing that works. They mentioned a torch—"

"A torch?" Zac frowned. "Did you bring any matches?"

"I don't think they meant that kind of torch," said Lu. "Remember how Dad always got so confused when we had a power outage, and Mum asked him where the torches were?"

Zac blinked as comprehension dawned on him. "You mean . . ."

Lu pulled a flashlight out of her backpack. "I'm sure real fire would work, but this is probably safer. And Penelope always carries one with her."

With a whoop, Zac threw his arms around her. "You're a *genius*."

"Dunno know about that," said Lu awkwardly. But when he finally let go, still beaming, she couldn't resist grinning as well. "If I'm wrong, we could become the manticore's dinner. But I might be right, too, I guess."

"It doesn't hurt to be optimistic every once in a while," said Zac as he started toward the trees. "Come on. I went that way this morning, and Penelope said I was too far south—"

All of a sudden, the ground began to quake, throwing Lu and Zac into a patch of wildflowers. In the forest nearby, several tree trunks crashed to the ground, and Lu screamed, throwing herself over her brother.

The sky, which had been a bright summer blue only a moment ago, darkened into black storm clouds, and a powerful gust of wind blew across the meadow. In the pasture, the unicorns began to rear and neigh anxiously, and Lu looked around, stunned.

"What's going on?" she cried as lightning exploded above them.

"I don't know!" Though Zac was shouting, she could barely hear him over the deafening thunder that followed. "We should go back!"

Terrified, she scrambled to her feet, struggling to stay upright as the earth continued to shudder. Grabbing Zac's hand, she pulled him toward the tree arch. This storm had to be magical, and if they could just get back to the real world . . .

But before they could take another step, a blinding light filled the air. And right in front of her eyes, a giant lightning bolt hit the ancient pair of intertwined trees, splitting them apart.

As suddenly as the storm had arrived, it grew quiet once more, and the sky returned to its bright, cheerful blue as the ground stilled. Lu barely noticed, however, as she stared at the charred remains of their only way out.

23

ZAC

IT HAD BEEN DAYS SINCE ANXIETY AND FEAR HAD last overwhelmed Zac, freezing him in place. But as he gawked at the destroyed tree arch, the edges of his vision darkened, and he could feel his chest tighten with panic.

No. No, no, no. They couldn't be stuck here—maybe they could still walk through the trees. But as he stumbled forward on unsteady feet and ducked underneath what was left of the arch, nothing changed. He was still in the Wilde-woods.

They were trapped.

"Breathe," said Lu as she joined him and rubbed his back. "It's just an anxiety attack. You're okay. Everything's okay."

"It's not okay," he wheezed, sinking to the ground. "It's not—it's not—"

He was hyperventilating now, his breaths coming in great gasping sobs. Vaguely he was aware of Lu wrapping her arms around him as he sank to the forest floor, but it didn't help. Nothing could help them anymore. Except—

"The—the phoenix," he managed. The phoenix would be able to fix this. He was magic. He would repair the tree arch, and everything would be all right, Zac tried to tell himself. Everything would be all right.

"We'll find him," said Lu, her voice sounding far off. "I promise, we'll find him."

Zac squeezed his eyes shut and drew his knees to his chest, his entire body trembling now. It would be okay. It would be okay. It would be—

Without warning, an image flooded his mind, displacing all his senses. He stood near the gnarled tree again, watching as the phoenix waddled past the trunk. Zac's heart leaped. "You're here!" he said, darting forward. "I thought you were ignoring me. The tree arch is destroyed, and Lu and I are trapped. Penelope's hurt, and Oliver . . ."

He trailed off. The phoenix didn't acknowledge him. He didn't even glance Zac's way. Instead he continued to waddle across the forest floor, as if Zac wasn't even there.

This was a memory, he realized, and all the hope

drained out of him. But why was the phoenix showing him this? It had to be important somehow.

As Zac walked alongside him, he spotted a strange bush nearby, directly in the phoenix's path. It wasn't very large, and the branches that covered it were scraggly at best, while the base seemed oddly twisted and darker than normal wood. Frowning, he moved closer. And only when he was a few feet away did he realize it wasn't a bush at all.

It was a cage. And inside, nestled among the leaves, was a purple phoenix feather.

"Wait," said Zac, trying to block his way. But with single-minded determination, the phoenix walked right through his intangible form, and Zac heard a soft purring as the bird approached the feather.

"No, look—it's a cage," he begged, but it was pointless. This was a memory. It wasn't happening in real time, and he watched, completely helpless, as the phoenix stepped right into the trap.

The cage door snapped shut instantly, and a triumphant crow echoed through the trees. Oliver emerged from a nearby copse, holding a thin wire that must have been attached to the door.

"Got you now, haven't I?" said Oliver with grim satisfaction. He picked up the cage, and inside, the phoenix squawked. "You're going to save my sister."

The phoenix tried to extend his wings inside the cage,

but it was far too small. Oliver wove a wide leather strap through the bars and secured it around his body, allowing him to carry the cage on his back. The phoenix began to cry out in earnest now, and Zac could feel the tension building in the summer air. And as the sky began to darken, the ground beneath him started to shake once more.

"What the—" Oliver jumped around a fallen log, nearly losing his footing. "What are you doing? Stop it!"

But the trembling grew stronger, and with a cry, Oliver darted away from the tree. And as soon as Zac lost sight of him, the memory dissolved.

"Zac? *Zac.*" Lu was shaking him now, her fear palpable. "Can you hear me? Are you okay?"

Zac nodded weakly, blinking as the forest and the charred arch came into view around him once more. "Oliver has him," he managed, his throat impossibly tight. "I saw it. The phoenix—Oliver trapped him in a cage."

Lu handed him his inhaler, but Zac refused to take it. This wasn't an asthma attack. "You're absolutely sure that's what you saw?" she said.

"Positive. That's why the storm happened, and the earthquake. It was the phoenix."

His sister exhaled sharply and eyed what remained of the tree arch. "Oliver can't hurt him while they're still inside the Wildewoods," she said. "That must be why the phoenix destroyed the exit—to buy himself time."

"But we're trapped here," said Zac as his breathing slowly eased back to normal. "Oliver is too."

"Only in this part of the Wildewoods. There's another exit, remember?" Lu pulled the useless map from her pocket. "See that symbol at the top?"

Zac squinted at the inky blotch on the northern border. "It looks like a smudge."

Lu frowned and peered at it again. "I don't think so. Look, down here—" She pointed to the bottom of the map, where there was another symbol, this one clearer than the first. "This is the tree arch."

He studied the mark. "Are you sure?" he said dubiously.

"Positive. See? This is the meadow, and up this path— I know it's blurry, but I think these are the grasslands and the lagoon. And I think these are the mountains we saw in the distance."

Though his hands still trembled slightly, Zac took the map from her, his eyes roaming over the distorted middle. "You think the other exit is north of here, in the grasslands?"

"Past the grasslands," corrected Lu. "Penelope said it was someplace dangerous. I think it might be in the Scorchlands, north of the mountains."

"Terrific," said Zac. "So all we have to do is cross the entire span of the Wildewoods, avoid getting eaten by dragons and an angry manticore and whatever else might be hungry, and hope we're going in the right direction. And if we aren't—"

"We could wait here for Oliver," she suggested. "He's trapped in here with us, after all. And I bet he knows where the other exit is."

Zac raised his eyebrows. "You think he'll let us tag along, even though we're trying to rescue the phoenix?"

She gave him a look. "Do you really think he'd leave us here to die?"

He hesitated. "I think he'll figure out what we're up to," he said slowly. "And I think he'll do whatever it takes to save Penelope."

Lu was quiet for a moment, and he knew she agreed. Or at least she wasn't willing to take that risk. "He doesn't have to know we're following him," she said. "If we hide in the trees, we can wait until he gets here, and—"

"Uh, Lu?" said Zac, catching sight of something over her shoulder. "I don't think that's going to work."

"What? Why not?" she said, whirling around. A moment later, her eyes widened, and she swore.

There, half-hidden behind a tree near the edge of the meadow, was Oliver. And he was staring directly at them.

24

LU

LU THOUGHT SHE WAS FAST. SHE'D BEEN ON THE track team at school, after all, and while Zac may not have been able to run, she could, and she loved it.

But Oliver was faster. While her sneakers barely touched the ground, he seemed to literally fly through the trees, weaving his way through the forest even with the cage strapped to his back. And before long, she'd lost sight of him entirely.

When she returned to the charred tree arch, Zac was standing, looking marginally better than he had minutes earlier. "Are you okay?" he said anxiously.

"Just annoyed," she said, leaning over to catch her breath. "He's really fast."

"So are you," said Zac, sounding impressed. "I didn't know you could run like that."

"That's because you and Mum never came to my meets," she pointed out. He frowned, and before he could say anything, she added hastily, "It's fine. I know why you couldn't. I'm only saying—you weren't there, so of course you didn't know."

"I'll come to the next one," he promised quietly, but his expression fell as they both seemed to realize that there wouldn't be a next one. One way or the other, they were stuck.

"We need to come up with a plan," said Lu. "If we can't follow Oliver, then we have to assume the map is accurate, and the second exit is north of here."

"What if it isn't?" said Zac, and she shrugged.

"It doesn't hurt to be optimistic once in a while, does it?" she said with a faint hint of mockery. "If we're wrong, we'll deal with it later. But that exit is our only way out now, and we have to at least try to find it."

They both studied the faded map again, though it wasn't much help. "How long do you think it'll take to get to the Scorchlands?" said Zac.

"I don't know," she admitted. He would have to stop

frequently, and she had no idea how far the Wildewoods really extended. Even if they managed to navigate their way over the mountains, they would still have to survive the dangerous creatures on the other side. "A few days, maybe."

Zac pursed his lips, and as if he could read her mind, he said, "How long do you think it would take if you didn't have to wait for me?"

She shook her head. "I'm not leaving you. We'll figure it out, all right? I'll carry you if I have to."

Zac snorted. "How? You're not that much stronger than me."

"I don't know," she said, frustrated. "But we stick together. This place is dangerous, and it won't matter how fast I can run if a rabid unicorn eats me along the way."

"You think I can save you from a rabid unicorn?" scoffed Zac, but when she looked at him, he was smirking. She smirked back.

"I think you're crazy enough to try. Now come on— if we want to have any hope of catching Oliver before he takes the phoenix out of the Wildewoods, we need to go. He was heading north toward the stream. If we can reach the mountains before sundown, we can find a cave and hole up for the night."

Lu started down the path, and Zac followed alongside her. "You know dragons live on those mountains, right?" he said.

"It's better than sleeping out in the open, where they can roast us from the sky and treat themselves to a midnight snack," she pointed out. In truth, however, she wasn't at all certain what they were going to do that night. They'd play it by ear, she figured. They had no other choice.

She found sturdy walking sticks for them both, and together they hiked toward the stream. The path seemed even longer than it had two days earlier, and they had to stop several times for Zac to catch his breath. His wheezing was getting worse, but he refused to rest for more than a couple of minutes. She kept an eye on him, letting him set the pace, and when they finally reached the edge of the grasslands, she wasn't sure whether to feel relieved or even more worried than she already was.

"Hold on," she said, and she darted toward a twisted tree. "I'm gonna take a look and see how far we have to go."

"You're going to what?" said Zac, but she was already climbing. This tree was even easier to scale than the one that Rufus liked, and she pulled herself up without breaking a sweat. Zac watched from the ground, and when she glanced down, she could see his mouth hanging open. Lu grinned. Apparently there was a lot they didn't know about each other.

Once she was as high as she could go without the branches giving way, she wrapped her arms around the rough trunk and gazed out across the Wildewoods. From this far up, they didn't look so big, and even the mountains that curved around the grasslands seemed closer than they really were. She spotted a unicorn herd nearby, and several miles away, tall grass rippled as if something large was moving through it. Her view of the lagoon was clear from here, too, though it seemed tiny compared to a vast lake to the west, nestled between the base of the mountains and the edge of the grasslands. That must have been on the part of the map that had faded.

"What do you see?" called Zac. "Is Oliver out there?"

She squinted. As good as her vision was, she didn't see any sign of him. But he could have easily been hiding in the trees, or taken another route they didn't know about. "No," she called. "He's probably still in the forest."

"Should we wait for him?" said Zac, and Lu considered it.

"I don't think so. There are miles of trees in either direction. He could come from anywhere, and we won't be able to catch him."

She climbed down, and when she was once more on solid ground, she wiped her palms on her jeans. "I think our best bet is to just go north. I don't see a shortcut to the mountains, unless you feel like swimming across a lake."

"Lake?" said Zac uneasily. "Like the lagoon with the mermaids?"

"Much bigger," she said, and he shuddered. "The long way it is, then."

As they set off across the grasslands with the sun beating down on them, Lu wished she'd brought a hat. Without the shade from the trees, the heat became almost unbearable, and by the time they crested the third hill, Zac was once again wheezing. While he sat and caught his breath, she looked around, surprised to find a chestnut foal with a tiny golden horn watching them nearby.

"Zac," she whispered, nudging him. He looked up, his chest heaving.

"Whoa," he managed. And as they both stared, the little unicorn trotted curiously toward them.

"Hello," she murmured, holding out her palm. The foal nuzzled it hopefully, and she grinned. "I'm sorry, we don't have any treats for you." They barely had enough food to last them the rest of the day. "Where's your family?"

"Uh. Right there, I'd guess," said Zac, and he slowly climbed to his feet. "Lu . . ."

An angry whinny cut through the breeze, and on the next hill over, a large stallion with an identical chestnut coat reared on his hind legs, his front hooves cutting through the air. Several other unicorns appeared behind him, their sharp horns flashing in the sunlight, and though the foal's ears pricked up, it didn't move back to the safety of its herd. Lu swallowed nervously.

"It's okay," she called, inching backward. "We're not hurting it. We're just saying hi, that's all."

The stallion snorted again, a clear warning this time. Lu took another step back and nearly lost her footing as the hill sloped downward. She caught herself, not taking her eyes off the unicorn stallion. If she looked away, she was sure he would attack.

"Whatever you do, don't run," she said quietly to her brother.

"No danger of that happening anytime soon," wheezed Zac. "If he comes this way, you go left, and I'll go right, okay?"

She nodded, but his words sounded like static as the foal trotted toward them once more, clueless to its sire's growing fury. Yet again, it tried to nuzzle Lu's hand, looking for food that wasn't there, and the stallion didn't waste any more time. With a battle cry that echoed across the grassy hills, he reared and charged straight for them.

Lu didn't think. With that horn only seconds away, she shoved Zac to one side, only to lose her balance and fall with him. And as the thunderous hoofbeats grew closer, the two of them tumbled down the side of the hill and into the gentle dip below.

"Ow!" cried Zac as they finally stopped rolling. "I told you to go left!"

"It was an accident," she said, glancing up at the top of the hill. The stallion now stood beside the foal, silhouetted by the bright sun as he stared down at them. With another neigh of warning, the unicorn shepherded his wayward young in the opposite direction, and Lu sat up, rubbing her stinging cheek. "Are you okay?"

"I think I cut my hand," he said, and sure enough, there was a small scrape on his unmarked palm. "You didn't happen to bring any bandages, did you?"

Lu pulled a package of Band-Aids out of her backpack. They were old and hot pink, but Zac didn't complain as she washed his cut with water from her flask and placed one carefully over the wound. "There," she said. "Other than that, you're not hurt?"

"Gonna have a few bruises tomorrow, but at least I'm not impaled," he muttered. "Are you all right?"

She nodded. She'd taken worse falls before, and she didn't mind a few scrapes. "Come on, let's get out of here before those unicorns decide we're too close again."

"I don't know what they're so upset about," grumbled Zac as she helped him to his feet. "The foal approached us, not the other way around. I guess all those fairy tales about unicorns being gentle were wrong."

"Can't really blame them when they were hunted for sport by monsters like Thomas Wilde," said Lu. "Besides, if I had a giant horn in the middle of my forehead, I'd have a short temper too."

"You already do," said Zac. Lu scowled, but with great effort, she let it drop. They were alone in the middle of the

Wildewoods, after all, and they'd nearly been killed by a unicorn. The last thing they needed right now was to bicker.

"Come on," she muttered, and she led the way up another small hill toward the mountains. No matter what happened, they had to keep going.

But despite her determination to reach the mountains before nightfall, the hills seemed endless as they crisscrossed them, searching for the easiest route that wouldn't wind Zac more than he already was. She wasn't sure how much longer he could keep this up, given the increasing volume of his wheezes, and when they reached a cluster of small trees, she insisted they rest and have something to eat.

"It's almost dinnertime, I think," she said as she handed him the pair of apples that had been on their breakfast tray. "We should camp here tonight."

"Are you joking?" said Zac, his chest heaving as he made himself comfortable in the shade. "We're completely exposed."

"We're not going to make it to the mountains before the sun sets," she argued, leaning against a tree trunk. "At best, we might reach the lake, but I didn't see any shelter on the shoreline."

"There isn't any shelter here, either, so we might as well walk as far as we can," he insisted. "Besides, there's no telling how far Oliver's gotten. If there's a shortcut, he must know it."

"I'm sure he does," she said, disheartened by the thought. "How else would he be able to reach the mountains every day and still be home in time for dinner?"

They lapsed into silence as they ate their meager meal. Lu was famished and would have killed for a giant bowl of macaroni and cheese, but for now, she had to make do with a granola bar and airplane cookies she'd found in her backpack.

As she chewed slowly, trying to make her food last, she spotted a pair of dark eyes peering at her from behind a thin tree trunk. She stilled. It was a red fox—a baby fox, from the looks of it.

"Zac," she whispered. "Don't move."

"What?" he said through a mouthful of apple. But he must have followed her gaze, because he froze a second later, and as they both watched, the little fox's nose twitched.

Moving slowly so she didn't scare it off, Lu broke off a tiny piece of her cookie and offered it to the little animal. At last the fox slowly stepped out from behind the tree trunk, but it wasn't a normal fox, she realized. It had two tails.

"There you go," she murmured in a low, gentle voice, the way she spoke to her feral kittens. "Come on—it's okay. We won't hurt you."

The fox crept even closer, sniffing the air between

them. To Lu's astonishment, it delicately ate the offering, and its ears perked as it waited hopefully for more.

Lu grinned and, still moving slowly, broke off another small bite. "It's a kit," she said to Zac. "A baby fox. Or—something close to it, anyway. You aren't allergic to foxes, are you?"

He shrugged. "I've never been around one before." But as far as Lu could tell, his eyes weren't watering, and he didn't seem to be sniffling more than usual. Both good signs.

"Where's your mother?" she said to the little creature. "And your littermates?"

"Probably lurking nearby, getting ready to attack," said Zac. He glanced around the hilltop nervously. "Why does everything in this place want to kill us?"

"Because everything here is wild," said Lu, delighted as the kit began to lick her fingers. Upon finding nothing else there, it climbed into her lap and nosed at the empty cookie wrapper, and Lu grinned. "Humans are the ones who don't belong in the Wildewoods. It's like—walking into a lion enclosure. That's the animals' territory, not yours. We're just visiting."

"I've never been to the zoo, remember?" he grumbled, but he watched in fascination as the kit played with the crinkly packaging. "I'm sorry we could never have a pet."

"What?" Lu looked up, surprised. "That's not your fault."

"I know, but—" He frowned. "You'd be happier if we had a cat or a dog. And I'm sorry we can't. I'm sorry I'm sick all the time and—and ruined your life."

She stared at him, the fox momentarily forgotten. "What are you talking about?"

He scratched his neck, his gaze trained downward as he picked at a blade of grass. "I'm not stupid. I know everything in our family revolves around me. My doctor appointments, my hospital visits, my medication, what I can and can't eat, what makes me sick and what doesn't—you said so yourself. Mum and I never went to your track meets."

"I don't care about that," she insisted. "I mean—yeah, it's not the best feeling in the world to have no one in the crowd cheering you on. But you can't help it. You didn't ask for this."

"Neither did you," he said. "And I think sometimes Mum and Dad were so busy making sure I could breathe and that there weren't any allergens in the house that they forgot to make sure you were okay, too."

As Lu stroked the kit's fur, tears welled in her eyes, and she said nothing for a long moment. He wasn't wrong. She'd felt ignored and forgotten in their family more times than she could count, but eventually it had simply become the norm. While their mum was busy hovering over Zac, Lu was outside, playing with friends and cats and everything her brother didn't have. Couldn't have.

"I never forgot about you," said Zac after a long moment, his voice small and barely audible. "I know it probably doesn't help, but . . . I didn't. And I never forgot about—about what it was like before you started going to school. About how much fun we used to have together, playing pretend and—and doing puzzles and stuff. I know you don't like me as much as Sophia or your cats, but— you've always been my only friend."

She hastily rubbed her eyes, feeling the emotional blow as keenly as she would have a fist to her gut. "I'm sorry for being such a bad sister," she mumbled, burying her fingers in the fox's fur. "I should have stayed home more and—and spent time with you, like Mum did. I should have played with you instead of going to the park, and I should have paid attention to your drawings, and—"

"I would have been really, really mad if you'd given up your friends because of me," said Zac. "I had Mum. She was with me all the time, and I was never alone. I promise."

But there was a difference between being alone and being lonely, and Lu knew the feeling all too well. She sniffed, and the fox began to purr. "I hate that we grew apart. I've hated it for a long time, but—I never knew how to fix it."

"It's fixed now," said Zac, and tentatively he brushed a single finger across the kit's cheek. "Mum dying was the worst thing that's ever happened to us. It probably always will be. But coming here, to the Wildewoods, and getting my sister back . . ."

He trailed off, but he didn't need to finish for her to understand. Wordlessly she twisted around and hugged him tightly. And though it was hardly the only time she'd done so since they'd arrived in England, this was the first hug that felt like it was for no other reason than the fact that she wanted to.

25

ZAC

WHEN THEY SET OUT ACROSS THE GENTLY SLOPING hills of the grasslands once more, Zac was sorry to leave that little grove of trees. A larger red fox—this one with three tails—had come to fetch the baby that had fallen asleep in Lu's lap, and to his surprise, there had been no growling or threats. The mother had simply walked right up to Lu and lifted her kit by the scruff of its neck before trotting off.

The sun was inching toward the horizon now, and Zac knew they had only a couple of hours of daylight left. "How far away is the lake you saw?" he said as they walked through grass that nearly reached his waist.

"I don't know," admitted Lu. "A mile, maybe two."

That was closer than Zac had thought. "If we can reach the south end, we can circle around to the mountains and walk along the opposite shore until we find a way across the range."

"Or until we find a cave," she said pointedly. "We need a safe place to sleep."

Zac couldn't argue with that. He'd never been so tired in his life. As they made their way through the tall grass, however, he saw something move only a few paces away. He froze, motioning for Lu to do the same.

"What?" she said. The grass shifted again as whatever it was moved closer, and she stepped in front of him. "Let me handle this."

"It could be another fox," he said, trying to see around her. "If it hasn't attacked us yet——"

"Doesn't mean it won't try." Lu gripped her walking stick with both hands, ready to swing. "Stay back."

But as she spoke, Zac noticed another rustle to his left—and then another to his right. Horrified, he stood there helplessly as the grass rippled in all directions, and multiple unseen creatures surrounded them.

"Lu . . ." He too clutched his walking stick, his back to hers now. They wouldn't be able to fend off all of them, but maybe a few good hits would scare the rest. "They're every-where. What do you want me to——"

"Oh!" said Lu suddenly, and Zac whirled back around,

ready to whack something with his stick. But instead she knelt beside a small brown rabbit with antlers sprouting from its head. "Look—it's friendly."

Zac narrowed his eyes. "That unicorn foal was friendly too," he reminded her as another creature approached him. This one was similar to the rabbit, though it had wings and, strangely enough, a squirrel tail.

"So was the fox," she pointed out. "And that turned out all right."

Two more odd rabbits appeared beside the first, each a different variation from the last, and Zac watched as several more approached. "What do you think they are?" he said, not daring to touch them. Not when there were so many. They might have been small, but if enough of them attacked, he and Lu wouldn't stand a chance against their sharp antlers and claws.

"I have no idea," said Lu, stroking the first one's fur. "I've never heard of these kinds of creatures before."

Another rabbit approached Zac, and this time it nuzzled up against the leg of his jeans. "Whatever they are, don't get too close," he said. "This one has fangs."

"They're fine," insisted Lu. "Look—"

A low, oddly human growl cut her off, and goose bumps formed on Zac's arms. He looked at Lu, whose eyes had widened, and for a moment, neither of them moved.

He knew that sound. It was the manticore.

"Lu," he said urgently, but she was already reaching for the flashlight.

"Don't move. Can you tell where it is?" she said, flipping the switch and sweeping the beam over the tall grass surrounding them.

"Facing me, I think," said Zac tightly. The manticore growled again, closer this time, and he could barely breathe. "There—it's there," he gasped, pointing.

"I don't see it," she said anxiously, though she was aiming the beam in the right direction. "Can you—"

All of a sudden, a roar filled the air, and the manticore flew out of the grass, launching itself straight toward them. Lu shrieked, but before Zac could react, his sister slammed into his side, all while pointing the flashlight directly into the manticore's eyes.

Zac tumbled into the grass, landing hard on his shoulder, but the pain barely registered as the beast screamed with fury. "Lu!" he shouted, scrambling to his feet. "What—"

"Don't move," she snarled, and to his astonishment, he realized she was standing three feet from the manticore, holding the flashlight like a weapon. The monster tried to flinch away from the bright beam, but every time it moved, she was there, the light focused directly in its eyes.

"It's working," he whispered, suddenly dizzy with relief. "It's actually working."

"Get behind me," said Lu. "*Slowly*. If you move too fast, it might decide to attack you."

He inched through the tall grass toward her, trying not to think about those sharp fangs or vicious claws, or the venomous stinger at the end of its scorpion tail. This time there was no hope of the phoenix saving them, and they were completely on their own.

"We're going to walk now," said Lu quietly, not taking her eyes off the manticore. "Follow my lead, one step at a time."

Zac tried to keep a lid on his mounting fear as he and his sister moved slowly up the hill and away from the manticore. The beast crept along as it followed them, trying to shield its eyes, but Lu kept the flashlight trained on it.

"How are we supposed to get away?" said Zac in a hushed voice. "We can't outrun it."

"Eventually it'll lose interest and search for easier prey. We just have to be patient," she said, though he could hear the uncertainty in her voice.

He grimaced. "Pretty sure those rabbit things wouldn't be nearly as satisfying as—"

Without warning, the beam went out, and Zac's heart nearly stopped. Lu immediately shook the flashlight, and it flickered. She swore, and the manticore growled again, its human mouth twisting into a nasty grin.

"Lu . . . ," said Zac as panic seized his insides once more.

"I'm trying," she snapped, shaking the flashlight again. The beam continued to flicker unevenly, and though the manticore flinched, it must have sensed the tide turning in its favor, and it began to close the distance between them.

Zac clutched his walking stick as a bead of sweat rolled down his forehead. "Whatever happens to me, you need to get out of here," he said, his voice cracking. "I can't run, but if I distract it long enough—"

"We're not having this conversation again," said Lu through gritted teeth as she continued to shake the flashlight. "I'm staying here."

"So what, we both die?" said Zac. "I'm useless anyway."

"You're not useless," she said fiercely. "You're my brother, and I'm not leaving you."

He opened his mouth to protest—they had no way to hold off the manticore, after all, and no weapons that could inflict pain inside the Wildewoods. If they both stayed, they would both die.

But then, in the dimming light of evening, the beam gave out completely, leaving them defenseless.

The manticore grinned again, saliva dripping from its fangs. Zac gripped his stick and tried to stand in front of Lu, but she forced her way to his side.

"We're a team," she said tightly. "We're doing this together."

And so they stood, shoulder to shoulder, waiting for the inevitable and ready to do whatever it took to survive. Zac's breaths came in tight wheezes, and his palms were already sweaty, but he planted his feet on the ground and stared the manticore down. If it wanted to eat them, it was in for the fight of its life.

The manticore roared and readied itself to pounce. But just as it was about to spring forward, the sound of hooves thundered across the hill, and a massive dappled gray unicorn appeared, its head lowered in a charge and its long silver horn aimed straight for the manticore.

"Hermes?" gasped Zac. Startled, the manticore shifted its attention toward the unicorn, but not in time to dart out of the way. The silver horn sank deep into its side, and the manticore's bloodcurdling scream cut through the warm evening breeze.

Zac stumbled backward, pulling his sister with him. Together they watched in awe as Hermes held off the manticore, artfully dodging the scorpion tail as the monster frantically thrashed around. But it didn't matter how hard it fought back—that first hit had been critical, and when the unicorn once again managed to thrust his horn into the manticore's chest, it was all over.

"Oh my god," whispered Lu as everything grew still, and the unicorn stood over the body of the manticore. "Did you see that?"

"Yeah," said Zac, too stunned to manage a quippy retort. "Hermes—are you okay?"

To his relief, the dappled gray unicorn looked unharmed. Zac approached him carefully, making sure the manticore was dead as he offered Hermes an uneaten apple from his backpack. It was gone in two loud crunches, and the unicorn dipped his head, bending his front legs and lowering his body.

"What's he doing?" said Lu as she shoved the useless flashlight back in her bag.

"I—I think he wants us to get on," said Zac. "Penelope said she's been training him to do this."

Lu eyed the manticore, giving it a wide berth even in death. "Might as well. Otherwise we won't get anywhere before dark."

Zac nodded, and with some effort, he managed to climb onto the unicorn's back. Lu clambered up behind him, and once they were both situated, Hermes rose.

"Steady," said Zac nervously, trying to find his balance as he gripped the silvery mane. Somewhere along the way, Hermes had lost his saddle, though the bridle still hung from his muzzle. Zac reached for it, trying to grab onto the thin leather strap. Hermes had other ideas, however, and with only a single whinny of warning, he took off at a run.

"Hold on!" shouted Zac, throwing his arms around the unicorn's neck and squeezing his eyes shut. Lu clung to him as Hermes galloped across the hills, and silently he prayed over and over that they didn't fall.

Like the first time Hermes had taken off with Zac on his back, seconds felt like minutes and minutes felt like eternity. He had no idea how long Hermes raced through the grasslands, his hooves churning steadily over the soft dirt. But at long last, the unicorn slowed to a trot.

"Where are we?" said Zac, his face still buried in Hermes's neck.

Lu gasped. "Look—it's the lake."

He glanced up. Sure enough, the lake was on their left, and beyond that, mountains rose up against the pink-and-orange sky. Farther east, cutting the grasslands off from the mountains, was a dense forest, and the tops of the trees reflected the colorful sunset. "The north end of the lake," he said, stunned. "Hermes brought us to the mountains."

"Almost," said Lu. "Do you think anything dangerous lives in that forest?"

"Probably," said Zac, and he scanned the lakeshore. The water glittered beneath the dusky sky, and he could have sworn he saw something massive moving among the waves. "But I'd rather not swim, if it's all the same to you. If we get eaten, I'm sorry."

Zac nudged Hermes forward, and the unicorn plodded toward the trees. Maybe it wouldn't be so bad. The dangerous creatures lived on the other side of the mountains, after all. And if Hermes could kill a manticore, he could handle whatever was lurking inside.

Zac was so lost in his thoughts as they entered the forest that he almost didn't notice the hush that fell. Not even the wind seemed to blow here, and the sounds of leaves and twigs cracking underneath Hermes's hooves somehow seemed magnified. And less than fifty feet in, the trees above them grew so dense that they cut out the rest of the evening light completely.

"Maybe this wasn't such a good idea," said Lu, her voice higher than usual.

"We're fine," insisted Zac, glancing around apprehensively. "Hermes wouldn't bring us here if it wasn't safe."

But even as he spoke, he heard another set of hooves nearby, though the second unicorn was cloaked in darkness. Another set joined the first, and then another, and another, until Zac was sure they were in the middle of an entire herd.

"You think that stallion found us again?" he whispered, twisting around to peer at his sister. Lu was pale, and she shook her head, her eyes locked on something to the right.

As Zac followed her gaze, he realized they hadn't been joined by unicorns after all. Instead, standing only a few yards away, was a burly centaur.

And he was pointing a spear directly at them.

26

LU

THE CENTAURS, LU WAS QUICKLY LEARNING, WERE not very friendly.

There were ten of them pointing their weapons at her and Zac—bows and arrows, spears, even a few crude knives. And as the burly one approached, she wrapped her arms tighter around her brother, as if she could somehow protect him.

"We're not here to hurt anyone," she said. "We're just trying to reach the mountains."

"This forest is closed to humans," said the centaur in a deep, booming voice that seemed to reverberate through the darkness. "You are trespassing."

"We didn't know," insisted Lu. "We'll leave."

"Trespassing," continued the centaur, as if she hadn't even spoken, "is punishable by death."

In front of her, Zac stiffened, while the other centaurs murmured their approval. Hermes pranced nervously as the sharp tips of their weapons drew closer, and Lu hoped with every bone in her body that the unicorn didn't take off. As bad as this situation was, she was sure the centaurs would relish the opportunity to hunt them. And while Hermes was fast, she had a bad feeling they could match his pace.

"Wait," she said as a nearby centaur aimed his bow for her heart. "Alcor—he'll vouch for us. We're not here to hurt anyone, I swear."

The leader's eyes narrowed, and he gestured for the archer to lower his weapon. "You are familiar with Alcor, son of Mizar?"

"Yes—that's him," said Lu hastily. "We met him a few days ago. He's—he's here, right?" He hadn't been in the stable yesterday.

"Alcor, son of Mizar, has returned to us, yes," said the leader, studying them with disdain. "You believe he will speak to your intentions?"

"He's our friend," said Zac, his voice cracking. Lu wasn't entirely sure she would have phrased it that way, but it gave the others pause.

"Very well," said the leader at last. "You will return with us. Should Alcor not be willing to take responsibility for your presence in our woods, you will be executed."

"Fair enough," said Lu, her throat tight. And while the centaurs led Hermes through the dense woods, she whispered in Zac's ear, "Maybe swimming was the better choice after all."

As they approached the center of the forest, Lu wasn't sure what she expected—a crude campsite, maybe. But when the orange flicker of a bonfire appeared in the distance, she spotted multiple large dwellings looming around it, nothing more than silhouettes in the low light.

"This looks like a town," she said, startled.

"Our kind did not build communities before the great migration," said the leader gruffly. "We preferred the freedom to roam. But we were hunted to near extinction, and we had little choice but to take sanctuary here. Now that our residence is permanent, we have adapted to the use of certain long-lasting structures."

Lu didn't know what to say to that, and so she kept her mouth shut. As they approached the bonfire in what seemed to be the epicenter of their community, she spotted a large statue of a centaur reared up on his hind legs. "Who's that?"

"Chiron," said the leader in a low snarl. "You have the curiosity of a jackalope that soon becomes dinner."

"Will you stop talking?" hissed Zac, and Lu pressed her lips together, swallowing her retort.

Surrounding the bonfire were dozens of other centaurs—

male, female, and even several children. Everyone was laughing and chatting and feasting on meat that was roasting over smaller cooking fires, and if it hadn't been for the fact that they all had the bodies of horses, it would have been a perfectly normal summer evening among friends.

"You will walk now," said the leader, and he brought Hermes to a halt.

"You're not going to hurt him, are you?" said Zac. "He didn't do anything wrong."

"We do not hurt the innocent," said the centaur. "He will be well cared for before we release him in the morning."

That was something, at least. Lu climbed off the unicorn, falling the last few feet and stumbling to regain her footing. It was only after she helped Zac down too that Lu realized how big the centaurs were—even the smallest children were taller than her. And as a male with cream coloring led Hermes away by his bridle, she stuck close to her brother, feeling like they'd stepped into a world of giants.

"Alcor!" boomed the leader of the hunting party. "We have found friends of yours."

At first there was no reply, and Lu gripped her brother's sleeve, hoping this wasn't the centaurs' idea of a practical joke. But at last, from the edge of the bonfire, a silhouetted figure limped toward them.

"Humans?" said Alcor with thinly veiled disgust. "You accuse me of befriending humans?"

Lu had no patience left for games, and she raised her chin, looking him directly in the eye. "You know us," she argued. "We met at the stable a few days ago."

The redheaded centaur moved closer, still visibly favoring his leg. "Ah, yes," he murmured. "You are the human children who caused rather a lot of trouble for your guardians. But I do not recall offering you friendship."

Lu felt like he'd slapped her in the face. She stared at him, fuming, as their last chance dwindled to nothing. "You knew our mother," she said sharply, speaking not only to Alcor now, but also to the rest of the gathered herd. "Josie—daughter of Alastair. You said she was your friend."

A soft murmuring rose from the crowd, and even some of the children stopped playing to watch. With his hindquarters to the bonfire, Alcor's expression was hidden in shadows. "You are correct," he allowed. "I did describe the friendship our herd once shared with your mother."

"You didn't just say that," insisted Lu. "You also said that if we ever needed a guide, you'd be honored to show us the Wildewoods. Well, we're here. And we need a guide, because if we don't find the other exit—"

All of a sudden, the earth began to tremble beneath their feet. Trees swayed high above them, and several of the children screamed as they ran for their parents. An especially strong jolt threw Lu to the mossy forest floor, and as Zac landed hard on top of her, centaur hooves hit the ground only inches from them as the herd struggled to remain upright. As she curled into a ball, branches crashed down around them, and one of the nearby structures wobbled, threatening to collapse.

At last, after what felt like ages, the trembling subsided, leaving Lu dazed and weak as the surge of adrenaline inside her waned. Several of the centaurs murmured their relief before trotting away to check on the buildings, but beside her, Zac was limp.

"Zac?" she said, touching his shoulder. Had he hit his head on the way down? "Zac, wake up!"

Suddenly his eyes opened, and he stared at her for a long moment, as if seeing right through her. "Oliver's in the mountains with the phoenix," he gasped. "A dragon was hunting them, and he had to find a cave to sleep in. The phoenix tried to escape the cage, but the bars—they're magical."

"You know why the earth shakes?" demanded Alcor, hovering above them. As Lu helped Zac to his feet, she glared at the centaur.

"Our cousin, Penelope, was stung by a manticore," she said. "She's dying. Her brother thinks phoenix blood can cure her, so he kidnapped the phoenix. That's why the earthquakes are happening."

Alcor stared down at them, his fury palpable even though she couldn't make out his features. "Your kin dares to threaten the magic of the sanctuary?" he said, his voice low and dangerous.

"We're trying to save it," she snapped. "That's why we're here—that's why we're trying to get over the mountains. The south exit was destroyed in a storm this afternoon. If we don't get to the north exit and stop Oliver from removing the phoenix from the Wildewoods, he's going to kill him, and if that happens—"

"The sanctuary will crumble," said Alcor gravely. "And us along with it."

All the blood drained from Lu's face, and suddenly she felt unsteady, as if the earthquake had started again. "You'll die?" she said, her voice breaking. "We thought—"

"We thought the borders would just . . . disappear," squeaked Zac, clearly as thrown as she was. "And then you'd all be part of the outside world again."

"Our existence is tied to the sanctuary," said Alcor, his thick brow furrowed. "If it perishes, so shall we all."

Lu felt sick to her stomach, and as members of the herd gathered around them, her entire body tensed with desperation. "Please," she begged, looking from face to face. "We want to stop him, but we need your help. Oliver and the phoenix are in a cave for the night. If you let us go, we might have a chance of catching him tomorrow. But if you execute us . . ."

She trailed off. The centaurs glanced at one another,

and Alcor stood still among them, with only his chest rising and falling. Lu clenched her jaw. If that didn't convince them, then nothing would, and the entire Wildewoods were doomed. And Zac and Lu along with them.

"Listen," she said, her desperation turning to anger. "You have two choices. You can kill us now and die tomorrow, or you can help us save the Wildewoods and live. That's it. Those are your only options."

Alcor sniffed. "You truly believe you can stop your cousin?"

"We're the only ones who can," said Lu stoutly, and beside her, Zac squared his shoulders.

"Optimistic words for someone so powerless," said another centaur, but Alcor silenced him with a look.

"Your bravery is admirable, daughter of Josie," he said. "Should the sanctuary truly be in peril as you claim, we would be fools not to heed your words."

"What?" gasped the lead hunter, and he gripped his spear. "Alcor, think rationally."

"I am thinking rationally. It is you who would rather have the thrill of the hunt than see the bigger picture. If the children are telling the truth—"

"They certainly are not," scoffed the hunter. "Their story is preposterous."

"And yet the ground shakes and lightning crashes as it never has before." Alcor turned toward the hunter, his face in profile against the bonfire. "In order to counter that which has never before happened, we must do what has never been done. We will shelter them for the night," he announced to the gathered herd. "We will feed them, and we will give them what counsel we can. Tomorrow, we will see them to the mountains. Beyond that," he warned, focusing once more on Lu and Zac, "there is little we can do to help. We do not venture into the Scorchlands, nor would we advise you to do so. The manticore is only one of many deadly beasts that lay waste to its dying grounds."

"The manticore's dead now," muttered Zac. "It attacked us in the grasslands. Hermes—the unicorn—he killed it."

Alcor sighed heavily. "Then tonight we will mourn. All life is a gift in the sanctuary, even that which is inconvenient to us."

"What about that rabbit?" said Zac, eyeing the roast. Lu noted it looked startlingly similar to the small creatures they'd encountered earlier, and suddenly her nausea returned.

"It is not a rabbit. It is a wolpertinger," said Alcor. "There are other similar beasts that roam our lands—jackalopes and rasselbocks, for instance. We kill what we must to survive, including that which preys upon us, but nothing more. Big or small, we are all the last of our kind here. Now come," he insisted, nodding toward the crackling fire. "Dine with us."

The other centaurs stepped aside, making room for them near the warm glow of the flames, and Lu and Zac exchanged a nervous look as they joined them. Considering the hunters had wanted to kill them only a few minutes earlier, Lu wasn't sure this was the best idea, but she and Zac didn't have many other options right now. Besides, the prospect of having a safe place to sleep was too alluring to turn down, especially after the day they'd had.

The food was another story, however, and when Alcor offered her a cooked leg, she politely refused. Zac, on the other hand, didn't seem to mind, and he took his portion with gratitude. Together they settled in beside the bonfire, and Alcor remained with them. If it hadn't been for the impending doom of the entire Wildewoods, Lu would have found the scene strangely comforting.

"How long will it take us to get to the Scorchlands?" she said. "Is there a shortcut?"

"I know of one not far from here," said the centaur. "A tunnel that cuts through the mountains, allowing quick passage from one side to the other. We often patrol the entrance to ensure dangerous creatures do not sneak into our forest. Unfortunately, we are not always diligent," he added, glaring at the pack of huntsmen nearby. "Especially when one's leader is recovering from an injury. I expect that is how the manticore passed into the grasslands, and you have my sincerest apologies. If we had not allowed it through, I expect none of this would have happened."

"It isn't your fault," said Lu. "You weren't here."

"But this is still my herd," he pointed out. "I must take responsibility for its actions. And that is why I will help you as much as I can. I do not wish to cause the doom of the sanctuary."

"That's what we're trying to stop," muttered Zac. "If Oliver finds the north exit before we do . . ."

"If the phoenix is taken from the sanctuary, there can be no hope for the rest of us," said Alcor with a heavy sigh. "Relations between centaurs and humans have rarely been cordial, let alone friendly. Your mother was the rare exception. And I hope you are both made of the same spirit and strength, son and daughter of Josie."

And as Lu stared into the fire, she could only hope they were too.

27

ZAC

THEY SPENT THE NIGHT UNDER THE STARS, PROTECTED by a herd of vigilant—and terrifying—centaurs. But as much as Zac disliked being treated like a prisoner, he was almost sorry when Alcor led them north the next morning, shortly after the sun had risen.

"The mountains are a treacherous place," warned the centaur as they walked together through the woods, Zac and Lu once again astride Hermes. "Dragons roam the cliffs, and you would be wise to make haste. Even inside the tunnel, there are many small breeds that inhabit the mountains, and their bites are no less vicious for their size."

"Great," said Zac, adjusting his grip on the burning torch the centaurs had gifted them when they'd left the camp. "Just what we need—something else with sharp teeth attacking us."

"That is why we have provided you with fire," said Alcor. "Like many creatures of darkness, they fear the light. As long as you keep it burning, you will be safe."

"Good to know," said Zac, glancing up at the crackling flame. Suddenly the torch didn't feel as heavy as it had before.

As the trees thinned and the stony face of the mountains appeared, Alcor slowed. "This is where we say our goodbyes," he said. "You will find the entrance to the cave in the fissure just ahead. I wish you good fortune and skill in your journey, son and daughter of Josie, and I hope we meet again under better circumstances."

If they didn't, it would mean they had failed to save the phoenix, though Zac tried to push that thought out of his mind. "We'll be sure to stop by for another bonfire," he said. "Thanks for the food. And the hospitality."

"It is our honor," said the centaur, bowing his head. And with that, he disappeared back into the forest, leaving Zac and Lu once again on their own.

No—not completely on their own. As they dismounted, Hermes remained with them, and Zac stood by his side, still holding the burning torch. "You think a unicorn can take out a dragon?" he said as Lu searched a thick cluster of bushes for the cave entrance.

"Maybe a small one," she said. "Not one as big as Devon and Surrey, though."

Zac ran his hand over Hermes's neck. As much of a comfort as it was having that sharp horn fighting on their side, he knew what he had to do. "You can't come with us," he said quietly. "It's too dangerous."

Hermes nickered and nudged his cheek. Zac grinned, but it faded quickly.

"I mean it," he insisted. "No matter what's inside that cave, we have fire. We'll be okay. But we can't protect you, too. And when we reach the Scorchlands . . ." His throat tightened. He was trying not to think about how they would navigate the most dangerous part of the Wilde-woods, but he couldn't ignore the problem forever. "You saved us from the manticore. You did your part. Lu and I will be all right."

"I found it!" she called, her voice muffled. "It's bigger than I thought it'd be. We can stand up inside."

Zac stroked the unicorn's muzzle, and when his fingers found the buckle to his bridle, he undid it. "There—you're free. Go back to the stable or rejoin your herd—whatever you want to do, it's up to you. But you can't come with us. I'm sorry."

The unicorn neighed louder this time, and Zac stepped

away, shoving the bridle into his backpack. Whether Hermes understood or not, he didn't try to follow, and instead he remained on the edge of the forest as Zac joined his sister.

"You'll see him again," said Lu. "We're going to find Oliver, and we're going to stop him."

"Yeah," said Zac hollowly, though he didn't have the confidence she had. Or was pretending to have, at least. "Come on—the faster we move through the cave, the sooner we can figure out how we're getting across the Scorchlands."

"Carefully," said Lu. "And with fire. If the manticore's afraid of bright light, maybe we'll get lucky and the rest of the animals will be, too." She pushed aside a curtain of vines, revealing an opening in the rock. "Go ahead," she said. "You're the one with the torch."

He stuck the flame into the fissure to ensure there was nothing waiting to eat them. The damp cave felt ten degrees cooler, and the walls were angled so they seemed to be closing in on him, but he took a breath and forced himself inside.

"I hope you're not claustrophobic," said Lu, eyeing him. "Have you ever been in a cave before?"

"You know I haven't." But as they walked deeper into the tunnel, the daylight from the entrance was choked off completely by the pervasive darkness, and he was suddenly glad he'd never done this before. If he had, he was sure he would have refused a second time.

They could have gone back. He was sorely tempted as he thought about the mountain surrounding them on all sides. What if there was another earthquake, and part of the cave collapsed? What if they found out the hard way that it had already happened? But the knowledge of what *would* happen if they didn't do this—if they didn't find Oliver in time—pushed him forward, and he focused on putting one foot in front of the other as the torch illuminated the way.

The smoke quickly began to tickle his lungs, but he refused to slow down. Occasionally smaller tunnels would branch off from the main one, far too narrow for Zac or Lu to fit through, and he worried about what kind of mythical creatures might exist that could. But as long as they were staying out of sight, away from the torchlight, it didn't matter.

"We have to be close by now, right?" he wheezed after what felt like miles.

"Definitely," said Lu, sounding sure of herself, but of course she had no possible way of knowing. She was just trying to keep him from panicking.

Behind them, however, he heard a faint skitter. "What was that?" he said as he spun around. The passageway was empty.

"Come on," said Lu, pulling at his arm. "We're almost there."

He hurried as much as he could without exacerbating his asthma, though with the smoke, it wasn't easy. The strange skittering sounded once more a few minutes later, and yet again, when he turned around, there was nothing there.

"Be careful," said Lu as the tunnel began to slope downward. "It's slippery here. I think there's water coming from somewhere."

Zac edged down the path, keeping a tight grip on the torch. "Do you think it's flooded?"

"Only one way to find out," said Lu, moving cautiously beside him.

She was right, Zac quickly realized—the wet rock was difficult to navigate, and he pressed his free hand against the side of the tunnel, struggling to keep his balance. Their boots splashed in the puddles, and somewhere nearby, he thought he heard trickling.

"Are you sure you don't want me to hold that?" she said. "Your arm has to be tired by now."

"I'm fine," Zac insisted, gritting his teeth. "I just need to—*no!*"

He lost his footing on another slippery patch, pitching forward onto the cave floor. To his horror, the torch landed in a puddle, and within seconds, it had sizzled out, leaving nothing but darkness in its wake.

"Zac?" said Lu, her voice sharp with panic. "Are you okay?"

"I'm fine," he said as he climbed to his feet, his heart pounding. "Where are you?"

"I'm here." Her hand landed on his outstretched arm, and he groped around until he found her elbow. "Come on. I've got you."

He followed her blindly down the tunnel, his anxiety screaming at him. He couldn't see—he couldn't think—his lungs seized up, and it took everything he had to keep moving. He couldn't stop. He had to get out of there.

The skittering echoed somewhere behind them, louder this time without the torchlight holding whatever it was back. "Lu," he said frantically, and her grip on his arm tightened.

"Go in front of me," she said. "Keep your hand on the wall. If anything attacks, I'll hold it off."

He didn't like that, not at all, but he didn't have it in him to argue right now. All he had was panic and the need to run, to escape that cave as quickly as possible, but his stupid lungs wouldn't let him. His chest felt like a vise now, so painfully tight that he wondered if his heart was about to explode. But the skittering grew closer, and when he felt Lu's hand on his shoulder, he summoned what little courage he had left and stumbled forward.

"Ow!" cried Lu, and he heard her boot make contact with something.

"What is it? Are they biting you?" he said frantically.

"They're scratching my legs," she said. "It's okay—just keep moving."

The water was gone now, and he thought the stone wall beneath his palm was growing warmer. Were they closer to the exit? Was there an exit at all, or had it caved in like he feared?

At last he saw the faint beginnings of light. He pulled his sister toward it as she continued to fight off whatever was attacking her, and before long, he also felt a nip at his ankles. The creature's sharp teeth were too short to make it through his rubber boots, though, and he kicked it away.

"We're almost there," he said, desperate now. His lungs were burning, but he managed to break out into a run. He would deal with the consequences once they were safe in the sunlight again.

As they dashed around a bend in the tunnel, daylight finally appeared, blindingly bright. Before Zac could celebrate, however, Lu's hand disappeared from his shoulder, and she screamed.

"Lu!" he shouted, whirling around. She was only a few feet behind him now, but at least half a dozen small, shiny black dragons crawled all over her, their wings spindly and talons sharp. One was even tangled in her hair, and it scratched her face in an attempt to escape.

"Get away from her!" cried Zac, and he launched himself at them, grabbing the first one he could find. He squeezed the bony creature as tightly as he could and threw it at the cave wall. It bounced back as if he hadn't even touched it, and horror washed over him as he remembered he couldn't hurt it.

Fine. He couldn't fight back, but if he could get Lu close enough to the sunlight, he wouldn't need to. Grabbing his sister's arms, he pulled her as hard as he could down the tunnel. She stumbled, nearly falling as the dragons crawled over her, but using all his strength, he caught and steadied her. She'd protected him countless times before. Now it was his turn.

As another dragon tried to attack her face, he grabbed it and once more threw it as hard as he could—but this time, he aimed for the daylight. The dragon shrieked and seemed to curl in on itself, and with an agonized cry, it bolted through the nearest crack in the rock.

Zac exhaled sharply. That was it. "Hold on," he said to Lu, and he grabbed another dragon and hurled it toward the light. It too screeched and fled to the closest exit. "Keep moving forward. I've got you."

At last—at long, long last—Lu stepped into the daylight, and the remaining dragons released her, skittering back into the tunnel. And as soon as she and Zac reached the mouth of the cave, Lu collapsed onto the ground, sobbing.

"Are you okay?" said Zac, kneeling beside her and checking her for injuries. There were scratches on her face and neck, and deeper cuts on her bare arms and the front of her jeans. But as far as he could tell, there were no bite marks or puncture wounds.

Her shoulders shook as she cried harder than he'd ever seen before—even harder than she had at the hospital the day their mother had died, when she and their father had joined Zac in a private counseling area away from the bustle of the emergency room. Now her entire body seemed racked with sobs, and all Zac could do was rub her back as he waited for them to fade.

"That was the bravest thing I've ever seen," he said quietly. "If it wasn't for you, we'd be toast right now."

She took several deep, shaky breaths, her body still trembling. "You—you threw them," she managed. "Into the light. That was—that was genius."

Zac grinned in spite of himself. "Can you say that again? I didn't hear you."

Lu swatted his arm weakly, and at last she lifted her head. Her eyes were red and puffy, and the cuts on her face were bleeding, but he could still see the spark that made her Lu. "You're okay?" she managed, and he nodded.

"Fine. A few scratches," he said with a shrug. Suddenly exhausted, he sat down beside her and took his first look at the forest on the other side of the mountains. They were higher up than they'd been on the other side, and Zac could see above the dark trees that populated the Scorchlands. While around half were still alive, several patches of blackened and burnt trunks stretched out before them, unmistakable evidence of what happened when dragons fought the dangerous mythical creatures inside this section of the Wildewoods.

"How are we supposed to cross without a torch?" said Lu, echoing the very fear that flashed through his mind. There was no going back now—nothing in the world could have made him return to that cave. But seeing the Scorchlands in person . . .

"Same way we crossed the grasslands," he said. "With a lot of luck."

But they couldn't rely on luck anymore, and they were running out of time. Oliver must have been halfway across the desolate forest by now, if not even farther. Zac hadn't had any flashes from the phoenix all morning, and it worried him. Were they already through the exit?

No, he and Lu would have known if they were. The entire population of the Wildewoods would have known. They still had time. But how much of it—that was the question.

A dragon's roar echoed from somewhere nearby, and Zac flinched. "We need to move," he said, standing and offering Lu his hand. He wanted to give her more time to recover, but they were too exposed in the mouth of the cave. "There has to be a path down the mountain from here. If we can find it—"

Suddenly the dragon roared again, directly above the cave now. Zac tensed, pressing himself against the rock. Around them, the wind picked up in great gusts as the dragon flapped its wings, and he felt Lu grab his sleeve. It would be okay, he told himself. As long as they stayed perfectly still, the dragon would fly off and leave them alone.

But instead another wall of wind hit them, so powerful it nearly knocked him off his feet. The dragon roared once more, and while Zac hid his face in his elbow to shield his eyes from debris, a hair-raising screech filled the air as talons scraped against the rocky mountainside only a few feet beyond the mouth of the cave.

The dragon had spotted them.

Beside him, Lu gasped. "Zac!" she said in a half whisper. "Look!"

Dizzy with fear, he forced himself to wipe his face and blink away the dust. Out of all the ways to die in this place, being burned alive by a dragon looking for its lunch was one of his least favorites. But as he looked at the dragon peering down at them with a curious gaze, his heart leaped with the first spark of hope he'd felt all day.

The dragon was violet.

28

LU

LU GAPED AT THE VIOLET DRAGON, HALF-CONVINCED she was hallucinating. "Is that—is that Devon?" she said, noting the red scales above the dragon's eyes.

The dragon dipped his head to sniff them, and a strange purring sound reverberated from its throat. "It's Devon," said Zac, grinning from ear to ear. "Remember us?"

Devon clambered into the mouth of the cave, forcing Lu and Zac to take a few steps back toward the darkness of the passageway. She shuddered, still able to feel the pin-prick talons of the small black dragons crawling all over her. She would much rather have taken her chances with this one.

"We don't have any treats for you," said Lu, showing the dragon her hands. "I'm sorry."

Devon didn't seem to mind. Instead he lowered his belly onto the ground, almost prone as he flattened his wings to his side. Lu frowned. What was he doing?

Zac took a careful step toward the dragon and ran his hand over the vibrant scales. "You wouldn't happen to know how to get to the other side of the Scorchlands, would you?" he said, and the end of Devon's tail flopped contentedly.

Lu watched the pair of them, her eyes narrowing. "I think he's doing the same thing Hermes did when he rescued us," she said warily. "Bending down so we can climb up."

Her brother stared at her. "Listen, I know we've both almost died about a dozen times this week, but *that* is actual suicide."

"Look at him," she insisted. By now Devon had also lowered his head and was watching them patiently. "I know it sounds crazy, but Hermes found us when we needed help too. The animals know what's going on. They know the Wildewoods are in trouble, and I think—I think they know we're trying to help them."

Her brother scowled, but rather than argue, he took a step back and gestured for her to go first. "If Devon doesn't eat you, I'll consider it."

Lu took a deep breath. After everything that had happened in the cave, her hands were still trembling, but they had no other viable way across the Scorchlands. She had to try.

And so, with courage she wasn't sure she actually possessed, she stepped up to the dragon and carefully climbed onto his back. Devon shifted beneath her, his muscles taut and his scales so smooth that they were slippery, but she managed to settle between two of the long spines that lined his backbone. It was a tight fit, but she didn't care about being comfortable right now, so long as she didn't fall off.

Rather than object, Devon eyed Zac, as if asking what he was waiting for. Lu saw her brother grin, and with less care than she'd demonstrated, he pulled himself up, settling between the long spines behind her.

"This is so cool," he said breathlessly. *"So cool."*

Lu's more tempered response disappeared in her throat as Devon suddenly launched himself off the small ledge, his wide wings stretching out on either side of them. Her stomach dropped, and she clung to the spine as they soared over the Scorchlands.

Behind her, Zac whooped, clearly having the time of his life. Devon flew lower, so close to the tops of the trees that Lu thought she could reach out and touch them. In the charred areas of the Scorchlands, she caught a glimpse of a creature that looked startlingly like a combination of a serpent and a rooster, and another that appeared to be a spider the size of a small house. She gulped, suddenly even more grateful to Devon than she had been before.

"Do you think he knows where the exit is?" she called to her brother, hoping her voice didn't get lost in the wind.

"Maybe," he shouted in return, though it sounded faint to her. "As long as we find Oliver, we'll be okay."

Forcing herself to relax as much as she could, Lu gazed across the landscape as they flew, letting herself take in the moment. It was terrifying, sure, but it was also exhilarating. If they made it out of the Wildewoods alive, maybe Devon would let them do this again. And maybe next time, she wouldn't be so scared.

At last Devon began to descend into what remained of a charred meadow. The forest seemed like it extended beyond their landing point, but Lu spotted a strange stone archway at the edge of the clearing.

"Zac!" she gasped. "The north exit!"

Part of her—the pessimistic part that was used to being disappointed—had questioned whether there was an exit at all. But now that they had found it, she could hardly contain her joy. As soon as Devon landed on the scorched earth, she slid off his back, giving his long neck a few appreciative pats before hurrying to the archway.

"Is that it?" called Zac, still astride the dragon.

"I think so," she said, touching the stone. She wasn't sure what she expected—a jolt of magic, maybe—but it felt as smooth and cool as the cave wall had. "I can't believe we made it."

"Me neither." As soon as Zac dismounted, Devon took a few steps back and launched himself into the sky once more, leaving them alone in the middle of the meadow. Lu wished he would stay, but they weren't trying to barbecue Oliver. They just needed to talk to him.

As eddies of ash and dirt swirled around them in the dragon's wake, Lu eyed the burnt trees. It would only be a matter of time before the deadly residents of the Scorchlands began to hunt them. "You should wait on the other side," she said to her brother. "I'll stay here and try to stop Oliver from leaving."

Lu expected him to protest—he always did, after all, when she tried to boss him around—but instead he was silent. She peered over her shoulder.

"Zac?" she said. He stood right where she'd left him, but there was something off about his expression. Once again, though his eyes were open, he wasn't seeing anything in front of him. Slowly she stepped forward, not wanting to startle him, but now was definitely not the time. "Zac," she repeated. "Snap out of it."

His entire body tensed. For a moment, their eyes met, and she thought he was about to say something. Instead he jerked forward, throwing himself directly at her.

That was when she heard it—a faint whistling sound.

In that same instant, as her brother crashed into her, the whistling was punctuated by a loud rip and Zac's agonizing cry.

Lu stumbled backward, fighting to hold him up. To her horror, blood began to stain his sleeve, and behind him, she saw something feathered sticking out of the ground.

An arrow.

Someone had shot Zac with an arrow.

No, someone had tried to shoot *her* with an arrow, and Zac had risked his life to save her.

"You're okay," she said, fighting to keep the panic from her voice as she tore off the bottom hem of her shirt to secure around Zac's bicep. "Don't move."

"I'm sorry—I wasn't trying to hit you," said a voice from the edge of the trees. Oliver limped into the meadow. He was dirty, and the knee of his overalls was torn and bloody, but the large cage was still strapped to his back, and Lu spotted the phoenix inside. "I was aiming between you. If you hadn't moved, no one would have gotten hurt."

"Your aim was off," said Zac, wincing as she tied the makeshift bandage around his bleeding wound. "The phoenix warned me. How did you get through the Scorchlands?"

Oliver frowned, studying his bow for a minute before nocking another arrow. "I walked. These monsters won't do anything to hurt their precious phoenix."

And only then did Lu realize they weren't alone. Lurking at the edge of the clearing, a small army of creatures surrounded them.

A chimera, with the heads of a lion and a goat and the tail of a snake.

A griffin, with the front of an eagle and the back of a lion.

A hydra, with three bobbing heads of a serpent.

Another manticore, this one stronger and better fed than the one that had attacked them.

Dark, knee-high creatures with mouths full of teeth. Scraggly chickens with the wings of dragons. Tiny dragons with the wings of chickens. A feathered snake with a scaly crown and its eyes missing.

But as Lu stood frozen beside her brother, none of the creatures approached them. And as she studied their gazes and the directions of their growls, she put the pieces together.

They weren't hunting her and Zac. They were hunting Oliver.

"I'm impressed you've made it this far," he said, cutting across the meadow to join them. "I would have appreciated your help along the way, but something tells me that despite how kind my sister has been to you, you don't have her best interests at heart."

Lu shifted until she stood between Oliver and Zac. "We want to save Penelope too," she said. "But you don't have to kill the phoenix to do it. You only need a drop of blood to cure her."

"I know," said Oliver simply. "I do have to kill the phoenix in order to break the curse, though."

Despite his injury, Zac straightened to his full height, his dark eyes flinty with fury. "If you kill the phoenix, the Wildewoods will be destroyed, and every single animal inside will die."

Oliver shrugged with the kind of cold indifference that came only from a lifetime of anger. "These creatures aren't even supposed to exist anymore. History has turned them into legends, but our family is still stuck here, generation after generation. This—the Wildewoods—is our only option. London? Forget it. Friends? Never for long. Parents who don't split up? Not in the cards." His voice cracked, and he shifted the weight of the cage on his back. "You've only been here for a few days. You have no idea what it's really like. But I've been here for years, and I will *not* sacrifice the rest of my life for some bloody ancestor's mistake. I will *not* sacrifice my sister."

"No one wants you to," said Lu, her mouth dry. "We're just asking you to give the phoenix a chance."

"The phoenix already had his chance," snapped Oliver. "He could have stopped Penelope from being stung in the first place. He could have removed this stupid curse centuries ago. But he chose not to, and now I'm choosing to save my sister's life—and mine." He drew back the arrow. "Considering what the phoenix did to your family, I would have thought you'd be on my side."

"What do you mean?" said Lu warily. "The phoenix is our friend."

Oliver stared at her for a moment. "You don't know, do you?" he said, amazed. "You just risked your life to save this stupid overgrown parrot, and you have no idea."

"What are you talking about?" said Zac, and as he shifted his weight to move closer to Oliver, Lu grabbed his shirt, holding him back.

Their cousin shook his head as if he pitied them. "Aunt Josie used to visit every year. She never stayed long—only a day or so—but every August, without fail, she visited the Wildewoods. She visited the phoenix."

Lu swallowed hard. "That's not true," she said. "She went to New York City every August, not England."

"Oh? Did you go with her, then?" said Oliver, raising an eyebrow. "Were you there every step of the way?"

Lu opened her mouth, but nothing came out. Their mother had always traveled alone.

"Just because we didn't go with her doesn't mean she lied to us," said Zac fiercely, trying to shake off Lu's grip. "She wouldn't have. She always told us the truth."

"Always?" said Oliver, his gaze heavy as it swept over both of them. "So she told you the truth about the

Wildewoods? The truth about the phoenix? The truth about where she grew up and why she never brought you here to meet your family?"

Panic fluttered in the pit of Lu's stomach, and she looked to Zac. Their mother had told them none of those things, of course—and if she hadn't told them that, then what else had she been keeping from them?

"Penelope said she knew Mum," said Lu, her voice sounding weak even to her own ears. "Remember? When we first met?"

She expected Zac to deny it—to insist that Oliver was trying to trick them—but instead he nodded, the gesture so minute that she almost didn't catch it. And though the anger on his face only grew sharper, she could see the hard truth settle into the furrow of his brow.

Their mother had lied to them.

"It doesn't matter where she went," said Lu, louder this time so Oliver could hear. "She loved us. A few secrets don't change that."

"Oh, but it does matter," said their cousin, with the smirk of a predator who knew he'd cornered his prey. "Would you like to know why she visited every August? Why she left you in Chicago while she traveled thousands of miles to a place you thought didn't exist?"

A block of ice formed in the pit of Lu's stomach, and a horrible thought slithered into her mind. But no—it couldn't be true. It didn't make any sense. "Mum wasn't cursed," she said, digging her nails into her palm. "She lived in Chicago with us."

"The phoenix certainly liked her better than the rest of us, and he let her leave for longer periods," agreed Oliver. "But she wasn't released from the curse—no one ever is. She still had to come back once a year."

This time it was Zac who spoke, his voice trembling. "You're a liar."

"I'm not," insisted Oliver, and there was something about the way he said it that convinced Lu he really was telling the truth. "You said so yourself—she had the same mark on her palm. She was branded, just like us. And every summer, she visited the phoenix. Except for last August," he added. "She was supposed to, of course, but she changed her plans at the last minute and didn't come."

Lu's entire body went cold, and suddenly she grew dizzy as the world spun around her. "He's right," she said tightly, barely able to speak. "Mum didn't go on her trip last year."

"What?" said Zac angrily, but when he looked at her, his eyes were red, and Lu knew he understood.

"The phoenix killed your mother," said Oliver plainly. "I'm sorry. I really am. But I can't let him kill my sister, too."

With his arrow now pointed directly at them, he

limped around her and Zac and headed for the exit. Lu gaped, her mind buzzing as she tried to make sense of it, and beside her, Zac was as still as a statue. Bound by their shock and grief, they watched as Oliver stepped through the stone archway with the cage still strapped to his back.

And when Lu blinked back tears, he was gone.

29

ZAC

It WAS HIS FAULT.

That was all Zac could think about as the sky turned black and lightning sizzled, striking the looming mountains. All around them, thunder reverberated through the air, and the ground shook beneath their feet, threatening to cast them into the very earth. But he didn't care.

It was *his fault*.

"Zac, come on!" shouted Lu, seemingly pulled from her misery by the destruction happening around them. She tugged on his good arm, but he couldn't move. His feet were rooted to the meadow, and all he could see was a memory of his mother sitting next to his hospital bed last August.

He'd been stung by a wasp and had suffered the worst case of anaphylaxis he'd ever experienced. He'd nearly died, he'd learned later—he had blacked out in the middle of it and still remembered very little about that entire day. But she had held his hand all week, and she hadn't left his side.

A searing pain shot through him, sending him crashing back to the present and he gasped and stumbled forward as Lu tugged on his injured arm.

"You aren't dying here," she said, and she shoved him toward the stone archway. "Neither of us is."

He felt the keen loss of magic instantly as he fell through and landed on the other side. That had been the only difference before, whenever he'd passed through the tree arch and reentered the real world. But on this placid summer day, as lightning crackled and trees crashed down inside the Wildewoods, the border between the two worlds couldn't have been starker.

The archway swayed, and Zac realized his sister was still in the Wildewoods. "Lu!" he shouted as she dove toward him. For an instant, he thought she wouldn't make it, but as soon as she passed through, the stone collapsed, and the horrific scene beyond disappeared.

They lay on the too-still ground for a long moment, both of them struggling to catch their breath. But at last, Zac forced himself to sit up, cradling his throbbing arm.

"It's true, isn't it?" he said hollowly. It wasn't really a question—he already knew the answer, after all. But she nodded anyway.

"I'm sorry." Lu's words came out choked, and Zac stared at her blankly. "It's my fault Mum stayed behind last year."

He blinked, his thoughts reeling. "No, it's mine," he insisted. "I was the one in the hospital."

"I'm the one who put you there," she said miserably, wiping her dirty cheeks. "I thought the air-conditioning was too strong, and Mum wouldn't turn it off because you liked it that cold. And I got mad, so I—I opened the back door. And I left it open. And that's how the wasp got inside."

They stared at each other, and Zac struggled to wrap his mind around what she was saying. He didn't remember being stung. He didn't remember any argument Lu had had with their mother.

But he did remember the look on Lu's face when the doctor had told them their mother had died. And he remembered the grief they had endured individually, too far apart after years of separation to come together even then.

"It wasn't your fault," he said softly. "You didn't know. Neither of us knew, and neither of us wanted her to die."

Lu swallowed thickly. "If I hadn't kept the door open . . ."

"And if I'd listened to Mum and carried an EpiPen like

I was supposed to, I bet I would have been okay," he said as tears stung his eyes. Lu said nothing, averting her gaze, and that was all the confirmation he needed.

"If it isn't my fault, then it isn't yours, either," she said, her voice hoarse. "It's the phoenix's fault. That stupid curse killed her, not one of us."

Zac looked away. She was right. But he stood anyway, his legs unsteady beneath him as he clutched his injured arm to his chest. "We're not done yet," he said. "There's still time before Oliver kills the phoenix. He'll do it at the manor—he needs special equipment, and besides, he'll need to get the cure to Penelope as quickly as possible."

Lu gaped at him. "You still want to save the phoenix?" she said, stunned. "But—"

"The curse killed Mum. I know. We can't turn back time, though. Mum loved the phoenix, and she loved the Wildewoods. And the Wildewoods loved her. We can't save her life anymore, but we can save the creatures she loved. We have to."

Lu opened and shut her mouth. "I—I don't think I can," she said quietly. "Oliver's right. The phoenix had a choice. And—and if you were the one who was stung, I would do anything to save you, too."

"No, you wouldn't," said Zac firmly. "Because you know there's another way. But if we're going to save Penelope *and* the phoenix *and* the Wildewoods, we need to go."

She looked torn, her brow furrowed and her face pale, but he'd already made up his mind. He gave her a few seconds before turning on his heel and walking away. If she wouldn't help him, then he would do it himself.

"Zac!" she called. "Please—come back!"

He ignored her. And though his beleaguered lungs had already survived more than he'd thought possible in the past few days, he forced himself into a jog, his arm protesting with every jolt. He didn't have much time, and he couldn't waste a single second.

He reached a familiar dirt road only a minute later, and he stopped, doubling over and clawing desperately through his backpack for his inhaler. His lungs were so tight that he could barely draw breath at all, and as he sucked in his medication, he realized with dismay that it wasn't enough this time. He still couldn't breathe.

Zac stumbled down the path, his head swimming. It was the same dirt road that led to the manor, which meant he was close. He'd been afraid there would be miles between the arches in the non-magical world, the way there had been in the Wildewoods, but both were on their property. He shouldn't have been surprised—of course the phoenix would have ensured that no one could stumble upon the entrances and accidentally destroy them. But that also meant that Oliver, even with his injured knee, had almost certainly made it back to the manor by now.

Any sane person would have stopped and let someone else save the day. Zac couldn't run. He could barely walk right now, and he'd missed his medication that morning, which only made things worse. There was no one else, though. Rowena, Conrad, Aunt Merle—they all loved Penelope, and he didn't doubt they would also choose her life over the phoenix's. But he couldn't stand by while every single creature inside the Wildewoods disappeared. He'd spent his whole life doing nothing while everyone else moved forward and made choices and lived. This time, it would be him.

And so he pushed on, walking as quickly as he could without causing his attack to worsen. His wheezes were so loud that he was sure Oliver would hear him coming, but he couldn't help that. The only thing he could control was what he did in that moment.

When he finally reached the manor, the front door was ajar. Pushing it open, Zac stumbled into the foyer, looking around for any sign of which direction Oliver might have gone. Upstairs, with Penelope? Into the kitchen?

"He went that way," said a voice behind him—Lu. She stepped into the foyer beside him and nodded to the right, and Zac was so relieved he could've hugged her.

"How—do you know?" he gasped. "Did the phoenix show you?"

"No," she said, a hint of annoyance flashing across her

face. "But that's where all the old equipment is. And that's where the tracks lead."

Zac looked down. Sure enough, muddy footprints led toward the abandoned wing of the manor. He followed them as quickly as he could, pausing only to take another dose from his inhaler. He wasn't supposed to do that, not so soon after the first, but right now, he didn't care.

As he and Lu burst through a pair of double doors and entered a long hallway full of dust, Zac pulled on one of the medical masks he'd shoved into his backpack the day before. His nose already tickled, but he couldn't let his sister do this alone. His eyes began to water, too, though miraculously he managed not to sneeze, and at last they reached a room toward the end of the corridor.

"This is it," whispered Lu. Soft light spilled out from underneath the door, and Zac heard faint thumping on the other side. "What's the plan?"

"You stay here," he said quietly. "I'll go in and try to free the phoenix, and—"

"Why am I staying here?" she said, before he could continue. "If we're going to do this, we're doing it together. We're a team, remember?"

"I remember," he wheezed, giving her a look. "I was going to say, if Oliver tries to take the phoenix and run, I'll never catch him. But you can."

Lu scowled, though after a beat, she nodded. "If he tries to hurt you, I'm coming in."

"I know," said Zac with a faint grin, and he opened the door and stepped inside.

He wasn't sure what he'd expected the room to look like. A creepy laboratory with potions bubbling over a fire, maybe, or some kind of dark lair with sharp objects scattered across tables. Instead he was faced with the skeleton of a dragon, and as he looked around at the other horrifying hunting trophies, it only got worse from there.

Swallowing his nausea, he crept toward the back of the twisted collection, where an array of old-fashioned weapons and instruments adorned the wall. Crouched on the floor next to a bookcase was Oliver, his shoulders hunched as he tore through journal after journal. The iron cage sat on a nearby platform, and inside, the phoenix ruffled his feathers, as if he were only mildly inconvenienced instead of on the verge of being slaughtered.

"Where is it?" muttered Oliver to himself. The instructions, Zac realized—he was looking for the instructions on how to kill the phoenix. But they were still in Lu's backpack, and unless Oliver had committed every step to memory, he was stuck.

It wouldn't stop him from trying, though, and Zac couldn't think of anything worse than both the phoenix and Penelope dying. With Oliver distracted, he inched forward, ducking behind objects and pedestals. But he could only go so far before his cousin was bound to see him, and what then? While Oliver wasn't armed at the moment, the bow and quiver of arrows rested on the wall beside the old instruments, only an arm's length away.

Zac got as close as he could, hiding behind the platform that held the dragon skeleton. He studied Oliver, considering his options. What could possibly keep him distracted long enough for Zac to steal the phoenix and sneak away?

On the other side of the room, the doorknob hit the wall with a resounding *crack*, and he jumped, shrinking even farther behind the platform. Lu stood in the doorway, her hands held loosely at her side, and to his shock, she was crying.

"What are you doing here?" said Oliver, startled, and he reached for his bow.

"You were right," she said hoarsely, wiping her cheeks. "About everything. About the Wildewoods, about the phoenix . . . Penelope shouldn't have to die because of that—that *monster's* selfishness. I want to help."

Oliver slowly turned toward her—and away from the phoenix. "Why should I believe you?" he said, stepping closer and aiming his bow at her. "How do I know this isn't some kind of trick?"

"The phoenix killed my mum," said Lu, her voice shaking with fury. "He destroyed my family. Because of him, I can never go home and see my friends. We'll never get to live with our dad again."

As she spoke, Zac seized the opportunity and darted on silent feet toward the phoenix's cage. Oliver was several yards away now, giving Zac the space he needed to maneuver. When he reached the iron cage, he offered the phoenix a small smile and pressed his finger to his lips. Whether the phoenix understood or not, he didn't make a sound.

"What could you possibly do to help me?" said Oliver. "All I have left is to extract the phoenix's blood. Once that's done—"

"You'll save Penelope," said Lu. "Except you haven't extracted the blood yet, have you? Because you don't remember how."

Zac picked up the cage with both hands, taking care not to let the edges hit the wall. It was much heavier than he expected, and as a jolt of pain ran down his injured arm, he winced, wondering exactly how Oliver had managed to carry it across the entire length of the Wildewoods.

Muscles, thought Zac. And good lungs. And lots and lots of hiking practically every day for the past two years.

"I remember," said Oliver with a snarl, and Zac slowly crossed the room, remaining behind him. "It's not that difficult."

"Yes, it is," said Lu. "Want to know how I know that?"

She pulled the missing journal out from behind her

back, and Oliver immediately lowered his weapon. "You have it?" he gasped. "But—how?"

"Long story. Doesn't matter," said Lu as she moved along the opposite wall. Oliver kept his eyes on her and, thankfully, his back to Zac. "What does matter is that I can help you. But I want something in return."

"Anything," said Oliver immediately, though he quickly added, "*Almost* anything."

"I want some of that blood for my brother, too," she said. "I want to cure him."

Only a few feet from the door now, Zac nearly dropped the cage, and he gaped at his sister. Was she joking?

"Cure him?" scoffed Oliver. "He doesn't seem that sick to me."

"You have no idea how bad it really is," she said. "When we were little, I used to stay awake half the night listening to him struggle to breathe. He's been in the hospital so many times that the nurses know him on sight. Our entire childhood was doctor appointment after doctor appointment, medication after medication, attack after attack. He's never been to public school. We can't go to the movies or the grocery store. And whenever he does leave the house, he has to wear a mask."

"He seemed fine in the Wildewoods," said Oliver, though he sounded uncertain now. "He made it all the way across with you."

"Because of the phoenix," said Lu. "Don't you get it? The magic that's going to save Penelope—it's been helping him. He's done more in the past few days than he has in his entire life, and if the Wildewoods are destroyed and the curse is removed . . . then I want him to still have that magic. I want my family not to have to worry about him every second of every day, because we know that if we stop—even for a moment—it might be his last."

Zac's throat was tight, and he lingered in the doorway even though he knew he had to go. Lu might have been pretending to be on Oliver's side, but everything she'd said was true. This *was* the best he'd ever felt, despite his persistent asthma. He'd never spent more than a few minutes outdoors since he was a toddler, but in the Wildewoods, he almost felt healthy again.

The phoenix blood *could* cure him, the same way it could cure Penelope. No more deadly allergies. No more asthma attacks that took away his ability to breathe. It was a dream he'd never dared to entertain, not even during his longest and most painful hospital stays.

It didn't matter how much he had to gain, though. He wouldn't let Oliver kill the phoenix.

He turned to slip into the corridor, his face hot. But as he did so, the edge of the cage caught on the doorway, and a loud metal clang echoed through the room.

Crap.

"Hey!" shouted Oliver, but Zac was already running down the hallway, nearly tripping over his own feet as he stumbled back to the main area of the house. He burst through the double doors, trying not to think about the fact that he'd left his sister alone in a room with Oliver and that bow, but as he turned the corner into the foyer, he nearly plowed straight into Rowena.

"Zacharias?" she gasped, her hand flying to her chest. "Where have you—and is that—"

He pushed past her, ignoring her questions. His only goal was to get outside and as close to the Wildewoods as possible.

"Zacharias!" she called. "Come back this instant!"

But he was already through the back door. As he stumbled across the garden, he felt his lungs seize, and his wheezing grew stronger until he could hardly suck in any air at all.

He just had to get to the forest. If he could hide long enough to unlock the cage, the phoenix would be able to fly away on his own.

The world began to spin, and Zac grew light-headed as he careened across the grass. Just a little farther now, he thought as he finally reached the trees. Just a little farther, and—

His foot caught on a root, and he pitched forward, landing hard in the dirt. The cage crashed to the ground beside him, and the phoenix squawked in protest, his wings catching on the bars.

"Sorry," he gasped, barely able to speak. He tried to climb to his feet, but his vision grew hazy, and he staggered and fell to his knees. He couldn't stand anymore. This was as far as he'd get.

With enormous effort, he managed to right the cage, and his clumsy fingers fumbled with the lock. But it was much more complicated than a regular birdcage, and white spots appeared in front of him. He couldn't breathe. He couldn't *breathe*.

"Did you really try to run?"

Oliver's voice sounded from the grass behind him, and Zac stiffened. There had to be a way to free the phoenix. It wasn't that difficult—he just couldn't *think*.

"You won't get it," called Oliver. "That's a phoenix trap—probably the last one in existence. They're smart, you know. They can open regular locks. But that one . . ." He let out a low whistle. "Thomas Wilde was a monster, but he was also a genius."

Zac didn't care. If he could open the cage, the phoenix could fly away, and then—

"Let it go," said Oliver sharply. "I won't ask again. My sister needs that blood."

"The animals," he gasped, the pain in his chest unbearable now. "They'll—they'll—"

"For the last time, I don't care about the bloody animals!"

Zac heard the creak of the bow as his cousin pulled back the string, and he squeezed his eyes shut, his fingers still fumbling with the latch. Oliver could do whatever he wanted to him. But he wouldn't let the phoenix die without a fight.

A twang echoed through the air as Oliver released the arrow, and Zac threw himself over the cage, shielding the phoenix from harm. No matter what came next, he hoped his family knew he loved them. And he hoped they knew he was trying to do the right thing.

But a second passed, and then another. Behind him, he heard a low, guttural gasp, and he opened his eyes, twisting around to see through his swimming vision what had happened.

Twenty feet away, Oliver held the empty bow in his hand, his face slack. Behind him, Rowena limped across the grass, racing as fast as her injuries allowed.

And in between Zac and Oliver, kneeling on the ground with an arrow sticking in her belly, was Lu.

30

ZAC

THE WORLD SEEMED TO CONSTRICT AS ZAC STARED at the arrow embedded in his sister's stomach.

Lu peered at the feathered shaft as well, mild curiosity mingled with surprise. "Zac?" she managed, her voice catching in her throat, and as she turned her head to look at him, she fell to the ground in a heap.

"Lu!" Zac half stumbled, half crawled toward her, dragging the phoenix cage behind him. "Lu—no—you're okay. You're okay."

He hovered over her, his own pain forgotten. Lu's eyes had fallen shut, and blood was spilling from her wound at an alarming rate. "Help!" he gasped through his tears, looking to Rowena and Oliver. "Please just—just *help her!*"

Conrad and Aunt Merle raced across the grass, and when their uncle reached them, he knelt beside Lu. "Don't touch the arrow," he said steadily, with all the self-assuredness of every doctor Zac had ever met. "I need to assess the damage."

"What did you do?" demanded Rowena as she rounded on Oliver. He was pale and trembling, but Zac had no sympathy for him. Not anymore.

"I had to," said Oliver, his voice breaking. "Phoenix blood can heal her. The equipment's in the trophy room. If I can just—"

He stepped toward the cage, but Rowena caught his arm. "You're not going anywhere," she growled. "Do you realize what you've done?"

"I had to," he repeated, the desperation in his voice mounting as he struggled against her unyielding grip. "Penelope's dying. I can save both of them. I know how to bottle the phoenix's blood, and if you'll just let me do it—"

"No," gasped Lu, and she cracked open her eyes. "Don't—don't kill the phoenix."

Tears streamed down Zac's face, and he took Lu's hand, afraid to touch any other part of her. "I won't let him," he said thickly. "Conrad will help you, okay? He'll save you."

Lu's unfocused gaze met his, and through her fear and pain, he saw an unyielding fierceness and strength that he'd never had. "Tell Dad—I love him," she said. "And you . . ."

"I know," said Zac, nearly choking on a sob. "But you'll be okay, Lu. I promise, you'll be okay."

That wasn't a promise he could make, though, and they both knew it. Lu managed a watery smile before her eyes fluttered shut once more, and Conrad swore under his breath. "There's no time to get her to a hospital. I need—"

"But the phoenix," said Oliver, distraught. "The blood—"

"That's not an option," snapped Conrad, his demeanor cracking. "I need my medical kit. It's in Penelope's room."

Zac tried to stand, but he felt like a fist was squeezing his lungs, and he stumbled back to the ground. Oliver made a motion to go, but Rowena held him in place.

"Not you," she snarled. "Stay right here. I'll handle it."

As Rowena limped back to the manor, the clang of iron caught Zac's attention, and he turned. Aunt Merle was crouched beside the cage, and somehow her nimble fingers had coaxed open the lock. "The phoenix is free now," she said as she opened the door. "You will not harm him."

The phoenix stepped out of his iron confines and ruffled his feathers. Aunt Merle gazed at him in wonder, and somewhere in the back of Zac's mind, he realized this was her first time seeing a mythical creature.

Rather than fly away, like Zac expected, the phoenix waddled up to him. The bird nudged Lu's cheek, and when she didn't respond, he tried again.

"There's nothing we can do," wheezed Zac. "Conrad's going to help her."

But their uncle's expression was grim, and despite his attempts to stop the flow of blood, there was an impossible amount now. Zac squeezed his sister's hand.

"Please," he whispered. "Please be okay. Please. I'm sorry—I'm sorry for everything. *Please.*"

The phoenix gently headbutted his injured arm. With great reluctance, Zac tore himself away from his sister, only to see the phoenix tugging at his plumage.

"What are you doing?" he said, startled. The phoenix ignored him, and after a moment, he managed to free a single feather. With his dark eyes focused on Zac, he held it in his beak and stretched forward, as if offering him a gift.

Zac took the brilliant orange and gold-tipped feather, not entirely sure what to do with it. It was beautiful, but what good was it now, when Lu was dying?

But as he stared at it, trying to understand, the world dropped away, and for a few precious seconds, he was back in the Wildewoods. His mother—only fourteen or fifteen now—leaned up against a tree, clutching her arm. There was a gash near her elbow, Zac realized, and though it wasn't nearly as bad as Lu's injury, she was also bleeding.

The phoenix hopped up to her in the memory, and just as he had in the present, he pulled out one of his feathers. Zac's mother looked down at him with a wince.

"I'm not taking that from you," she said firmly. "I'm okay."

But the phoenix nudged her leg insistently and let out a muffled cry. His mother sighed, and finally she accepted the feather.

"You're almost as stubborn as I am," she grumbled before putting the shaft between her lips. And as Zac watched, astonished, the gash on her arm started to heal itself, and the broken skin closed until there wasn't even a hint of a scar left.

He came crashing back to reality with such force that he nearly blacked out. Frantic now, he inspected the feather again, and this time he noticed a tiny drop of blood in the shaft.

Phoenix blood.

He gasped. "You want me to——?" he managed, and the phoenix bobbed his head.

Zac didn't waste another moment. He leaned over Lu, and with a gentle pinch, he pushed the single drop of blood out of the feather and into his sister's mouth.

For several terrifying seconds, he waited. What if it was too late? What if Lu had lost too much blood?

But at last, as Zac watched in bewilderment, the arrow began to work itself out of her body. Conrad sucked in a breath and snatched his hands back. "What did you do?" he said, astonished.

"The—the feather," said Zac, reeling. "It had a drop of phoenix blood."

Conrad said nothing, and together he and Zac took in the impossible sight of the arrow falling out of Lu's body, and the wound in her stomach magically closing on its own. Her color returned slowly but surely, and finally, *finally* her eyes flew open.

"What happened?" she gasped, trying to sit up, but Conrad eased her back onto the ground.

"Lie still for a moment," he warned. "I don't know if you've healed completely."

"It was the phoenix," blurted Zac, petting the bird. "He—he gave me a feather, and there was a drop of blood in it."

Lu's eyes widened. "You saved me?" she said to the phoenix.

He made an odd purring sound and nudged his head against her cheek again. This time, Lu grinned and reached up to stroke his neck.

"Thank you," she said. *"Thank you."*

Zac couldn't even manage to say that much as his throat tightened and his eyes threatened to overflow. The phoenix had saved her. Oliver had nearly succeeded in killing him, but the phoenix had still saved Lu.

The bird ruffled his wings again, and he dug his beak into his plumage once more. This time, his dark gaze focused first on Zac's heaving chest, and then the injury to his arm as he offered Zac the feather.

Zac took it in his shaking hand. As badly as he wanted healthy lungs, and as much as he hurt right now, he knew what he had to do. "Can I give it to Penelope?" he said quietly. "She's going to die if I don't."

"I'm sorry," cried Oliver. "I'm so sorry. Do whatever you'd like to me, but—please, just—just help her. *Please.*"

Zac glared at him before returning his attention to the phoenix. "Oliver doesn't deserve your help, but Penelope loves the Wildewoods. And she would never have wanted any of this to happen because of her."

The phoenix scrutinized him for several seconds, but at last he bobbed his head again. Beside Zac, Conrad exhaled sharply, his own eyes watering as he took the feather with its precious drop of blood inside. "Thank you," he said hoarsely, and he stood, swaying slightly on his feet. "I am so sorry for what my son tried to do. I want to believe his intentions were good, but regardless of that, it will never happen again."

With that, he sprinted across the lawn, heading straight for the manor. And as Oliver sank to the ground, burying his face in his hands, Zac helped his sister sit up.

"Are you all right?" said Lu, studying his face. "You're wheezing. Where's your inhaler?"

Zac let out a choked laugh. Lu was the one who'd been shot in the belly only minutes ago, not him. "I'll live," he managed. "You're really okay?"

"I feel like nothing even happened," she said. "And look—the scratches from the cave are gone."

"The cave?" said Aunt Merle as she gave both of them a once-over. "You've had quite an adventure, haven't you? We've been worried sick about you all. Rowena wanted to go in after you, but of course, with her injuries and only the north entrance still standing—"

She stopped suddenly, a strange look passing over her face. As Zac followed her gaze, he realized the phoenix had waddled past Lu and was approaching the patch of grass where Oliver now sat alone, shaking with silent sobs. And to Zac's surprise, the phoenix gently nudged his arm.

Oliver looked up, his eyes red and swollen. Instantly he jerked back, as if afraid the phoenix might burn him, but the bird only tilted his head inquisitively and tried again.

"When one is offered the gift of forgiveness," said Aunt Merle, "I have always found it best to accept, even when one has not yet forgiven oneself."

Oliver's chin trembled, and for a long moment, he stared at the phoenix like he didn't know what to do. Zac couldn't blame him. Less than ten minutes ago, Oliver had been intent on draining the bird's blood, after all. But the phoenix continued to watch him, his curious gaze never wavering, and at last Oliver reached toward him with a shaking hand, gently stroking his feathers. "I really am sorry," he said in a broken voice. "I only wanted to help my sister."

"But—that wasn't the only reason," said Zac, not wanting to sound like he was accusing Oliver of lying, but this was too important to ignore. "You can tell him the truth. He already knows, anyway. You hate it here, and you want to go back to your friends and your mum. It isn't fair that you had to leave them all behind because of something Thomas Wilde did centuries ago. And it isn't fair that his descendants are cursed when we haven't done anything wrong. Some of us love the Wildewoods," he added, glancing at Lu. "But forcing us to stay here won't make anyone's life better."

Oliver's Adam's apple bobbed, and he cleared his throat. "I wanted my life back," he finally admitted, so softly that Zac could barely hear him. "I've wanted it back even before I really lost it, ever since I found out what would happen when we turned thirteen. I love London. I love my friends and my mum, but—" His voice caught, and he blinked rapidly. "But I love my sister more. And as long as she's okay, then I'll find a way to be, too."

Several seconds passed, and no one moved. At last the

phoenix seemed to sigh, and he headbutted Oliver's palm before finally turning away and waddling back toward the rest of them. Zac didn't know what it meant, or what the phoenix had been trying to convey, but either way, Oliver took a deep, shaky breath and hung his head, alone once more.

"What a wonderful creature," murmured Aunt Merle, and ran her fingers gently over his feathers. "It has been the honor of my life to meet you, little one."

The phoenix trilled, and he tilted his chin to allow her to scratch the underside of his long throat. Aunt Merle laughed, delighted, and she bent down to kiss the top of his head.

As Zac focused on his breathing, Lu elbowed him lightly in the ribs. "Look," she said, nodding toward the manor. Conrad was crossing the garden slowly, his arm wrapped around—

"Penny!" Oliver scrambled to his feet and hurried toward his sister, limping across the grass as fast as his knee allowed. Shortly before he reached Penelope, however, he stumbled to a stop, hesitating.

Zac couldn't hear what she said to him, but after a few somber words, she caught her brother in a hug, burying her face in his shoulder. And as Oliver once again broke down, he returned her embrace.

Footsteps sounded as Rowena approached Zac and Lu.

Leaning heavily on her cane, she lowered herself onto the ground beside Aunt Merle, and she held out her hand to the phoenix. He eyed her suspiciously, but that didn't seem to bother Rowena in the slightest.

"You didn't have to save either of the girls, but you did," she said quietly. "I am forever grateful."

"We all are," said Aunt Merle, stroking the phoenix's tail. He seemed to relax at this, and finally, with a soft purr, he nuzzled Rowena's palm. Aunt Merle beamed and threaded her fingers through Rowena's, offering her a kiss.

"Wait," said Lu suddenly. "The creatures in the Wildewoods—what happened to them? Are they okay?"

"What are you talking about?" said Rowena, startled.

"The second exit was also destroyed when Oliver brought the phoenix into our world." Lu looked at the bird. "Can you fix them?"

The phoenix seemed to huff, as if insulted she even had to ask. Stretching his wings, he launched himself into the air, a bright orange streak as he flew through the forest toward the tree arch. Lu helped Zac to his feet—which was bizarre, considering her shirt was still soaked in her own blood—and together they followed.

Even on this side of the arch, the entwined trees were little more than a charred tangle of branches, and by the time Zac and Lu caught up, the phoenix was perched on top of them, studying the mess the lightning storm had left behind.

"When we found it like this, we thought all three of you were goners," said Rowena thickly, as she and Aunt Merle joined them. "We had hope, of course, that Oliver would find you and help you to the other side, but how you survived the Scorchlands . . ."

"It was Devon," said Zac. "He found us, and he flew us to the stone arch."

"Devon? Our dragon, Devon?" said Rowena, dumbfounded. "Well. I suppose he's earned a few treats the next time he stops by."

"Maybe you could bring his hatchling out to play with him and Surrey," suggested Lu, and as her eyes met Zac's, she grinned. "I bet he'd like that."

"Perhaps so," said Rowena, shaking her head in disbelief.

As they watched, a shimmering halo appeared around the phoenix, making him seem as if he were glowing. He let out a deep, resounding note, and without warning, a blinding flash of gold engulfed him. Zac shielded his eyes, but something warm washed over his skin, as if he were bathed in sunlight. And as the light faded, he finally lowered his hand.

The tree arch was mended.

Aunt Merle clapped in delight. "How extraordinary!"

But then, slowly, her expression shifted, and her mouth dropped open. "Is that—is that a *unicorn*?"

Zac craned his neck to see around her. Sure enough, a bay unicorn with a diamond horn stared through the archway back at them.

Rowena gasped. "Did the phoenix mark you?" she said urgently, grabbing Aunt Merle's hand and examining it. Her palm was blank, and so was the other. Rowena frowned. "But how . . ."

Zac looked at his own hands, and to his shock, he saw nothing but dirt and a bit of blood. Where there had been a distinct *W* only a few minutes earlier, there was now only smooth, unmarked skin.

"Lu," he said, but she was already studying her own palm—and just like his, her mark was also gone.

"What on earth . . . ?" Rowena trailed off. There was no mark on her skin either. But instead of relief, like Zac expected, she limped hastily toward the tree arch, nearly losing her footing on the uneven ground. "Have we been banished? Is this a punishment?"

"A punishment?" said Zac, surprised. "I thought you didn't like the Wildewoods."

"No, no," she said, waving her hand dismissively. "I have always hated the curse—the compulsion, of course, and the way it has torn our family apart. I have never resented the Wildewoods or the creatures that need our help." She stopped at the edge of the tree arch, as if she were afraid of finding herself barred.

The phoenix trilled, and he flew down from the twisted branches to land on the path beside her. Without hesitation, he waddled over the barrier and paused, peering back at Rowena as if waiting for her to follow.

Taking a deep breath, Rowena stepped forward. Nothing stopped her. There was no invisible barrier. Instead the air shimmered as she returned to the Wildewoods, and as she glanced over her shoulder at the rest of them, a wide smile spread across her face.

Zac took Lu's hand, and they walked inside together. "It's all still here," he said, amazed. "Do you think the creatures are okay?"

"The phoenix wouldn't have let anything happen," said Lu firmly, and she reached up to stroke the bay unicorn's muzzle. "All he ever wanted was to protect them."

Rowena set her hand on the trunk of a nearby tree, her brow furrowed with confusion. "Why now? After all Oliver tried to do—why did the phoenix choose this moment to release our family from the curse?"

"Isn't it obvious?" Aunt Merle stepped through the tree arch to join them, her eyes shining with tears of joy. "Zac and Lu were willing to sacrifice their lives to protect him, and they both nearly did. The debt is paid."

Kneeling beside the bird, Zac ran his fingers through his

feathers, and his voice caught in his throat. "Thank you," he managed. "For everything."

The phoenix trilled affectionately, headbutting his hand, and Zac grinned.

The debt was paid, and at last, the curse was broken.

EPILOGUE

LU

OVER THE PAST THREE MONTHS, LU HAD DISCOV-
ered she didn't like riding unicorns nearly as much as she
thought she would.

Maybe horses were different, she figured, bouncing in
the saddle as Hermes pranced through the forest, all too
happy to be out in the afternoon sunshine. It had rained the
day before in the Wildewoods, and he was a ball of energy
after being cooped up in the pasture.

"You can teach him not to jolt you around so much,"
said Penelope with a grin, riding beside her on Athena. "He
should know better by now, anyway."

"He's never going to learn when Zac lets him do whatever he wants," said Lu as her teeth clicked together.

Penelope laughed. "Maybe I'll have another unicorn trained especially for you next time you visit," she said with a mischievous smirk. "There's a chestnut I've had my eye on—the one with the sapphire horn. I think you two would be a good match."

Lu smiled, but inwardly her heart sank. This had been the most amazing summer of her life, and today, their father was due to pick them up and bring them home to Chicago. When they'd arrived in May, Lu would have given anything to go home. Now that their vacation was over, however, she would have given anything to stay.

As they neared the gnarled tree, Lu spotted her brother sitting beside the trunk, drawing with intense focus as the phoenix preened beside him. He was lost in his own world, and Lu hated to interrupt him. But it was time.

Penelope slowed Athena down to a walk. "I'll leave you to it," she said, and Lu nodded. As Athena trotted away, Lu urged Hermes closer, and the unicorn snorted.

All summer, Lu had tried to spend time with the phoenix. But whenever she'd gotten close, she remembered what the curse had done to her family, and she just . . . couldn't. She knew it was unfair. The phoenix had saved her life, after all, and she owed him some gratitude. But the curse had still killed their mother, and that gratitude had a limit.

She couldn't steer clear of him forever, though. Besides,

it seemed rude to leave without saying goodbye, and as she and Hermes approached, she cleared her throat. "Did you finish?" she said. Zac didn't bother looking up.

"Yeah, this morning. I'm doing another drawing now."

Lu climbed out of the saddle and dropped to the ground. "Dad's going to be here any minute. We really have to go."

Zac scowled, his pencil moving as steadily as it had before. She sighed and sat on his other side, averting her eyes from the phoenix.

He was drawing their mother again—one of the dozens of pictures he'd completed during their long summer days in the Wildewoods. It was beautiful, and Lu felt a sudden surge of jealousy. It was the same jealousy she'd felt before, when she'd discovered the phoenix was showing Zac memories of their mum. Part of her had hoped that after the curse had been lifted, the phoenix would show them to her, too. But how could he when she'd been so diligent in avoiding him?

"Rowena will be furious if we're not back soon," she said after another minute or so. "Besides, you don't want Dad thinking we've forgotten him, do you?"

Zac sighed, and reluctantly he put down his pencil and began to pack his things. "I think he's forgotten us," he mumbled. And though Zac was obviously exaggerating, he wasn't completely off.

Their father had called only a handful of times over the

summer, and during each conversation, he'd sounded distant and had only been able to talk for a few minutes. Again and again, Lu had tried to figure out why. Did he prefer to be alone now? Did he no longer love them? Did he still want to be their dad?

Of course he still loved them, but it was the last question that had kept her awake at night. What if he didn't show up? What if he changed his mind?

She wouldn't complain about living in England now. She loved the Wildewoods, and she hated the thought of leaving. But after all they'd been through, if they lost their father, too . . .

Lu felt a soft nudge against her knee, and she blinked at the phoenix, surprised. His eyes looked like a puppy's, and there was a fleck of gold in the otherwise dark irises. She hadn't noticed that before.

"Hi," she said quietly, gently running her fingers down his long neck. The phoenix continued to stare at her, and though a lump formed in her throat, she didn't look away. What else was she supposed to say to the creature who had inadvertently killed her mother?

Suddenly the forest around her shifted. It didn't fade, exactly—she was still in the same place under the gnarled tree—but it *felt* different. Beside her, Zac gasped, staring at something nearby, and Lu turned.

There, not five feet away, was their mother.

She was younger—maybe in her early twenties—and she sat on the ground beside the tree, her shoulders shaking with grief. The phoenix stood beside her, his worry clear, and he tentatively nudged her elbow. When she didn't move, he tried again, and at last their mother looked at him, her eyes red and puffy.

"Cal's leaving," she whispered in a tear-choked voice. "He got a job offer in Chicago, and he's moving as soon as we graduate next week. I'll never—I'll never see him again."

The phoenix made a low humming noise and ruffled his feathers, and though Lu wasn't sure what that meant, she thought he looked upset. Her mother's chin trembled, and as the spring breeze rustled the leaves, she twisted something around her finger.

"He wants me to go with him," she whispered. "He even gave me this."

She held out her hand to the phoenix, and a flash of silver caught the sunlight. Lu recognized the piece of jewelry instantly.

"It's an engagement ring," said her mum, managing a watery smile as the phoenix inspected the simple band. "I know it's impossible, but . . . I didn't have the heart to tell him I can't accept. Not yet. Not when we're so happy together. I just—I just want a few more days to be with him. To pretend that maybe we could have a future together after all." She wiped her eyes, and her lower lip quivered. "I love him so much."

She broke down into sobs once more, and the phoenix stood perfectly still, seemingly contemplating something Lu didn't understand. But as she watched, the phoenix let out a mournful note, and he dipped his head as a soft golden glow appeared in a halo around him.

Her mother jerked as if she'd been burned, and she unfurled her fingers, staring at her palm. "What—" She looked from her hand to the phoenix and back down again. "But—"

The phoenix purred and inched closer to her, his dark eyes wide. Her mother began to tremble, and she threw her arms around him, hugging him gently and stroking his magnificent plumage.

"Thank you," she cried. *"Thank you."*

And as the edges of the forest began to dim, Lu caught sight of her mother's palm. Though there was a bit of dirt on the heel, that was all she could see.

The *W* was gone.

The memory faded, and soon it was replaced with another. Their mum was a little older this time, and she looked tired. Her hair was cut short like it had been when Lu and Zac were babies, and she crouched low to hug the phoenix once more.

"I've missed you," she murmured, her face buried in his

feathers. "The babies came in October. Twins. A boy and a girl—Zacharias and Tallulah. They're so beautiful," she said, her eyes shining. "I can't wait for you to meet them."

"The phoenix knew about us?" said Lu, dumbfounded. "Mum told him?"

Beside her, Zac nodded, and she clutched his sleeve as if she could anchor herself to this moment somehow. But just like the first memory, this one also faded, and it was yet again replaced with another.

Their mother sat on the ground beside the tree, showing the phoenix pictures. It was another sunny day, and in the dappled light, Lu caught sight of her own young face in one of the photographs.

"They're the smartest kids I've ever known," said their mum, glowing with pride. "I want them to meet you. I want them to meet the whole family. I tell them stories about the Wildewoods all the time, and I can't wait to see their faces when they discover they're all real."

The phoenix purred, and he studied the pictures as if memorizing them. Their mum smiled and ran her fingers over his feathers, though after a moment, she opened her palm and gazed at the spot where the white mark had been only a few years earlier.

"I miss it," she said quietly. "I miss having a reminder of you. Seeing a blank spot where your mark once was, when you're still such a huge part of my life . . ." A beat passed, and she hesitated, clearly nervous. "I know I don't have the right to bear the mark without the responsibility. I know I gave up that privilege when I left and married Cal. But every time I look at my hand, I miss you more and more, and lately—it's been unbearable."

The phoenix eyed her, and before she could say anything else, yet again he began to glow in that soft golden light. A moment passed, and when the halo disappeared, their mum gasped, staring at her palm once more.

"Really?" she whispered, her voice catching. The phoenix nudged her elbow, and she wrapped her arms delicately around him. "Thank you. I'll never forget what it means, I promise."

Lu's thoughts raced, but before she could make sense of it all, the image faded once more. This time, when their mother appeared, she looked like she was in her mid-thirties. She looked as old as she would ever get to be.

This must have been her last visit with the phoenix before she'd died, Lu realized. It was his final memory of her.

"I have to go back," said their mother. "Zac and Lu need me. But I'll return next summer, I promise. And before long, you'll get to meet them. They'll get to meet *you*."

The phoenix ruffled his feathers and shifted his weight from one foot to the other, clearly upset. Lu watched, her heart breaking. Did he know what would happen? Did he know this was the last time he would ever see her?

"I always hate leaving you. This is my home, and you're my family. You're *our* family." Their mother dropped a kiss on the crown of his head. "I love you. You know that, right?"

The phoenix let out a sorrowful note, and their mother stroked his wing.

"None of that from you," she murmured. "When you meet them, you'll see that this was all worth it."

The memory began to fade, slower than before, and Lu stared at her mother's face, desperate to hold on to this moment. But finally, as the past dissolved and the present took its place, all she could hear was her voice.

"They're the best things in my life," said her mother, sounding far away now, "and I know they'll love you every bit as much as I do."

Lu blinked hard, not at all surprised to discover that her cheeks were wet. Beside her, Zac was also crying silently, and she groped around for his hand.

"The curse didn't kill Mum," she said, stunned. "She only had that mark because she wanted it. The phoenix released her."

Zac shook his head in disbelief. "It was just—it was just an aneurysm, then. It was just some stupid, random aneurysm."

Beside her, the phoenix made a questioning sound, and Lu wiped her eyes. "Thank you," she mumbled, kneeling down to hug him the same way her mother had. "Thank you for showing us. Thank you for letting us see your memories of our mum."

The phoenix rested his head on her shoulder, and Lu found herself not wanting to let go. But at last it was Zac who touched her arm, his other hand running over the phoenix's feathers.

"Come on, Lu," he said quietly. "Let's go home."

The tires of the taxi crunched on the gravel drive, and Lu stood nervously beside her brother. What were they supposed to say? There was no good way to start a conversation after three months apart, especially when their father was the one who had abandoned them in the first place.

"We don't have to forgive him," mumbled Lu as the car pulled to a stop.

"Yeah, we do," said Zac. "You know we do. He's our dad, and he's made plenty of mistakes. But I don't think this was one of them."

Lu stiffened as the passenger door opened and their father stepped out. And while Zac bolted forward, leaving her standing beside Aunt Merle, she wondered if he was right after all. If their father hadn't brought them here, they wouldn't have discovered the Wildewoods. They wouldn't know Penelope and Aunt Merle and Rowena and Conrad and Oliver. And they wouldn't have those memories of their mother. They would never have found the answers to questions they hadn't even known to ask, and the scars they both carried would have remained open wounds for a very long time.

But as Zac caught their father around the middle, she realized that they wouldn't have had each other, either. She and Zac would have spent the rest of their lives drifting apart. Maybe their father knew that deep down—maybe he realized that forcing them to spend the summer here, together among strangers, would give them the chance to fix the bond between them that had been in danger of fading completely.

Or maybe that was giving their father way too much credit. Regardless, the results were the same, and after all their little family had been through, she could find it in herself to forgive him and wipe the slate clean. If not for his sake, then for Zac's, and for their mother's.

As their dad hugged Zac tightly, Lu approached, hating herself for feeling shy about it. But when their father's gaze met hers, the ice inside her melted.

"My baby girl," her father murmured, and he reached for her. Lu's feet closed the distance between them without her telling them to, and suddenly she was burying her face in his chest, clinging to him and Zac like they were the only lifelines she had left.

"I missed you," she mumbled, and she was surprised to discover it was the truth.

"I missed you both too," he said gruffly. "So much I could hardly stand it. I'm sorry for leaving you here. I'm so sorry."

Lu shook her head and sniffed. "It's okay."

"No, it isn't." He pulled away enough to look at them, and grief flickered across his face. "I lost myself when your mother died, and that had nothing—*nothing* to do with how much I love you, all right?"

"You missed her," said Zac simply, and their father nodded, his eyes growing red.

"I didn't know how to be your dad, not without her. And when your aunt offered to take you for the summer . . . I shouldn't have said yes, and I will forever regret that. But I'll never leave you both alone again, all right? I promise."

Lu hugged her father once more, and Zac joined in, wrapping one of his arms around her, too. A few seconds later, however, Rowena coughed politely on the steps behind them.

Their father straightened, letting them go, and he hastily wiped his face. "You must be Rowena," he said. "It's a pleasure to meet you. Thank you for taking care of my children when I couldn't."

"They're a bit of a handful," she said, eyeing the pair of them. "But we enjoyed every moment. Well, almost every moment."

Their father managed a smile, and beside Rowena, their cousin waved in greeting. "I'm Penelope," she said. "Thanks for letting us borrow them for the summer. They saved my life."

He chuckled nervously, clearly not sure how to take her comment. "Your father lives here with you, doesn't he? And your brother? I wanted to thank them, too."

"Dad's on the land," said Penelope with an apologetic shrug. "And Oliver lives with our mum in London now."

"Oh. Well. Please thank them for me, then. And thank you especially, Merle, for all you've done," he added, offering their aunt his hand. But she stepped past it, instead catching him in a warm hug.

"Anytime you'd like to visit, you're always welcome," she said. "And I do hope you'll all visit often."

"We'll talk about it," said their father with a sideways look at Lu and Zac.

"We want to come back next summer," said Lu firmly, climbing the steps to join them. "We want to come back *every* summer."

"And holidays, too," said Zac as he followed her. "Whenever we can."

Their father blinked, clearly taken aback. "Well—I suppose we could arrange something," he said slowly. "You really like it here, huh?"

"It's our favorite place in the world," said Lu with absolute sincerity.

Rowena cleared her throat. "Lunch should be ready soon. I assume you'll be joining us."

"Oh, no, I couldn't intrude," said their father. "Besides, we need to get going."

"Your flight doesn't leave until nine, and I absolutely insist," said Rowena. "Children, while Merle and I finish cooking, why don't you show your father around?"

As Lu met her eye, Rowena offered her a wink. "We can do that," said Lu with a grin, and she glanced at Zac. "Think he'd like the forest?"

"The forest?" said their dad. "But your brother—"

"As long as we walk slowly, I'm okay," he said. But suddenly, as if remembering something important, he tore open his backpack and dug around inside. "Wait," he said to Rowena, and to Lu's surprise, he pulled out one of his sketchbooks and offered it to her.

Their aunt took it, the lines on her forehead deepening. "Your drawings?"

"My graphic novel," corrected Zac. "I finished it this morning, and I want you to have it."

Rowena opened the cover, and she slowly turned the pages one by one. "This is lovely," she said roughly. "Are you sure you want to part with it?"

"I want it to stay here," he said. "With the Wildewoods. Besides, what's the point if I keep it to myself?"

Aunt Merle wrapped her arms around Zac. "Thank you, darling. We will treasure it always."

"Yes, thank you," echoed Rowena, and though Lu couldn't be sure, she thought she saw her blink away tears.

As soon as their aunt let him go, Zac took his dad's hand. "Come on," he said. "The forest isn't far."

Their father seemed baffled by the whole exchange, but he allowed Zac and Lu to lead him away, across the grass and up the path that cut through the woods. "Did you kids really enjoy staying here?" he said.

"Yeah," said Lu honestly. "Everyone knew Mum, and it was nice hearing more about her. She loved this place."

"I know," he said, his eyebrows knitting together. "She used to talk about it endlessly when we were both university students in Manchester. I always wanted to visit, but she insisted her family didn't like strangers. This place really is quite something, isn't it?"

"You have no idea," said Lu. The tree arch came into view, and she took their father's other hand. "Do you want to see the coolest part?"

"Uh . . . I suppose," said their dad warily. "As long as it's safe."

"It's safe as long as you stick with us," said Zac from his other side. "You can't freak out, though, all right?"

"I'll do my best," he said. "But no promises."

The twins exchanged a smirk, and with their father between them, they stepped through the tree arch and into the Wildewoods together.

ACKNOWLEDGMENTS

A resounding thank you to my agent, Rosemary Stimola, and my editor, Karen Wojtyla, for believing in this story. And my undying gratitude to the team at Margaret K. McElderry Books, especially Nicole Fiorica, Debra Sfetsios-Conover, Irene Metaxatos, Bridget Madsen, Elizabeth Blake-Linn, and Shivani Annirood, for seeing it safely onto shelves and into readers' hands.

Thank you to Sara Hodgkinson, Jennifer Rees, and especially Caitlin Straw, all of whom helped shape this story along the way.

Thank you to Vivienne To, who created the beautiful artwork on the cover.

Thank you to Nigel Johnson and Devon Erps, two of the most enthusiastic and patient sounding boards on the planet.

And thank you to Andrea Hannah and Becca Mix, for their unrelenting support and friendship.

ACKNOWLEDGMENTS

Writing a book is never easy, but this one was uniquely difficult for me. My acknowledgments for *Curse of the Phoenix* go beyond the writing and publishing process, and they extend to the people who helped me and my family when, like Zac and Lu, I lost my mother suddenly as a kid. My deepest gratitude to Helena Mõtus-Puusepp, Elke Schmidt, Janne Eljas, and Chantel Ashley, all of whom were there for us when my mom couldn't be anymore.

And most of all, to my dad, who is an amazing parent and will never give himself the credit he deserves. Love you most.